THE
PEACEMAKER

Aidan de Vries

THE PEACEMAKER

Erser & Pond

Cover design by Benjamin Beaumont

Printed in the United States by Erser & Pond Publishers, Ltd. 1096 Queen St., Suite 225, Halifax, N.S., Canada B3H 2R9

Library and Archives Canada Cataloguing in Publication

De Vries, Aidan
      The Peacemaker / Aidan de Vries.

ISBN 978-0-9781761-5-0

      I. Title.

PS8607.E975P42 2008   C813'.6   C2007-907612-2

10 9 8 7 6 5 4 3 2 1

First Edition

*This book is dedicated to my wife,
my children, and my grandchildren.
May they live in a peaceful world.*

*If you wish to be brothers,
let the arms fall from your hands.
One cannot love while holding offensive arms.*

Pope Paul VI

CHAPTER ONE

Ivan Welland was just beginning his second year as National Security Advisor to the President of the United States. He and his wife, Marina, had bought a house in Georgetown, close to downtown Washington D.C., and had started their family with the arrival of little Julia. It was Ivan's habit to walk every morning to his office in the White House, which gave him both exercise and time to think.

In keeping with the national anthem, Ivan usually started work by the dawn's early light. Anyone awake at the break of dawn might have observed his 6' 7" frame, topped by a shock of hair that bounced with each step of his purposeful, loping gait as he moved through the quaint streets, an expression of deep thoughtfulness on his handsome face. Ivan had tried all his life to tame his hair, but those on his head fought back with cowlicks and those on his face, with a five o'clock shadow.

The streets were deserted at 6:00 AM. They gave off a sweet, fresh odor after the night's efforts to clear the city air of its remnants of the previous day's human detritus. On this particular morning Ivan was remembering the welcome but anticlimactic feelings that had led up to the present. The memories of his adventures in Chechnya were quickly fading into the past. He had only a dim recollection of how he had shot the imam in Grozny, how he had decoded the terrorists' communication system, and how he had planned the raid on the secret sanctuary of the caliphs under the Kabah in Mecca. Months later he had saved an ocean liner from a determined terrorist plot to destroy her at sea, which had resulted in his receiving many accolades from his confreres in the halls of government, but these were only memories now.

Ivan was absorbed by the idea that he might be missing the excitement of being on the front line of the battle against violence. He hoped that he had enough common sense not to become a danger junky. It would certainly have been out of character for a peace-loving Harvard PhD to need frequent doses of life and death situations in order not to be bored. Now that he was a husband and father, his grasp on his own life should be even firmer.

Involved as he was in this line of self-analysis, he didn't notice the nondescript car that was following silently behind him. As he approached the employees' entrance to the White House, he became aware of a man in a dark, unbuttoned overcoat walking toward him. He was keeping his coat closed with one hand as he drew near. Noticing that the man was overdressed for the weather, Ivan assumed he was a derelict or a homeless person.

When they were within a few feet of each other the man opened the right side of his coat, exposing an automatic weapon that had been suspended on straps over his shoulder. In an instant he had swung the weapon around, using the swivel that connected it to the harness as a fulcrum, and quickly moved the gun in an arc that lined up with Ivan's chest.

Ratta-tat-tat.

The sound broke the morning silence. The bullets struck Ivan's chest and he was knocked backward to the ground.

The Marines on guard at the entrance to the White House had been watching the tall, familiar figure of Dr. Welland as he approached. When the shots rang out, they were immediately galvanized into action by the noise of the gunfire in this most unexpected location. The tan car that had been following Ivan suddenly gunned its engine and screeched to a halt so the shooter could climb in. The nearest Marine removed his weapon from its holster, raised it, took aim and fired at the assailant, who had just reached the car and had his hand on the door handle.

The man dropped in his tracks. The driver saw him go down and sped off, never even glancing back to see what had become of him.

"Take care of Welland. I'll look after the shooter," the senior Marine shouted to his buddy.

The gunman was already dead. The Marine's bullet had hit him in the back of the head at the cerebral cortex. The Marine dragged him to the curb, speaking loudly into the mike he wore to communicate with the security detachment leader inside the White House.

"Code Red. Shots fired. Dr. Welland down. Send medic to employees gate." To the other Marine he said, "How's the doc? My guy's dead."

"Welland's alive. I'll try and find out how bad he's hit," the Marine yelled back.

"I'm okay," said Ivan breathlessly, trying to get onto his feet. "I'm wearing a vest. I got the wind knocked out of me, that's all. Help me get inside the grounds. Tell your buddy to drag the shooter inside, too. We can't let the press get hold of this."

He tried to stand up. His chest hurt like blazes. By this time several other Marines had shown up. Two of them took Ivan's arms over their shoulders, and he staggered into the West Wing between them. He gestured for them to sit him in a chair. The watch officer in charge of the detachment ran up to him, followed by the medic on duty.

"Get a stretcher for the body," Ivan said to the medic. He pointed to the corpse. "Take it to the infirmary. Don't let anyone touch it. Wait for further instructions. I'm okay. Don't look at me that way. Now get on with it."

He opened his shirt and his Kevlar vest to see what was hurting him so much. The watch captain approached to see if there was anything he could do to help.

"Come close," Ivan said in a low voice. "Listen, we're lucky this happened early in the morning, before the press corps could get wind of it. Let's keep it that way. Have your men clean everything up and get it all back to normal out there. Tell them it's top secret. I don't want anyone talking about this."

He pointed in the general direction of the entrance gate. "Your men did a good job. We don't need the reporters coming in and saying the Marines could have prevented this incident, and they should have done such and such, now do we?" The watch captain nodded and went off to do as he was told.

Ivan couldn't see any blood on his shirt or on his chest, but he could see three red bruises that would soon be black and blue. He stood up stiffly and headed for his office. As he walked slowly along, he wondered how he would keep his wife Marina from seeing his bruises. Naturally she'd worry if she saw his chest, and it wouldn't be hard for her to imagine what might have happened if he hadn't been wearing the bullet-proof vest.

Brooklyn, his administrative assistant of many years, was already at her desk. She believed that part of her job called for her to watch his back, and she certainly couldn't do that from her bed.

"What on earth happened to you?" she said, when he came into the office. "You look like you were in a fight in a biker's bar, and you lost."

She knew her boss always arrived at work looking neatly turned out, perhaps a bit too conservatively for her taste, but looking smart nonetheless. She also was aware that he had a morning meeting with the President every day, so there could be no neglecting the haberdashery department, which only made his present state the more remarkable. At that moment his suit was dirty from being on the sidewalk, and his shirt and tie were untidy.

Ivan winced as he sat down. He explained to Brooklyn what had happened outside on the street, and why he wanted to keep it a secret. He was always entertained by his assistant's New York accent and her spunky attitude, but he also had the greatest possible appreciation for her talents.

"This attack on me proves that the work we've been doing is succeeding. We're on the path to something big. I think we're getting close, and we're not going to back off. Let's call the team together this afternoon for an information exchange and strategy meeting. Tell them how lucky they are not to have to find a new boss. In the meantime, if you'll excuse me, I'll change my clothes."

Ivan kept a packed suitcase and a change of clothes in his office, because on more than one occasion in his capacity as the ranking presidential security advisor, he had had to depart at a moment's notice for unexpected destinations. The worrisome part of the incident that had taken place that morning was its location – Washington, D.C. – in front of the gates to the White House. There was little doubt in his mind that both the target and the scene of the crime were to be a metaphor in support of the message that no one was safe anywhere or at any time. The attempt to kill him in front of the White House, one of the most secure places on earth, had to be part of a greater plan.

Ivan's mind was locked in on solving the why problem as he dressed himself in his spare clothes. He would be able to determine who was responsible for the attempt on his life if he could discern why he had been chosen to be the victim. The where and when elements of the equation were already known. He still had a few minutes to mull over the events before his daily meeting with POTUS.

"Damn it Ivan, we can't have my Security Advisor knocked off right in front of the White House!" The President had already heard about the attempt on Ivan's life. "How the hell would that look in the newspapers of the world?"

"Right, sir, or for that matter, how would it play at *my* house? Fortunately I was able to limit the news of the incident to just the few Marines on duty at the time."

"Are you sure the press corps didn't get wind of this?"

"Yes. No one was on the street at 6 AM. It all happened so quickly. I was knocked down, and before I could get to my feet the Marines shot the shooter and killed him. The boys got me inside the building immediately, and carried the gunman's body inside, too. His corpse is in the infirmary as we speak."

"How do you plan to proceed from here?"

"Well, Mr. President, it's obvious that whoever wants me dead wants it to be a national event. Why else would they do it here? I don't think we should give them the satisfaction. Let's not even mention the affair to anyone at all except to those who have a need to know and have top-secret clearance. I'd like *my* staff to handle the investigation as far as possible. We know what we've been working on, and we're the ones who should develop a suspect list. We're also capable of keeping it quiet."

The President sat back in his chair, stroking his chin while he pondered Ivan's words.

"I suppose since you were the intended victim, you're the one who has the most motivation to find the perpetrator. Even so, I encourage you to use the services of the FBI and the Secret Service. No sense being a lone wolf when there's so much help at hand."

"Yes, sir. I intend to work closely with the directors of those agencies."

"Good. Then I'll put you in charge of the investigation. By the way, which of your projects is the most likely to have made someone mad enough to want you dead?"

"Arms control," Ivan replied.

The President smiled. "My predecessor told me you were a pisser, and he was right."

"Yes sir. Thank you."

Ivan stood before the team of elite investigators and called the meeting to order. He had worked with them before, and he considered each one to be a close friend. But this was not the time for friendly chatter, and the group seemed to know it. All eyes were fixed on him as he began to speak.

"Brooklyn has already described to you the close call I had early this morning," he began. "It was an eye opener, I can tell you. Those of you who may have doubted the efficacy of the Kevlar bullet-proof vest can gather round and see the benefits of modern science first hand."

Ivan opened his shirt to reveal the angry bruises left by the bullets that had struck him. He did this to impress a visual image upon his team, so they wouldn't forget the seriousness of the matters they were dealing with.

"The President," he went on, "has given me permission to lead the investigation into the facts concerning this attack, and to bring the people responsible for it to justice. I'd like each of you to take an active part in this inquiry."

His listeners had all been introduced to him years before by Simeon Montcalf. This man, who had chosen to dub himself *God's Personnel Manager*, wasn't improperly named as far as Ivan was concerned, although he would never have admitted it to Montcalf himself. Simeon was retired now and living with his wife Julia, the former Secretary of State.

Ivan and Marina owed much to this couple. In a way Montcalf had been responsible for Ivan's meeting Marina, for he had sent him to Chechnya where she was a professor at the university. Montcalf had identified Ivan as someone special when he was just a young PhD student at Harvard, and had also been instrumental in arranging to get Marina and Ivan out of Chechnya and back to the U.S. He had been a witness when Ivan and Marina were married, and the other witness was Julia, the Secretary of State at the time. She was the woman who had kick-started Ivan's career, and the one for whom his daughter was named. In one of life's peculiar turnabouts Montcalf and Julia had developed an attraction for each other at Ivan and Marina's wedding, which eventually led to a wedding of their own. The foursome had become the best of friends, and now they were neighbors living in Georgetown.

Ivan still hadn't figured out how Simeon Montcalf's early identification system worked. All he knew was that if you were looking for a budding genius with a specific set of skills, Montcalf had the uncanny ability to cause the perfect candidate to suddenly materialize in the flesh. As far as Ivan could tell, Montcalf was incapable of doing anything himself, but he unfailingly came up with the ones who could.

One of Montcalf's finest recruitment jobs turned out to be David Feingold. The specifications for the search had been to find a super computer nerd with a PhD in math or statistics. Feingold was a product of the City University of New York. He loved to construct statistical models, computer algorithms, and computerized analysis tools, which skills had several times resulted in the saving of human lives in their thousands. He was Ivan's alter ego, but he also came equipped with neuroses. Getting him to move out of his parents' home in Brooklyn and move to Washington, D.C. was as troublesome as relocating the Statue of Liberty. Finally when that was accomplished, Ivan was free to address David's pathological fear of flying, which was a job akin to trying to stuff a recalcitrant Saint Bernard into a travel cage – lots of flying fur, foaming at the mouth, and gnashing of teeth. Feingold was truly fond of Ivan, however, and never hesitated to do anything for him once the trauma caused by the hated changes were subdued by the passage of time and the establishment of new replacement routines.

Another one of Montcalf's wunderkinder was Damian Rutledge, who, though no longer a *kind*, was still a wonder. Damian had been working in the CIA as an anti-terrorist analyst. Gradually his synthesis of historical terrorist events had been categorized and worked into a computer data bank that cross-referenced every known terrorist attack, using hundreds of pieces of data and relating each against all other such acts. It was amazing how often the details of one type of attack could be lined up with another, which inevitably led to the discovery of suspects and tactical trends. His knowledge was widely appreciated and used by Homeland Security agents from all the government agencies such as the CIA, FBI, ATF, DEA as well as T Men and military Intel officers. It took a presidential order to have him seconded to Ivan's group, but once the two began to work together it would have taken an act of Congress to separate them.

Then there was Abdul, the eldest son of a Yemeni tribal sheikh who had been sent to study linguistics at Yale. He had chosen to remain in the United States and had become a citizen after being infected by the viral twins, freedom and democracy. He served in the group as the Arabic language and cultural expert. His father had recently died, and by the Sharia laws of inheritance, he was now Sheikh Abdul. Many security workers were shocked into silence when they heard his title for the first time, but they had always known that he was one of the good guys who redeemed the reputation of Islam and gave hope that religious freedom could one day co-exist with the Arab world. His assistance had been invaluable in the affair of the caliphs in Mecca, for which he and Ivan and the others in the group had received presidential citations.

As for Ivan's assistant, Brooklyn, she was a long-term employee of the State Department and had been assigned to Ivan when he first arrived in Washington. She was selected to be Ivan's assistant because she was available, having run out of male bosses who could put up with having an assistant who was smarter than they were. But Brooklyn didn't have that problem with Ivan. Her brash manner, feisty personality and unrestrained impatience had made her a formidable legend in Washington government circles, enabling her to get just about anything she needed from recalcitrant civil servants who had the temerity to try to block her path. She was the only daughter of German-Jewish immigrants who retained a personal interest in Israel, so she had zero tolerance for political correctness when she was facing off against jihadist murderers. She didn't like having her boss shot, either.

Ivan was inclined to agree with his assistant on that one. It occurred to him one day to explore the idea of purchasing all the weapons in the hands of illegal arms traffickers, using U.S. defense funds for the purpose. He was so pleased with this notion that he decided to put his elite little group to work on a feasibility study. They weren't quite sure where their boss was going with this one, but they obediently rolled up their sleeves and divided up the work according to their various skills and experience.

Ivan hoped they'd come up with some suggestions for new policies that the President could implement in order to ease the situation in the Middle East. The options of killing and fighting had to be removed from the equation so that substantive peace negotiations could be given a chance to work. The situation was extremely vexing, for in the past every time a leader in the Arab world had shown even the slightest interest in a negotiated settlement of land issues in Palestine, the leaders of the Islamic extreme right would launch a massive attack that simply could not be ignored by the Israeli politicians, and negotiations would be broken off in favor of reprisals.

Ivan planned to get an update on the progress his team had made. He also intended to assign them an important second project, the results of which would, he hoped, supply the tools to develop a lasting peace once the opposing sides permanently stopped killing each other.

"So, as I was saying when I called this meeting to order," Ivan said as he buttoned up his shirt, "the President indicated to me that he wasn't happy that his National Security Advisor was shot on the very doorstep of the White House. And it obviously doesn't say much for the efficiency of the Security Advisor himself, if he permits such a thing to happen. What it does say clearly, however, is that the target and the location of the attack were chosen by the perpetrator to make a point. So let's take a minute to examine what the motivation of such a man, or men, could be. Who wants to begin? David, who do you think was responsible?"

"The obvious answer would be an Al Qaeda cell group, but that almost sounds too simple to mention."

David Feingold was Ivan's statistical and computer expert. He was Jewish and had family connections in Israel. He was always trying hard to be evidentiary in his thinking, and not just prejudiced against Islam. But working with Ivan had done little to improve his opinion of the Arab jihadists.

"Damian, what are your initial thoughts? Ivan asked.

"To me, this attack has the fingerprints of a gangland hit. You know, walk up to the bastard and pump him full of lead."

"I see, and in this case I would be the bastard."

"Correct," Damian smiled.

"How about you, Abdul? Who do you say should be given the credit or the blame?"

"Much as we Arabs would like to blame either the Jews or the Americans, in this case I find myself leaning towards a more specific conspiratorial group. One whose interests are more related to the current investigations that we're probing."

"Okay. And Brooklyn, what's your best guess?"

"I'd prefer not to guess, but if you insist, my opinion is a combination of Damian's and Abdul's conjectures. I think the shooter was a professional hit man who was working for one of the many enemies that you've managed to accumulate in the short time you've been here."

"Thank you for your valued opinions," Ivan said. "The President is allowing me to head up the investigation, and I'll need your support, as usual. I find it impossible to believe that the target and the venue of the crime were merely random or coincidental. The Security Advisor to the President of the USA would never be shot in front of the White House by accident. I think we can also assume we're doing something very annoying to someone important. I think we can take comfort in the fact that they didn't succeed. I know *I* do. It's a truism that in the security business if someone doesn't want to kill you, you're probably not doing your job properly."

"How come you were wearing a bullet-proof vest at six o'clock in the morning, anyway?" David asked.

"I could tell you I had a supernatural feeling that someone was going to take a shot at me," Ivan replied, "but that would be a lie. Or I could say my fantastic analytical abilities enabled me to predict an oncoming attempt on my life, but that would be a lie, too. The truth is, Brooklyn won't let me into my office unless I'm properly dressed for the occasion."

"Do you have the feeling they'll try again?" David asked, when the chuckles died down.

"I'd love to know the answer to your question," Ivan said. "But the more important thing is that we've struck a nerve with someone who wants us to discontinue our work so badly that he, or they, are willing to kill to stop us. We aren't going to let that happen. In fact we're going to intensify our efforts. And to respond to David's query about another possible attempt on my life, I'll be meeting with the Director of the Secret Service later to work out whatever preventive measures need to be taken to ensure there's no reoccurrence of this morning's incident. Now let's get down to business. I'd like to have a complete run-down on where we stand with our weapons project. We have a lot of work to do, so let's get started."

CHAPTER TWO

The meaning of his name was *One Who Pretends to be a Prophet*. In spite of his name, however, Maulana al-Matanabbi was revered in Islamic religious circles, but not because of his scholarship. During the time he was in public school he was intellectually unable to compete with the best students, who were all studying to be scientists, engineers, or businessmen. So he was sent to a Madrassa school operated by Wahabists, and was made to memorize the Koran, which was the only textbook used in the school. His soft, chubby face and body did not help to mark him as an outstanding person. As with so many other boys of the time, those who couldn't make it in one of the practical fields were slated to train for a career in religion.

Unfortunately for Maulana, and subsequently for the rest of mankind, his ego exceeded his abilities by a very wide margin. His academic failures ate away at him. Because of his poor performance at school, he knew he was destined to become the imam of a small neighborhood mosque in Egypt like his father before him, but his ambition made him wish to achieve much more than that. He had to work within the religious framework of the culture, however, because he was educated for nothing else. In his youth many of his peers found him to be conceited, interested in his own progress to the exclusion of everything else, and a narcissist of an undeniably high order.

Fortunately for him he became a large man, and his beard covered some of the weakness in his face. He worked in front of a mirror to develop a steely cold expression in his black eyes. He aspired to be a man to be reckoned with, whose personal standing would never be questioned – a man who would be instantly respected as one to whom wisdom and power had been given by divine authority.

When it came to thinking about himself, his appearance, his reputation, and how he could make the most of his career as a scholar of the Koran, Maulana was something of a genius. He worked consciously on his preaching skills. He adopted a cold, lofty manner that headed off anyone's assumption that he was just an ordinary country cleric. His narcissism allowed him to minimize the accomplishments of others and extol his own. He thought incessantly about how the Prophet Muhammad had used religion to gain temporal power.

When the Arabs had suffered defeat at the hands of the Israeli army it was too much for him to bear, and he became more and more radicalized. Gradually his rhetorical abilities and his superior bearing found him gaining the adulation of the public, and he was given ever more important positions in the jihadist movement. His ability to learn by reading and listening was impeded greatly by his need to be revered.

Maulana didn't have to create a unique Islamist philosophy, as it had already been done for him by his countryman, Sayyid Qutb, during the decades that Egyptian President Abdul Nasser held him prisoner. Qutb had founded the Muslim Brotherhood, which eventually gave rise to al Qaeda and the other violent practitioners of Islam, and these elements adopted Maulana as one of their own.

Like all solemn egomaniacs, Maulana was a skillful blame shifter. He was an expert at finding ways to blame the failures of Islam and the Muslim people on everybody but themselves. Over the years his impatience at the progress of Islam in the world, and consequently his own progress, led him to violent jihad as a way of bringing down those who opposed him. He regarded anyone who got in his way as an enemy of Allah, and had no compunctions at all about issuing fatwas condemning individuals, nations, or other religions to a fiery death.

Maulana reveled in the perks of his position. He loved the robes, hats, and even his own dark full beard that covered his ordinary Semitic features. He took pleasure in the enthusiasm of the crowds when he addressed them. His self-righteous statements affixing blame squarely on the Western democracies and on American ignorance and arrogance were capturing the hearts and minds of the believers. He was reaching an ever-increasing audience of fanatical young males who were disillusioned with the lack of hope and opportunities in their own society.

Moderate Muslims were severely criticized for being too cowardly to join Allah's great jihad, therefore many were embarrassed into supporting his growing militia of young fighters. His vitriolic, outspoken messages of hate were being subsidized by the local government authorities who feared that his growing power might be turned against them. They found it expedient to be supportive of his tirades against the West and any of his other targets, as long as he didn't put the blame for the sad state of Islam on them, the temporal leaders.

At the same time Maulana was distilling the firewater of jihad, Sheikh Mansurallah was using it to irrigate and grow his own terrorist organization. Mansurallah had fought as a jihadist all his life. He was what the Western devils referred to as an insurgent. He could afford to support himself using the inherited wealth left to him by his father. Thus he was that rare idealist who could fight purely for Islamic principles with no concern for the material spoils of war. He and his trusted comrades went wherever they were needed to fight for Islam, comfortably blending in with the local population regardless of national borders.

As he became more experienced in the guerilla style of urban warfare and the politics that surrounded it, he began to realize that Osama bin Laden's personalized style of putting a face to the message had only resulted in the leader's becoming a mark and a fugitive. Mansurallah's black-as-tar facial hair covered his features so completely that he would probably no longer even recognize himself if he were clean-shaven, but then neither would his enemies. His beard was a pan-Arab passport for him. Osama, however, was a prisoner of his own rhetoric and the fabrication of an Islamic public relations machine that portrayed him as a hero to the Arabs, but Public Enemy Number One to the West. Mansurallah, on the other hand, consciously used anonymity as his most important weapon for carrying out Allah's work.

Mansurallah's main wish was to be a man of action, not a figurehead. He wanted to actually fight, and his long lean body craved combat. He understood the tremendous costs in security measures that Osama bin Laden's inspiration had exacted upon the American economy, but Mansurallah simply couldn't shake his personal vision of himself and his cause. He would do the fighting and let Osama do the leading while Maulana did the preaching. His name, Mansurallah, meant *The Victory of Allah,* and he was firmly determined to live up to his name. He would emulate the Prophet Muhammad, praise be unto him, and strike all infidels and their sympathizers with the sword of Allah.

Circumstances had created a confluence of these two stars of the militant Muslim world, but in their opinion the rest of humanity was destined to end up in a black hole. The influence of some 1,300 years of socially accepted brigandage was on the side of ambitious men like Maulana and Mansurallah, who saw only that the West was richer than the Arab world. Custom and practice in the Middle East was simple – anyone not from your family, tribe, nation, or religion was fair game. Centuries of kidnapping, assassinating, murdering, pillaging, enslaving and robbing infidels was in-bred by the time their generation came along. Leaders like Maulana had no problem convincing their minions and cronies that Allah wanted them to cleanse the world of unbelievers. Likewise, warriors like Mansurallah had no trouble influencing young men to take up arms to bring the foreign devils to their knees.

It wasn't long before some prominent men in the Muslim Brotherhood arranged for these two very different leaders to meet to discuss ways that they could cooperate in ridding the Middle East of the Christians and Jews. After the ceremonial kissing, the two men sat down in the back room of Maulana's mosque.

"Welcome, my brother," the cleric said, deigning to bow slightly. "I have heard good things about you and your wish to serve the will of Allah."

"I, too, have heard how you inspire our people to seek justice and avenge the atrocities of the enemies of the Prophet, praise be unto him," Mansurallah replied, pleased to note that his brother Maulana had recognized the importance of his own position.

"Our mutual friends from Al Qaeda have long wished for us to meet and form a bond that would have synergisms for both our followers, as we try to evict the infidels and rid our lands of the home-grown puppets who govern us and cooperate with the Western devils," the imam remarked.

"I'm told," the desert warrior said, "That you have created a militia, and that you have many candidates for martyrdom. I can readily see the mutual benefits of combining our efforts in the holy name of Allah."

"That is true," Maulana agreed. "I can support your hard work with recruits and with funding. The young men in our Wahabist Maddrassah schools have been trained ever since childhood to seek martyrdom by giving their lives for Allah. They are waiting for their call, and many are impatient for their turn to come. It would not be wise for us to let their enthusiasm grow cool."

"That shall never happen to any young men in my training camps," Mansurallah assured him. "Send me the recruits and the funding, and I shall turn them into manly warriors who will prove themselves to be heroes on the battlefields of all the infidel countries of the world. The

Jews will be pushed into the sea, and the Zionists who support them will regret that they were ever born. But before they die, my jihadist armies will make them bow to the power of Allah, praise be unto him."

The conference continued in this vein, with both men vying for position while at the same time eagerly making promises for mutually beneficial ways to cooperate with each other. Neither the jihadist warrior nor the cleric was at a loss for flowery, self-congratulatory words to describe the epic success ensured by their faith in Allah.

The tea flowed as boasts and compliments were exchanged with unbridled enthusiasm. In the end it was decided that they would combine their efforts. Maulana would lead the way in spiritual matters, and Mansurallah, for his part, would bring glorious victories to the followers of the straight path.

CHAPTER THREE

Bradley was named after his grandfather, who had been a famous general in World War II. His mother had married Henry Burke, an Irishman with a silver tongue who had talked himself into a golden career on Wall Street. Bradley Burke inherited both the family solidity of an American military legend and the blarney-based wit of his father.

Brad was a popular student at Yale. A member of the Skull and Bones Society, he was connected to the top echelons of the University hierarchy from the time he was a freshman. His performance at Yale was not outstanding as far as his grades were concerned, but his popularity was second to none, and his glib tongue and debating skills were renowned among members of the student body.

Brad Burke was taller than average, and had the fine, blond, straight hair of a young man. He had a high forehead, intense blue eyes, a long straight nose, and an upper lip that bore the scar of a surgically repaired harelip. As soon as puberty was kind enough to give him whiskers sufficient to grow a moustache to cover his scar, he took advantage of that circumstance and was never again seen without his bushy lip protector. Over the years he learned to trim his moustache in different styles until he finally settled on the full model whose bottom edge paralleled his lip, extending the whole width of his mouth.

When he graduated from Yale University he decided to get an MBA and go into business. He was accepted by the

Harvard Business School, and it wasn't long before he found his particular métier. He was a negotiator. He could bring two divergent sides to the table and put together a deal no matter how far apart they were when they began. Brad was encouraged by his professors to stay on at Harvard and do a PhD. Professors always liked to have bright students enter the teaching profession because it bolstered their opinion of their own career choice.

Brad was not persuaded to follow this advice for several reasons, the first being that he was developing certain tastes that were very expensive. But almost equally important was the fact that academia was not exciting enough for him. Why teach others how to be successful competitors?

He was excited by the idea of making billion-dollar deals, and he wanted his business career to provide him with the opportunities to make such deals. Many Fortune 500 companies interviewed him, but he decided that big oil was to be his ticket to fame and fortune. So when he was offered a negotiator position with Paramount Petroleum, he snapped it up without a moment's hesitation.

In the first few months of his employment with the firm he was sent to various locations to deal with wildcatters. His skill in negotiating brought the company rights, leases, and agreements that were very lucrative, and he was rocketed up the corporate ladder. He was amused by how easy it had all been.

Along the road to success he became friends with a geologist who worked at a competing company and was a bright star in his own right. Peter Dunbar was a Canadian, educated in Alberta and working for a smaller competitor. Brad Burke and Dunbar had originally been opponents, each trying to get an oil exploration company in the Canadian North to consign future oil shipments to their respective refineries.

As they hung around in the tiny mining town waiting for the company to make its decision, they shared a bottle of Scotch and developed a healthy respect for each other.

Dunbar was not a particularly persuasive negotiator, but he was an extremely knowledgeable geologist, who, it was rumored, could smell oil under the ground or at the bottom of the ocean. The two of them realized that their skills complemented each other's, so one day Bradley told Peter that he would get Paramount to make him an offer of employment that he wouldn't be able to refuse.

The Canadian oil exploration company eventually opted for Peter's deal. It was one of the only times that Bradley hadn't come home with the bacon.

"Don't be glum, buddy," Peter had said. "The only reason I got the deal is because we Canadians are kind of envious of you guys south of the border. You're brash and smart and damn successful at everything you do. So all things being equal, if we have to choose between a Yank and a Canuck, we'd rather deal with fellow Canadians instead of always being overshadowed."

"Boy, that explanation was as smooth as butter," Brad laughed. "I'd say there's a good chance that you have negotiator's genes in you somewhere. There's hope for you yet, even if you are a Canadian."

"Get outta here," said Peter, taking a swipe at him.

Brad didn't really mind losing the transaction with the Canadian oil company, because when Peter finally decided to accept the job at Paramount Petroleum, Brad was convinced that they got a better deal by far than the small Canadian contract that he had lost. The two men became business associates and closed many highly profitable deals working in concert with each other.

The friendship they developed together extended to other very personal matters as well. Brad's silver tongue, forward manner, and excellent sense of humor were attractive to women. Peter Dunbar, although he was every bit as handsome as Brad in his own way, was shy around women, especially when he first met them. He came to rely on Brad to introduce him to girls, and Brad was a very dependable friend in these matters.

In time Peter began to grow envious of Brad for his success with women and for his success within the corporate hierarchy as well. He hid his feelings perfectly, however, and Brad was never really conscious of his secret jealousy. Negotiating was a field made for aggressive people who could search out subtle weaknesses in the people across the table. Brad was intelligent enough to recognize flaws in others, although he hadn't yet developed the strength of character to correct his own defects. The secret of his success lay in the fact that he could quickly determine the personal human desires of most people. His job, like those of his opposing negotiators, was to achieve a sweet deal that favored his company.

Seldom was there a deal in which the stakes and benefits were exactly equal. Brad's normal tactic was to give ground on the personal requests, but he usually would make up for that by gaining the corporate high ground. Sometimes it was as simple as losing at golf. More often than not it had to do with supplying favors to opposing negotiators, their bosses, or their stockholders, and quite frequently it called for procuring women for them.

Arab oil executives were especially vulnerable to this type of bargaining chip. Brad could never quite understand why guys who already had four wives wanted this kind of incentive to make deals. He supposed it explained why blondes had been invented.

Early on in his career he realized that the best source of beautiful young women suitable for entertaining his friends, clients, and negotiating adversaries was the film industry. This realization had occurred to him at the same time as his company had acknowledged his particular perspicacity by granting him a huge expense account.

The first time that he had understood the value to him of a Hollywood connection occurred while he was negotiating an offshore deal in Southern California. He was never sure whether the money boys of Hollywood had discovered him, or it was the other way around, but it became a marriage made in hell. Filmmakers were always on the lookout for investors to help them with the seed money to finance new productions. When the producers discovered that Brad held the keys to the oil vault and could be a large investor, he became the target of many petty financiers in the cinema business.

Along with money deals came the sleazy behind-the-scenes sex aspects of movie production. After a while it would have been easy for Brad to spend more time making movie deals than negotiating oil deals. He never lost his perspective, however. He could negotiate a one-billion-dollar oil deal in an afternoon, whereas film moguls spent years putting together a film project, and no film had ever yet grossed a billion dollars worldwide.

Selling stories and sex appeal was a big business, but the oil business was still king, and Bradley never forgot that. He was impressed by the symbolism of the Michelangelo painting on the ceiling of the Sistine Chapel, with God touching man with his extended finger and instilling life into his creation. Brad didn't quite think of himself as God, but he did feel he was giving the finger of life to the film producers.

His efforts at financing films were becoming quite sophisticated, and he was actually making money in his expense account. He doubted that very many corporate executives were showing a direct profit in their own expense accounts, and he was right about that. Naturally he kept his name, and his company's name off the list of credits that followed the showing of every film, but Bradley Burke was the *eminence grise* behind a large number of famous movies. He was also behind the making of a good many film stars, and an even greater number of fallen stars.

Since the earliest years of their production, Hollywood movies had been a hypnotic lure to young women seeking to make it in show business. From every place big enough to have a cinema, pretty girls who thought they had talent were being enticed into acting as a career. Brad guessed it was the ultimate trip for a narcissist. To see one's face on the big screen and to enjoy the attendant fame and money was irresistible to many incipient Miss Americas.

But the odds of making it in Hollywood were far worse than those of a wildcatting driller finding oil, and the odds of that were already bad enough.

It was a cliché – small town girl full of hope, and full of herself, comes to Tinsel Town to set the place on fire. In the end it eventually becomes clear that she has put herself on the down escalator to dissolution.

It all begins with a girl meeting someone who claims he can help her get a part in a movie, and it quickly proceeds to the casting couch. It results in her getting into bed with a show business figure that claims to be able to help, but can't or doesn't. This then leads to jobs as an escort, model, porn actress, prostitute, and eventually to becoming a drug addicted floozy. Bradley Burke understood the reality of the world of make believe. He could have found his way to the top of that fetid pile, but he chose a different path.

Cynical opportunists who preyed on the hopes and dreams of small town girls never gave up their feeding frenzies around the latest crop of show business groupies. Brad was a more capable of turning aspiring actresses into victims than were any of the usual show business types, but his moral make-up didn't permit him to intentionally do evil things.

Ironically Bradley was closer to movie star quality in appearance and demeanor than most of the scruffy, poorly-educated, self-appointed star-makers that exploited such women. His Ivy League education, suave personality, and the fact that he actually had money and connections, assured his success with women. As the stand-out performer in the group of stage door johnnies, Brad had the pick of the litter whenever he entered the market. In a few cases, after they had served his purposes, he had actually furthered the careers of budding actresses.

There were sadder, more frequent cases, however, that ended badly for the women with whom he became involved. On two separate occasions when he had arranged for some OPEC delegates to meet young starlets, the men liked the girls so much that they kidnapped them and took them back to the Middle East with them in their private aircraft. Brad didn't approve of these tactics and wanted no part in them, but with Arab royalty the harem was always beckoning.

Doris Brightman was one of those hopeful Hollywood girls that Brad introduced to Peter Dunbar. Unfortunately for Peter, she was the one he chose to marry. She came to be known as DeeDee, and she was an underhanded, calculating, envious woman who had it in for Brad since the beginning, after he rejected her overtures and passed her off to Peter.

She really should have had no complaints. Peter took care of her royally. Although he was always just one step behind Brad at the company, he still earned a paycheck in the seven figures. She lived in a mansion and lacked nothing materially. Nonetheless, DeeDee coveted Brad's position for her husband. She resented Brad for having spurned her, and it was always secretly gnawing away at her.

When Bradley Burke eventually became the Chairman of Paramount Petroleum, the Hollywood connection began to pay off in other ways. With Brad's encouragement, movies favoring the political positions of big oil were written, produced, and targeted to specific audiences. Subtle, soft messages were being subliminally inserted into commercial films, and the results were better than any previous public relations campaigns.

The unlikely partnership of oil and movies was taking on proportions never before conceived of by either industry. Until Brad's ascension to the top job at Paramount, no previous CEO had ever played so successfully with the principles of the law of supply and demand. His uncanny ability to read the secret desires of men and women extended to the subsequent effects that the fulfillment of their personal covert cravings had on the international market for oil. Thus if the pursuit of power was the principal motivator of those in charge of a particular petroleum region, Brad was able to interpret the effects that gaining or losing control of their resources by certain local players would have on the greater market for oil products.

Over the years Brad became the man whom the leading Arab government and oil business officials preferred to deal with on the most important matters. His colleagues in the Oil Producer's Association used him as a living resource when it came to knowledge of the political and economic situation in the Middle East.

Nowhere was a negotiator appreciated as much as in the Arab world. For centuries all business had been conducted in Muslim countries as a face-to-face bargaining session. Whether buying a watch or a multi billion dollar oil field, the transaction was the same as it was in a bazaar. This kind of negotiating was not every American businessman's cup of tea. Brad, however, had made himself the master of this sort of dealing, and was greatly respected by the most important Arab figures.

Mostly the issues came down to a balancing act between the availability of crude oil and its price per barrel on the world futures market. The Saudi six thousand member royal family, which sits both literally and figuratively on a large portion of the world's oil supply, was a case in point. Before foreign geologists discovered oil, the Arabs were just a bunch of tribal marauders operating in the desert. When Western engineers showed them how to extract, process, export, and finally how to sell their product to an oil-thirsty world, they proved to be very fast learners. Gradually they realized the power and influence they held by virtue of just sitting atop the greatest pool of black gold in the world.

Step by step the Saudis learned the fine art of modern day financial marauding from the British and American oil pioneers. The Saudi royal family eventually nationalized the oil business in their country and took over control of it, injecting into the struggle the old, arcane tribal elements of family conflicts. Matters of royal succession to power were conducted through factional alliances, assassinations, and religious manipulations on a scale unknown since the days of the prophet Muhammad.

Eventually, by resorting to price-controlling threats and maneuvers, they managed to bring a number of other oil-producing nations into the OPEC cartel, through which they managed the world economy by manipulating the supply of crude oil in such a way as to control world prices, thereby enriching themselves to an incredible degree. They spread the responsibility for oil price increases by inviting other oil-producing nations into the organization, thus taking the general focus off the obvious geopolitical aspirations that were growing behind the scenes.

Using the powerful tsunami of incoming currency from the petroleum business, they entered into a cash caliphate that has had enormous influence in the growing economy of the world. During the splashy beginnings of Arab royal financial decadence, the Sheikhs arrived on American and British shores to buy fleets of Cadillac cars and warehouses full of merchandise. They took over entire floors of our medical facilities to house their entourages while a royal patriarch underwent surgery, or with their acquisitive natures they bought not just the goods in stores, but the stores themselves. In time, however, the fires of overt greed were subdued by excess. Their sins became subtler and therefore more serious.

The next wave of their financial attentions was directed toward high finance. They began to use their enormous oil revenues to buy up shares in solid international companies. Little by little their wealth was diversified in investments throughout the economy of the West.

Sharia traditions recommend partial ownership as a means of debt repayment instead of interest charges. The Prophet warned of usury, but didn't specifically proclaim against dividends, stock splits, and the many other corporate instruments of modern high finance that euphemize our greed so that it resembles ordinary business conduct.

In the big picture, however, the love of money had once again found the loopholes in the laws and reestablished its hegemony over yet another tribe of humanity. No race of people knows how hard it is to manage great wealth in a holy way until they first have it.

Bradley Burke, because of his excellent connections, straddled the petroleum world and found himself in bed with the most venal partners that history had ever evolved. His chief financial officer had been warning him that mysterious Middle Eastern investors were acquiring large blocks of shares in Paramount Petroleum via the stock markets of the world. The number of investors with exceedingly large dollar holdings was steadily increasing as the overall number of investors was decreasing, and yet no single investor in a publicly-traded stock ever managed to possess the 10% maximum ownership allowed without registering the fact with the regulators.

According to the CFO at Paramount, Brad Burke's tactic of floating occasional new stock issues, which should have widened the stockholder base, only worked temporarily. It did increase the overall value of the company, but the long-term results of selling these stocks didn't change the ownership demographics, and the largest blocks were still held by the same Arabs who were now hiding behind corporate entities. Most of the largest and most successful companies in the world could have noticed the same pattern on their stockholder registers.

Foreign investments in major Western economies were beginning to flow in at an unprecedented rate. Government economists decided to congratulate the free enterprise system for encouraging foreign investment, and Wall Street happily received the new money, flattered that market economics was succeeding so well.

The motivations of the new Arab investors, however, were neither theoretical nor benign. They had studied the rules of the game, and being interested in winning, they used the regulations to ensure that they ended up with all the marbles.

If Islam could manage to conquer the infidel world by economic means instead of by military victories, then why not use financial tactics? Secular Islam's script for the fall of the West called not for a massive financial crash but a steady draining of the blood of the American economy.

The greedy, impatient hotheads who couldn't stand the anonymity of an economic conquest and couldn't wait for the inevitable peaceful financial takeover, formed the terrorist groups that wanted the glory of a bloody victory and the personal fame that would go along with it.

Wiser heads were patient, but also traveled incognito. The smart ones, the real movers and shakers, permitted the wild insanities of the militants because they were moving things in the right direction. Their violent activities also kept these extremists busy enough to distract them from turning their attention toward their own nefarious schemes.

The logic of the elders of Araby was not to pay with Arab blood to attain Allah's revenge on the infidels – not when they could buy their capitulation in time and use the infidel's own resources to pay for it.

Many cynical leaders in the Western world embraced the callous belief that nothing else mattered as long as the system lasted to the end of the present generation, since they personally would not be around to see the results of the fall of the American economic empire.

The loss of religious faith on the part of most Europeans and many North Americans had removed the moral spine from their governments. Materialism, short-term gains and hedonistic pleasures were substituted for the principles that had once made them great.

Behind the daily struggles was a continuing spiritual battle of monumental proportions. The hearts and minds of men and women were being forced to choose between good and evil, between freedom and submission, and between responsible decisions and cowardly inaction.

No leader had come forward to conduct the democratic world out of the ferment.

CHAPTER FOUR

Ivan Welland's elite little group had gathered around the coffee table in his office to discuss his strategy for dealing with the latest problems emerging from the enemy camp. They sat waiting for him to gather his thoughts, poised to receive one of their boss's "big picture" speeches. They were about to get a snapshot of one of the biggest.

"No one has the right to take a human life," Ivan began, pausing for a moment to look at the alert and expectant faces of his friends seated around him. "Even Isaac Asimov's robots had this declaration programmed into them. If we substitute a person for a robot in Asimov's first law of robotics, we get this statement: *A person may not injure a human being or, through inaction, allow a human being to come to harm.*

"Why, then," Ivan asked rhetorically, "can't mankind learn this lesson? How is it that a man can feel free enough to walk toward me, look me in the eye, and shoot me? Since it is God who made us, and not we ourselves, how do we get permission to kill a creature that *we* didn't create? Although we're not theologians by any stretch of the imagination, we're still going to come face to face with this question and others like it as we proceed with the enormous project I have in mind. I intend eventually to install a plan that owes its origins to Asimov."

The team had grown accustomed to being summoned on short notice like this to attend one of Ivan's meetings. These conclaves were always exciting because their boss was a man who liked to challenge them with his original, creative ideas for solving problems. Not only that, he was not afraid to walk into hell for a heavenly cause, as Don Quixote had once put it. Undoubtedly there were powerful people in the world who had no interest in reducing violence and achieving peace, no matter how strong the logic of the peacemakers. These were the real enemies, and it was far from easy to tell who and where they were, even those in the U.S., and there were many.

"What do you think is the primary purpose of our work in this department of the government?" Ivan asked them that day. "Anybody?"

Each of them imagined that his piercing eyes were staring at them personally, and it made them uneasy. It was Damian who finally answered.

"We've all been given a mandate to advise the President on how the government can make its citizens more secure."

"That sounds about right," Ivan agreed. "So how do we accomplish that?"

This time nobody replied.

"Okay. Then let me tell you a story. When I was a little boy, maybe ten years old or so, something happened that may be instructive in this case. I was outside, playing with some neighborhood friends. We'd just seen a movie about the Three Musketeers, and we were dueling with a bunch of sticks we'd found lying around. Eventually, of course, one of the boys got poked in the eye. It was pretty awful for all of us.

"Anyway, the injured boy was taken to the emergency room of a nearby hospital. When we got home, my mother was furious. She ran around and collected the sticks from all the boys and burned them in our fireplace. Then she gave us a stern lecture, and warned us never to even *consider* doing anything like that again or we'd have *her* to deal with. I'd never seen her so mad before in my whole life.

"In case you're wondering, the boy didn't lose the sight of his eye. But he was very lucky, and so was I. As you may have guessed, I was the kid with the longest arms, and I was the one who poked him.

"So to sum it all up, my plan to make American citizens more secure is based on this childhood incident. Simply put: no weapons, no injuries."

"Then if I read you correctly," Brooklyn remarked, "you're talking about some sort of arms control."

"That's partly right."

"But we already have a nuclear arms control pact," Damian commented.

"Right again. And has it worked?"

"Yes, for those nations who signed on."

"Well, how many people have died as a result of nuclear weapons since the agreement went into effect?"

Damian thought for a moment, "Probably none."

"I'd have to say, then, that the agreement was worthwhile. Wouldn't you?"

"I guess so, but I'm not really sure if it was the agreement itself, or the threat of reprisals from the United States that kept the nuclear peace."

"Does it matter which?" Ivan asked him. "The important thing is that we haven't had any loose nukes flying around the planet. But you've brought up two important points, Damian. First, why haven't all the nations signed on? Second, if the fear of U.S. reprisals is the only deterrent – the only reason why nations aren't using weapons of mass destruction – then is this a good thing or a bad thing?"

"I think I know what you're getting at," David replied. "It's dangerous to put all our eggs in one basket and depend on one nation to provide security for everyone in the world. But nuclear weapons aren't the only problem. We've had millions of deaths for one reason or another through the use of masses of destructive weapons, if not weapons of mass destruction."

"My point exactly," Ivan said. "When we outlawed nukes, most of the belligerent nations in today's world were miles away from having any. Now we have Iran, Korea, and others carrying on as though they invented them. Meanwhile they're doing a terrific job of making do with conventional weapons."

"So what are you proposing, boss?" Brooklyn asked.

"For purposes of review, and in the simplest of terms, our challenge comes in two parts. Part A is how to remove all the killing tools, and Part B is how to provide the world with a peaceful alternative to the violent resolution of conflicts. So we have to put our thinking caps on, and we have to do this right. No errors, no loose ends. We'll have to sell it to POTUS first, and then to the world."

"How are we going to do that?" Abdul wanted to know.

"I thought you'd never ask," Ivan smiled. "What we need is a completely new universal weapons policy. I'm suggesting that we formulate such a policy and submit it to the President as soon as possible."

Brooklyn had been Ivan's assistant for several years now, and they had developed a system of communication that worked for them. Every now and then it called for her to act as a straight man, and she was pretty sure that now was one of those times.

"I don't suppose you have any ideas about how we can begin to create such a policy," she said.

The idea had been percolating in Ivan's head for some time now, ever since he had come across a comment that had been attributed to Albert Einstein. He quoted it for the team.

"I don't know what weapons we'll use to fight World War III, but World War IV will be fought with sticks and stones."

"Albert Einstein was supposed to have said that," Ivan continued, "but I'm not altogether sure he was right. Many people harbor this fear, but I'm not inclined to agree with their position. Of course, Einstein was a lot closer to it than I was because I wasn't even born till after 1945, and the same is true for most of the hotheads who are rattling their centrifuges now. Anyway, I think for the moment we should focus our attention on cutting back on conventional weapons rather than nuclear weapons. If we do it right and don't mess up, the nukes will take care of themselves by following their non-nuclear brothers into obsolescence.

"Great thinkers of the past were not omniscient," Ivan went on, "any more than the people of our day. I don't believe that World War III is inevitable, and I don't think, either, that on the continuum of the creation cycle it's going to be necessary to start all over again from scratch in order to make progress. Mankind is traveling lineally from one age to another – it's not marking time or going back over the same ground. What I *do* worry about, though, is that the threat of a nuclear holocaust will be sufficient to frighten mankind into giving up its loftiest ideals, its precious freedoms, and its hope for an honorable peace.

"All eyes at the various security agencies are focused on the nuclear threat. Developments in uranium enrichment in Iran and North Korea have galvanized the world into a perpetual state of paranoia. The government and the media seem jointly to believe that the refusal of these countries to accept arms inspectors equates with having nuclear bombs at their fingertips. It's just as likely that these rogue nations refuse inspections because they're afraid to let anyone know how inept their nuclear efforts really are."

Ivan, in his position as National Security Advisor to the President, was vigilant. But he also suspected that the main threat to the United States was not necessarily nuclear in nature, but might come from other weapons of mass destruction or from the employment of the incredible masses of conventional weapons that exist in parts of the world where they do the least good. Diverting the attention of the audience is a magician's main trick, and Ivan suspected that these nuclear necromancers actually had other plans.

"Why would a country like Iran, with its enormous oil deposits, bother to build expensive nuclear plants when they could just as well have oil-fired facilities at a fraction of the cost? Obviously, Iran's national goal is to attain hegemony over the Islamic world. If it can divert the world's attention to the proliferation of nuclear weapons and keep the specter of the horror of the irreversible effects of radioactivity in the forefront of the minds of the diplomats, Iran can make a political and religious power grab in the Middle East with conventional weapons which they have in profusion, rather than nuclear weapons, which they may not have anyway.

"All Iran has to do is convince the world that they *might* have nuclear weapons, and the world would be so grateful to them for not using these weapons that they would be seen as heroes instead of fanatics. Then they could use the money they save by *not* going nuclear to purchase other cheaper, less detectable weapons of mass destruction, or to buy more conventional weapons to arm the masses of Islam in their own country and in other countries as well.

"If Iran can convince the Americans and the Israelis that they have nuclear research facilities deep under the ground, then they don't really need to have them in their arsenal to receive the benefit of pretending to have them. It's a typical, classical propaganda tactic, but I seem to be alone in these suspicions. My doubts that the attacks that have been promised by the terrorists would be nuclear in nature don't preclude our being alert to other types of attack. The heads of other government agencies disagree with me, and the funding and energies of their departments are mostly being directed to prevent a nuclear conflagration, or if such a catastrophe happens, to deal with the aftermath.

"Nuclear bomb development requires large investments in machinery, and time-consuming enrichment procedures using expensive uranium derivatives. These items, and the enormous amounts of money they cost, can't be hidden from view. It's just about impossible to conceal radioactivity from the sensitive detection equipment that we have on hand today. Delivering nuclear weapons requires expensive, technologically advanced missile conveyance systems."

Ivan paused for a moment to take a drink of water, then he continued his presentation.

"No doubt there's a great deal of interest in these matters in the Middle East and Asia, but at least in Islam the preferred standard operating procedures have so far been very efficient, very secretive missions involving people as weapon deliverers such as the would-be assassin who shot me. Expensive missile development with inertial guidance systems is sophisticated technologically and therefore very impressive, but attacks with this kind of weapon might as well have their return address pinned to them. It's simply impossible to launch long range or inter-continental missiles without exposing the launch site to counter strikes.

"It's much more in keeping with jihadist psychology to win by using treachery. It's a whole lot cheaper, and it has the added attraction of making the victim feel stupid for having allowed himself to be tricked. The idea of making the infidels appear naïve and dumb has always enhanced the pleasure of the extremist Islamist conspirators. There's also the practical side of it, too. Unidentified suicide bombers are not so easily traced back to their sources. For this reason the Islamists have always opted for small, secret investments with large-scale payback potential. Changes in Islamist jihadist operational philosophy would make me very suspicious, but I haven't detected any such changes yet.

"What if these guys have decided to concentrate their talk on nuclear attacks while they put their efforts into something else entirely? The lemming-like preferences of the media for stories about nuclear preparations on the part of Iran and the North Koreans raises questions in my mind.

"Is there a reason for the media and for some government spokesmen to espouse an almost unanimous desire to emphasize the dangers to America from nuclear attack, to the exclusion of all other possible methods of aggression? What ever happened to biological weaponry as a means of attack? Is the threat of anthrax poisoning dormant now? Only a few years ago it was hyped by the media, but you never hear anything about this sort of thing any more.

"Maybe we're going overboard with our technological prowess. Maybe it's time for us to take another approach. If you think back to the 9/11 attacks, it's obvious that they were successful because they were simple and audacious, and in keeping with the marauding mindset of Al Qaeda, not because they were technologically sophisticated. So perhaps we should concentrate our attention on conventional weapons, rather than on nuclear ones."

"Excuse me Ivan, but wouldn't it be even harder to halt the spread of conventional weapons than it would be to stop nuclear proliferation?" Damian asked. "I mean, there's so much money to be made in providing weapons to both sides of any conflict. It's hard to put a lid on all the greed."

"That's an excellent question," Ivan replied. "Should we be trying to put a lid on greed? Should we be trying to appeal to people's higher nature? I'd like to hear from all of you on this subject. Let's get down to the nitty gritty and have a general discussion."

Ivan smiled to himself as he caught a quick glimpse of what appeared to be relief on the part of his audience. He knew very well that his team members were bright young people who found it hard to sit still for long introductions. But he wanted them to feel that they were part of the solution he was seeking, not just a group of yes-men following his lead. And this, Ivan knew, would require a careful build-up and a fair bit of patience on his part.

"There are conventional weapons all over the Middle East," David moaned. "Home made bombs, automatic rifles, rocket launchers, you name it. Every household has a store of them in the basement."

"Every mosque, too," Abdul pointed out. "Weapons are as common as flies, and probably more accessible than food or water."

"Where do all these weapons come from?" Ivan asked.

The answer seemed so obvious that nobody ventured to say anything. They all felt as if they were back in school again, being lured by the teacher into some embarrassing situation by a trick question.

"There are arms dealers everywhere, in every country of the world," Damian said, to keep the discussion rolling. "It would be hard to shut them all down, too, even if we knew where they were."

"You're right," Ivan agreed. "You're absolutely right. So let's scratch that idea. Let's just put ourselves in the shoes of your average young jihadist warrior for a minute. What happens when he runs out of ammunition?"

"I see where you're going with this," said David, his eyes lighting up. "We should take away the ammunition and leave the guns alone. There are many fewer explosives manufacturers than there are gun makers, so the chore of locating and closing them down would be a whole hell of a lot easier."

"There you go, David," Ivan said. "Why don't we put some numbers on it? Find out if this works demographically like crime, where 10% of the criminals account for 80% of the serious crimes. Brooklyn, get hold of the military budget and see how much we spend on explosives and ammunition. Abdul, put on a blitz and find out everything you can about illegal arms smuggling. Damian, you help Abdul. We need to know the identities of the largest smugglers, the routes they generally use, and the financial side of this dirty business, and anything and everything else we need to know to shut these people down permanently. Abdul, put your ear to the sand and find out what type of weapons and explosives the terrorists are acquiring, and the latest info on the progress of nuclear weapons development in Iran."

Ivan looked with satisfaction at his little team as they scrambled to take notes.

"David and I will work together to create the algorithms," he continued, "and we'll set up the software that you'll need to analyze the data. Concentrate your efforts on the explosives and the ammunition manufacturers and get me a detailed overall picture of the munitions industry, but try to keep a low profile. It seems to me that the people who make explosives would be singularly averse to any nearby explosions that could ignite their factories. Brooklyn, you act as secretary-facilitator to the team. Handle all the coordination with the other government agencies and help me pull all this information together so we can evolve a program for violence containment that we'll soon be able to present to POTUS."

The meeting lasted most of the afternoon, but when it was over the team was focused on the huge job they had in front of them. With the work assignments made, Ivan began to think about the other aspects of his developing plan. All sorts of questions arose in his mind about where the opposition to his plan would come from, and what incentives could be offered to make people, corporations, and governments wish to cooperate. Everything so far had to do with Part A of his plan. He had not yet begun to think about Part B.

CHAPTER FIVE

The meeting between Maulana al-Mutanabbi and Sheikh Ibn Mansurallah had been long overdue. Separately these men had been fighting Allah's battle against the infidels for years. Each man was using the tools he had been given by Allah to pursue Islamic hegemony throughout the world. Maulana employed the pulpit to incite his vast captive audiences to strike out against the infidel dogs. Mansurallah utilized modern military weapons, tactics, and explosives to proclaim Islam by terrorizing its enemies into the submission required by the Koran.

Together with their minions the two terrorists comprised formidable forces, but until this meeting they were separate and uncoordinated in their efforts. Linking the power of the word with the power of arms would bind Islam together, and that was the purpose of the meeting of these two personalities. Since both men professed to have but one purpose – to bring the world to its knees before Allah – there was little reason for them not to reach an accord.

The most extreme interpretation of the Koran was the one espoused by these two leaders of the jihad in the Middle East. When Sadat, Begin, and Carter reached their infamous and disgraceful accord, both Maulana and Mansurallah had been children, but children who were students of the imams on the far right. They had gloried in the assassination of the Egyptian leader, Anwar Sadat. Their teachers had filled their heads with hatred for any who would make peace with the hated Jews and their supporters, the satanic Americans. They believed that this particular agreement was the work of the Great Satan, and must be abrogated in order to harness and consolidate the power of Islam and restore Palestine to its rightful Arab owners.

Any Muslims who didn't agree with the jihadist extremists were deemed to be cowards, worthy of summary execution. Arabs not actively fighting for Allah were expected to give financial aid to the cause, as well as any other support that might be sought from them by the warriors. This assistance might take the form of silence, shelter, food, information, and cover stories, and if refused, would not be forgotten or forgiven. Penalties for failure to back the jihad were as likely to be exacted from the families of the reticent, as they were from the overtly uncooperative ones themselves. Overbearing duress was applied to any Arab not enthusiastically in support of jihad in its most extreme form.

A particularly sore point with Maulana was the Al Aqsa Mosque in Jerusalem. That the third holiest site in Islam should be in territory controlled by the Israelis was simply unthinkable for him. That the Dome of the Rock should be located on land shared with the infidels was a perpetual irritant, since it was the holy place from which Muhammad and his horse had journeyed to the skies in order to instruct the other prophets of Allah at their meeting in heaven. The fact that the Al Aqsa Mosque had originally been part of the Hebrew Temple of Solomon and then remodeled as a church *before* it had metamorphosed into a mosque was something that Maulana never calculated into his reckonings. For many centuries the mosque had been a derelict building, until the moment when Israel became a nation. Never mentioned in the Koran, Al Aqsa (its name translates to *the furthest*) only became a religious focus for the Arabs *after* the Israelis reclaimed the Great Temple of Solomon.

The Islamic clerics created the legend of its holiness to instill the power of religious fervor into their political claim for the territory that is now Israel. It was not so amazing that the infidels didn't agree with this view of proprietorship, but any land, building or object that had ever belonged to an Arab, even the *furthest*, was an Arab possession for eternity according to Islam, and was therefore a non-negotiable item for them. Al Quds, the Arabic name for Jerusalem, belonged solely to the Palestinian Arabs, and they believed that no Arab should rest until it was theirs once again. The world seemed to forget that for hundreds of years the Arabs hadn't cared a whit for the Palestinians, until the foundation of the nation of Israel. Then, and only then, did Islam discover the religious significance of Palestine.

Whether the mosque had been returned to Islam via war, terror, bargaining, or by theocratic fiat, both Maulana and Mansurallah wanted to keep it in their possession to an equal degree – the nth degree. Maulana preached that Muhammad wanted the mosque to be a Muslim shrine like those in Mecca and Medina, and therefore since the Jews wouldn't give up their claim to it, they must be put to the sword. The logic of Mansurallah's arguments, although more militaristic than Maulana's theological ones, led to the conclusion that the Jews must be driven into the sea, and the State of Israel wiped off the map. If the two men could achieve their goal by cooperating with each other, there would be glory enough to go around.

It was hardly any wonder that the meeting of Maulana and Mansurallah went so well. Their minds worked as one. They were soul brothers. During their conference their tenets, their objectives, and their methods were meshed together. There was a good deal of swaggering and posturing in their Arab rhetoric, but there was no doubt that either of these men would have gladly died to achieve the holy objective of the universal ascendancy of Islam. The end result of their talks was a single overall strategy, but one that left lots of room for independent tactical creativity. They knew that they were facing a massive, worldwide enemy that could not be crushed in a single battle. They were aware that their greatest weapon was patience. They would stay on the offensive, but they would pick their fights so that they always had the advantage of surprise.

They kept Muhammad's dictum in the forefront of their minds, namely that whichever side was the most committed always wins the battle, in spite of the relative size of the forces of the combatants. Maulana's sermons fired the spirits of their adherents, and Mansurallah's generalship employed them as warriors for Allah. They were indeed a strong team, and their commitment to victory was total.

Mansurallah wanted to ensure Allah's supremacy in the world in order to have the honor of living up to the meaning of his name, *the victory of Allah*. Some days after his meeting with Maulana, the Arab terrorist had entered the lobby of the Palm Desert Resort on the shore of the Red Sea, not too far from the Israeli city of Eilat. Mansurallah and his cadre of killers in gas masks were anything but relaxed. They had shot and killed two civilian guards that had been stationed on the periphery of the resort. The silencers provided by an arms smuggler had substantially quieted the shots, and Mansurallah hoped that no one inside the building had heard the noise.

The gas-dispersing equipment had evidently worked, as there were now several unconscious bodies strewn about the lobby. The assailants immediately began placing their charges according to the verbal directions of the demolition expert in their midst. They were hurrying as fast as they could go, while Mansurallah and some other heavily-armed jihadists impatiently stood guard, looking like alien beings in their gas masks. They were to deter any people who might approach the resort, or shoot anyone inside who woke from their induced sleep before the terrorists finished their lethal assignment.

The armed attackers were trying to move silently. They wanted to transact their deadly business and head back to the desert as soon as possible. They didn't want to be involved in a loud gunfight that would alert people in the resort just down the road.

When they were finished they quickly filed out of the building, running to the desert's edge a few hundred yards behind the building. The chief demolition expert handed the small radio-controlled detonator to Mansurallah so that he, as their leader, could be the one that destroyed the infidel house of sin. Mansurallah depressed the button, setting off a series of explosions that rocked the night and filled the sky with orange fire, lighting the desert sands with bright flashes and sending smoke billowing high above the building. The assailants walked away like crabs, scuttling diagonally so they could watch their handiwork while they moved quickly toward the safety of the desert.

It seemed to them as though the roof had lifted off the eight-story building, but in actuality what had happened was that the charges had blown the vertical supports from under the roof, and for a second the roof stood unsupported until it collapsed on the rubble beneath it. There was no sign of life, no screams – just the blinding fire, the deafening noise, and the acrid smell of the burning buildings with the nuanced roasted odor of flesh from the burning corpses.

Mansurallah was disappointed. Obviously the mission had been a success, but he felt that the hated Jews, who were enjoying their vacations and sleeping their ugly heads off, should have been made to suffer. This manner of killing was too kind to an enemy that deserved no consideration. He tried to console himself with the thought that they had probably killed everyone in the building. It had been estimated that there would be 175 guests and a few resort employees inside. If they made their escape safely with no casualties in their own ranks, their attack would place them in the top ten terrorist strikes of all time.

It would also mark the advent of a new weapon in Allah's arsenal: the sleep eradicator. Mansurallah was proud of his invention, for it would save the lives of many of the faithful soldiers of Allah. In appropriate future missions they wouldn't have to attack directly. If they could get access to the ventilation system of a targeted building they could put all the inhabitants to sleep, then they could destroy the building and kill everyone in it with no interference from anyone.

He resolved to begin training some of his men to be both air conditioning and ventilation mechanics at once. Placing them with firms in the HVAC repair business all over the Middle East would give him access to hundreds of targets. Yes, this little raid launched from the Sinai would presage many larger and even more successful ones in the near future, if he had anything to do with it. But first he must concentrate on making his escape from the vaunted Israeli Defense Force.

CHAPTER SIX

O n the recommendation of his staff, Ivan Welland had arranged to meet Brad Burke in his office at 6 AM in order to accommodate the oilman's scheduled trip to the Middle East. He would try to cover what was on his mind as quickly as possible so that Burke could be on his way. The two men shook hands, took seats, and looked each other over. Brad led off with a quip designed to show friendliness and respect.

"What incentives did you use to get your secretary to come to work before six in the morning?"

"The usual ones," Ivan said. "I wave the flag, and tell her that Uncle Sam needs her."

"And that's all it takes! I must try that on my people."

"Well, let's see if it works on you first," Ivan smiled.

"Fair enough. So… what can I do for Uncle Sam?"

Brad leaned comfortably back in his seat. He had heard reports that Ivan had carried out some incredible feats of bravery, even heroism, coupled with some brilliant strategic calculations during his tenure with the State Department. Now, as National Security Advisor to the President of the United States, he was expected to accomplish even greater things for his country. It seemed to Brad that he was very young to have had such a stellar career in the White House, where competition was furious and back-stabbing was the order of the day. This guy either knew the right people, or he was a budding genius.

"Well, to start with you can hear me out," Ivan replied. "Then you can give me your honest opinion of a plan that

I'm hoping will have a positive effect on reducing the violence in the Middle East and elsewhere."

"A worthy ambition. I'll do my best."

"I'm afraid I'll have to ask you to keep our conversation in the strictest confidence, at least for a little while."

"I can be trusted."

Sensing that Brad was going to be able to put patriotism above price gouging and profiteering, Ivan decided to go on. It was possible that Islamic terrorism, along with the chaos it created, worked to keep oil prices at an all time high, and this was obviously good for the petroleum business.

Ivan decided to watch Brad's face carefully as he outlined his plan. He was hoping to detect his inner thoughts by reading his facial expressions, which was exactly what Brad was hoping to do with Ivan.

Looking Brad straight in the eye, Ivan began to explain his idea that the secret of a successful peace arrangement in the Middle East involved first and foremost a complete halt to the shooting.

"I'm told that you're a very good negotiator," Ivan said. "You've struck many deals with the Arabs, and you've even managed somehow to get them to hold up their end of the bargains."

"That's a fair statement," Brad admitted.

"As one of the government's security policy advisors, I'm charged with the responsibility of making worldwide conditions safe for our citizens and their interests. It seems to me that for a long time now we've been putting our energies into the wrong tactical areas. I'm not referring to geographical areas so much as the timing and methods of our actions. We're being reactive rather than aggressively proactive, and I believe we've spent incredible amounts of money trying to defend ourselves when we should be in the attack mode."

Ivan leaned back and contemplated his guest. Brad was about to say something when Ivan began talking again.

"By now you probably think that I'm the biggest hawk in Christendom," he went on, in a slightly apologetic tone. "But that's not it at all. I don't want to just treat the surface of the problem, I'd like to go after the root causes, but first we need a complete end to the use of massive quantities of weapons. If we can remove the weapons from the negotiating table we can get serious about the discussions, and hopefully make some long overdue progress."

"And how do you propose to do that?"

"I'd like to put a blanket over the production of all the chemicals needed to make ammunition and explosive weapons. There are too many guns in the world, too many gun runners, and too many people willing to use guns to force their evil desires on the rest of us. But here's where it gets interesting," said Ivan, leaning forward and speaking in a low, conspiratorial voice. "These weapons are useless without ammunition, and there are not that many large producers of ammo. My plan is based on the theory that without gun powder you can't have bullets, without explosives you can't have IEDs, and without uranium there can be no nuclear weapons." Ivan paused to catch his breath and observe his guest's reactions.

"Sort of like *Praise the Lord and cut off the ammunition,*" said Brad with a wink.

"Exactly."

"Go on, your idea is promising, though I'm not sure how you're going to get any chemical manufacturers to relish the idea of shutting down their businesses, especially those that are not located in the States."

"I've thought about that, of course, and I've devised a sort of carrot and stick approach to the problem. I'd like to get your view of its viability."

"Okay, shoot," Brad said, then clapped his hand over his mouth. "Whoops, I didn't mean to say that," he added, with a twinkle in his eye.

Ivan smiled and continued. "We begin by closing off the manufacture of all chemicals needed in making ammunition and explosives in the U.S. We require the same shut down of all similar companies throughout the world. The stick is that we will shoot a missile in their front door if they fail to conform to our request. I don't believe we'll have to fire too many missiles before the bad boys realize we're serious, as an explosion in an explosives factory can't be kept quiet."

"And the carrot?"

"The carrot is that the U.S. Government will purchase all their current inventory, and all their usual production during a one year period, during which time they can find some other products to manufacture."

"And where do we come up with the financing necessary to cover these purchases?"

"It comes from the Defense Department's budget. I think, on the basis of my preliminary research, that it's far more cost effective to spend money on peaceful disarmament measures than on trying to kill our enemies after they're armed. My department is busy studying this issue as we speak, and early indications are that it's likely, over the long term, to represent an amazing savings to the American taxpayer, and it's no more costly in the short term."

"That's quite a statement," Brad said. "I'll have to see your figures to believe it, but if you're right, Dr. Welland, you may be in line for a Nobel Peace Prize."

"Thank you, but I'll take the peace and the President will get the Prize, *if* our plan works."

"Back to my first question – what does Uncle Sam want me to do?"

"My staff thinks you're the best negotiator in the business. We'd like you to present this idea in concept form to a few of your Arab friends. Will you do it?"

"Wouldn't it be better if this came from the government itself, rather than a private citizen like me?"

"It will come from the government when we're ready, but for now we need someone to float the balloon to get an early reaction to the idea. If your spade work and our research gel into American foreign policy, we'll still have to get Congress to back us and our allies to support us."

"Quite a task you've set for yourself, Dr. Welland. Quite a task indeed."

"Yes, it truly is, and I'm fully aware of the difficulties. But to me it seems pretty clear that if the U.S. is forced to be the policeman for the world, we should try to spend our money for crime prevention, rather than run around the rest of the world, where we're clearly not wanted anyway, trying to arrest foreign criminals."

"You're springing this on me, you realize, and I haven't had time to digest it all, but it certainly is an interesting and different approach. I'm willing to float your balloon, but what can you give me to establish my credibility? After all, I'm not a State Department officer, am I?"

"That's the beauty of my scheme – you bring your own credibility with you. As the CEO of Paramount Petroleum and its subsidiary, Paramount Chemicals, and as the Chairman of the Petroleum Producers Association of America, your support by being the first explosives company to voluntarily shut down its production of war materials in direct accordance with the President's peace plan, would give your company an enormous amount of good publicity, as well as all kinds of cachet with the peace movement, and this can't fail to benefit your business."

"Why don't I feel like the best negotiator in the business right now?"

Ivan ignored that comment. "With the booming economies of India and China using ever growing quantities of petroleum as fuel, won't the world end up being totally immersed in smog if we don't do something quickly?"

"Are you saying that by discontinuing making petroleum based explosives, our fuel oil supplies will last longer?"

"It's just one part of the picture."

"Yes, but what a potentially messy picture! And the biggest question is, who's going to pay?"

"The Defense Department," Ivan said.

"How do you figure that?" Brad asked.

"Well, if our plan to prevent the killers from using their weapons is successful, we'll have a lot more defense money to spend on other things, won't we?"

"Such as?"

"Why not spend some of it on developing clean energy sources? And why wouldn't Paramount Petroleum be the very one to lead the way?"

"Now you're talking my language. But how do we get the money away from the Defense Department?"

"Now you're talking *my* language. That's the investment grant program that the government will be glad to institute once the security of the world is assured. It's the other end of the carrot, the long, thin end that's the root, and the connection with the earth."

"The negotiator in me tells me I can float your weapons balloon. But I'm warning you, it better not be filled with hot air."

"It won't be," Ivan assured him. "It will be filled with hydrogen."

The meeting broke up a few minutes later, with Bradley promising to try out Ivan's idea on some of his Arab contacts, and to report back as soon as possible after returning from his trip. Brad had a good deal more respect for the government as a result of his meeting with Ivan, and Ivan felt that even a business warhorse like Bradley Burke could be inspired to do the right thing under the proper circumstances.

Laura Murphy had scheduled a meeting with Jane Player, the most vocal and most feared advocate of the environmentalist movement. This meeting was set to occur before the opening plenary session of the Society of Environmentalists conference in Washington D.C.

Nearly everyone hated Jane, and she made the most of it. She operated under the dictum that any publicity, even bad publicity, was better than no publicity. Laura was not in favor of Jane's methods, but she felt that at least they were on the same side. At school Jane had been a hippie wannabe, but she was too young at the time to make the grade. Later she rose in the ranks of those who protested. She had made a whole career out of protesting. Her causes were numerous – war, any war anywhere, women's liberation, racial equality, abortion rights, same sex marriage, and especially gay rights.

Lately she had welded herself into the protests against globalization, and as an outgrowth of that, the environment and global warming had shown up on her radar screen as promising areas for her strident protestations. Laura was a quiet, almost introverted intellectual, and Jane was by comparison a wild mountain woman. They really had little in common as people, but as a hockey team needs a player policeman to keep the other team's tough guys in check, so the environmental movement needed Jane Player, for she was that kind of a player.

Jane lived in the Berkshires, whence she would swoop like an eagle on any worthy fight that was ebbing and needed to be reenergized. In her case the cause was not as important as the fight. She had met Laura twice before, but only casually. Jane had decided to make the environment her next battleground. Apparently she thought that living in the woods made her an expert on the natural world. She had no academic knowledge of the subject of environmentalism, but Babe Ruth probably had no technical knowledge of the physics of hitting balls either, but he was, as Jane was, a hard hitter nevertheless.

A large, thick woman with no discernible curves, Jane was blocky, masculine, and resembled an Auguste Rodin statue of a nun. When she spoke, any mental picture of a nun went quickly out of the hearer's mind and was immediately replaced by that of a stevedore, for she was brash, coarse and loud. Jane was a popular lecturer at a small avant-garde northeastern college that specialized in women's studies. The college had been one of the first to admit women on an equal standing with men, and on the strength of this, had built its reputation as a leader in the fight for equality of the sexes. Nobody seemed to care whether the battle was about equality in gender, race, or opportunity, as long as equality was involved.

Laura had courteously agreed to meet Jane at the latter's request, even though they had almost nothing in common. In fact, Laura disliked Jane's strident, combative way of handling every situation. Laura had been raised as a Quaker pacifist, but time and maturity had relaxed some of the more extreme personal restrictions of her faith. It seemed to her that Jane had no scholarship in her methods, and therefore she could never win any really intelligent people to her cause. The only ability that Laura was willing to accord to Jane was that if you sided with her it would quickly be apparent who your enemies were because they would be the ones hollering back at Jane.

They met in a booth in the far corner of the cafeteria that was in the lobby of the hotel in which most of the guests at the conference were staying. It was only seven AM, but Jane was already in the mood for making war, not love.

"Hello Jane, it's nice to see you again," Laura said. "Please have a seat."

"Hi Lauren," she replied in her deep, husky voice. "Man, I need coffee, like *now*." She had intentionally called Laura *Lauren* as if to say, "you ain't nearly as important as you think, professor."

"And you shall have it right away," said Laura. Her reply was an attempt to make light of Jane's brusqueness and her imposing size.

"Listen Lauren, are we going to let these rich corporate jocks poison the air we breathe forever? Or are we going to actually *do* something about it?"

"I think we *are* doing something about it. Isn't that what this conference is all about?"

"Yeah, yeah. Talk is cheap, especially when you're talking to the choir. What we really need is a home run media event to wake up the zombie women of America who are cringing in submission to their horrible hairy husbands. They've got to be told to stop sending their meal-tickets off to the auto plants and the refineries. They think they're putting food on their plates, but all they're doing is pumping more poison into their precious little rug rats. Anyway, I've got a plan to get this movement off the pot. Ha, ha, so to speak. I want to know if you'll support it by being our statistical research person. We need a few dramatic facts to hammer into a creed, and a slogan to give continuity to our marching orders. Are you willing to help?"

"Tell me your plan, and I'll think about it."

"What's to think about? Oh well, if you want to play hard to get, I'll tell you all about it. I want to organize the most powerful protest the country has ever seen. I want to bog down the whole damn system until they make cleaning up pollution the principle policy of this administration."

"How are you going to do that?" Laura inquired.

"Simple, the women who are dissatisfied with the progress being made to get a clean environment are going to drive their jalopies to their kids' school, or their congressman's house, or wherever we tell 'em to go. They'll leave their vehicles there in a jumble, with the motors running, creating as much exhaust as possible. If these bastards are going to choke the life out of us, we'll give them a taste of their own poison."

"And what happens when the cars run out of gas?" Laura wanted to know.

"They'll still be blocking everything up. They'll have to be towed away, or fueled up for free in order to move them out of the way. At the same time we'll hit the politicians with our manifesto. From the President of the United States down to the lowliest clerk in the highway departments of every State, we're going to make it clear. *Clear the Air, or Clear Out.* That's our slogan to galvanize these sloths into action."

Laura had to admit that Jane's plan, if implemented, would be hard for politicians to ignore. However she had just arranged a meeting with a certain Bradley Burke, the current Chairman of the Petroleum Producers Association, in which she felt they had agreed to attack the problem in a sensible, non-confrontational, co-operative manner. Working with Burke to clean up the environment steadily, and in a non-disruptive way, was much more her style for solving problems. Laura felt that a new arrangement of voluntary concerned parties working together could accomplish more than a hate and blame fest like the one Jane was proposing. If this calmer, more serious, genteel effort of hers and Brad's could be made to work, fine. If it didn't produce results, then it might be time for Jane's approach.

"Well, are you in or out?" Jane asked her, with a tone of unashamed belligerence.

"I'm afraid I can't support your initiative right now," Laura answered pleasantly. "I'm working on a solution of another kind, which I'll announce in the near future. If this fails, then I might reconsider."

"A typical gutless academic attitude," said Jane, in a tone of undisguised anger and disappointment. "You ivory tower types are like gentlemen guerillas – you want other people to do your fighting for you."

She left the table in a huff, leaving Laura to pay the bill.

CHAPTER SEVEN

Ivan Welland was in his office when he received the news of the horrible bombing at the resort on the Red Sea. There were seven Jewish Americans among the dead. They had evidently been sharing a holiday with their relatives, and had become innocent victims of yet another shameful terrorist slaughter. He was certain the Israeli authorities would do their best to catch those responsible, and of course America would help in any way it could.

Ivan felt sure that the Israelis were already planning some sort of retribution. The preliminary report of the event contained only one surprising detail. The Israeli Defense Force had found two exterior guards that had been shot to death, but there were no bullet wounds on the burned bodies inside the building. They had all been killed by the explosion or by the subsequent building collapse. He thought it strange that not a single person was awake to challenge the intruders.

It was time for him to go home. He packed up his attaché case with some work he would try to do at home after baby Julia went to sleep. He said goodnight to Brooklyn and headed to the motor pool. Since the shooting incident he had permitted himself to be driven home in one of the armored cars that were chauffeured by secret service men. He still wore his Kevlar vest every day.

Progress in the investigation of his shooting was moving slowly. The body of the would-be assassin had been identified only as a probable Latino, based on its appearance and a scrap of paper with some Spanish scrawl written on it that was found in the pocket of the dead man's jacket. The FBI fingerprint files did not match with the dead man's prints. One glimmer of light was a positive ID of a DNA match with some unsolved drug-related crimes in Chicago. Matching a hair from the head of the Chicago murderer meant that the attempt on Ivan's life might be laid at the feet of the Colombian cocaine cartel or some other criminal drug dealers out of the Mid West.

Needless to say, Ivan had no connection to drugs or dealers in drugs. He had never even smoked a joint in his life. He'd gone over all the details of the shooting with both the FBI and the Secret Service investigators. Eventually they were forced to admit that more than likely the attack on Ivan had been made by a professional hit man who did contracts for anyone who could pay his fee. It was concluded that the Chicago crimes were just coincidental and unrelated. Ivan felt uneasy about that idea, but it was just a feeling, and there was no proof.

As he rode along in the back seat of the ordinary-looking black sedan with the dark tinted windows, Ivan mulled over the facts once again. The Chicago criminal had used a .38 caliber handgun. Ivan had been shot with an AK-47 assault weapon. There was no match there. The man in the Windy City was known to be a mid-level figure in the heroin and cocaine trafficking trade. He dealt in drug quantities large enough to make a boss or another dealer mad, if the product or the money to pay for the dope made an untimely disappearance.

Ivan was sure people in that line of business would know how to find a hit man in order to solve problems of this sort. He could understand why the idea of killing a DEA agent might occur to an operative in the drug trade, but why try to kill a government employee from a department that had little to do with drugs? Yet there was no doubt that the killer had been dispatched to kill him. The hit man hadn't hesitated even for a moment. He had recognized his target and had gone right to work. Ivan was alive only because he had thought to wear his vest, and not because the would-be murderer had confused him with someone else.

His mind returned to the subject of the weapons. What was a hit man doing with an AK-47? How hard was it to obtain such a weapon in the U.S.? What if the gun came from some other country, and was brought to the U.S. specifically to make it seem as though a foreigner had committed the crime?

This line of reasoning made a bit more sense to Ivan. The Russian-made gun, the weapon of choice of extremists in the Middle East, would certainly point the finger at a terrorist. His job as the Security Advisor to the President would make him a more likely target for a terrorist than a drug dealer. So are we looking for an Islamist fanatic, or a drug dealer's hit man? Perhaps neither. What if someone far more devious wanted him dead, and had thrown in a couple of red herrings to complicate matters?

Ivan had gone this far in his musings when the driver pulled up in front of the house he had rented in Georgetown, not far from his friends Julia and Simeon Montcalf.

He hopped out of the car, walked to the door, put the key in the lock, and went in.

"I'm home, if anybody cares."

"We care very much," came a voice from the dining room alongside the entrance hall, and his wife Marina stepped out holding their toddler by the hand and shooing her along towards her father.

Ivan rescued the wobbly-legged child from a fall.

"Hello, Button, have you been a good girl for Mommy today?" he asked her, as he picked her up and nuzzled her.

The child countered by pounding his chest and shoulders with her little hands, saying *Dadda* and giggling with delight.

"I'm glad Daddy's wearing his Button-proof vest," Ivan said, with feigned relief.

"Me too!" Marina exclaimed. "You must always wear vest when you are in such dangerous home."

"This little girl packs a wallop," Ivan said, hugging Marina with his free arm. "Are you giving her karate lessons?"

"Yes, of course! She already has diaper with black belt. She will soon become famous security officer."

"Just as I thought."

He switched to Russian so he could keep up his speaking skills, and also because it helped Marina to feel less estranged from her native land.

"What's new, my darling?" he asked.

"Not much. I taught my classes, but football heroes in front row are teasing me, so I put them on straight path again. After I give heroes extra homework, I came home again and relieved Mrs. Johnson of babysitting chores. I wrote little bit my book while Julia napped, and then we made dinner together. Incidentally, we eat tonight baby-tossed salad and clay patty cakes, ya?"

Ivan smiled. "Nothing else to report?"

"No, snoopy husband who wants to find out everything about innocent wife." She hesitated a moment and continued. "Man came by here about one hour ago. He said he was from Telephone Company. I refused to admit him to house. I told him we had no trouble with telephone, and he must have wrong house. So he looked at clipboard and asked am I Mrs. Daniels. I told him that no I am not this Mrs. Daniels, so he apologized and said he did have wrong house."

As Marina finished her story Ivan was already on his way to the phone. He took the instrument apart, looking for any sign of tampering. He reached into his jacket pocket for his secure cell phone and pushed *three, talk.* It rang on the desk of the Chief of White House Security. Ivan proceeded to tell him the story of Marina's encounter with the phone man. Ivan's end of the conversation went silent as he listened to what he was being told. After a minute he said "Okay," and hung up.

"What is wrong, Ivan?"

"It may be nothing, but I didn't like the sound of your telephone man."

"He is not my telephone man. I already told you, I send him away."

"You did exactly the right thing. Now call Auntie Julia, and ask her if she would like to have the Welland family as house guests tonight. The Secret Service is going to stake out our house. In about fifteen minutes the house will be crawling with handsome agents, and I've got to get you both out of here before you fall for one of them."

Marina quickly called her friend, the former Secretary of State, and made the arrangements. She had learned that when her husband went into the mode he was in, it was best to follow her marriage vows and obey him at once.

Ivan asked her to pack enough clothes for herself and the baby for a few days. While she did that he secured the house, activated the silent alarm system, closed the drapes over the windows, and a few minutes later he opened the garden door to admit four armed secret service officers. He smuggled Marina and his child out the back and helped them into the waiting car. The driver took them quickly to Aunt Julia's, where a security agent was already standing guard.

The Secret Service men back at the Welland house were busily engaged in figuring out how best to capture any intruders that might attempt to breach the security of the residence. They were highly motivated to arrest someone for the attempt on Dr. Welland's life. Their failure to apprehend the culprit would be a blot on their professional escutcheons.

Everyone concerned with the investigation felt that the visit of the phony phone man to Welland's home was related to the shooting. The indications were that somebody wanted Welland out of the way badly enough to make a second attempt on his life. Pride in their ability to protect a senior member of the government was motivating the agents to be thorough in their preparation for any eventuality. When they felt totally sure that they had everything under control, they sat down to wait for their quarry to show up.

The Welland family was received by Julia and Simeon Montcalf with great affection and hospitality. The toddler came in for a great deal of warm, avuncular attention from Simeon. Ivan felt deeply touched by his display of affection, for he never would have ascribed such feelings to his old mentor from his first assignment back in Chechnya.

Julia had always, since the first day of their acquaintance, been a role model for Marina and an incredibly strong supporter of Ivan's abilities, and for this reason they had named their child after her.

Neither Julia nor Simeon even asked why the Wellands had wanted to move in with them on such short notice. Whether it was because they knew that Ivan's work was top secret and he couldn't discuss it with anyone, or whether it was simply because they trusted him so completely, it didn't matter, for that was the kind of faithful friends they were.

Ivan explained to Marina that the Secret Service always took extreme precautions to protect those in their charge. The suspicious visit of the man using the telephone ruse was enough to galvanize them into action. He tried to make their emergency reaction seem more routine than it really was. He couldn't help being proud of the Secret Service agents' prompt response to his call. If the life of his family had to be put in jeopardy, then these were the people he trusted to protect him more than anyone else. Still, he couldn't sleep well because of his concern for his family's welfare, and because he didn't know what was going on in his house. Had he known, he would have slept even less.

The agents had tried to make everything seem normal in the house. The lights and the TV were turned on and off as though the Wellands were at home. From eleven o'clock on they had turned all the lights off as though the family had gone to bed.

At three AM a barely audible noise was heard at the front door. Inside the house the agents silently assumed the positions they had chosen for themselves in the event that an intruder attempted to enter the house.

The youngest agent, perhaps because he was the quickest, moved stealthily to the door. He listened for a few seconds, then threw the door open, hoping to catch someone by surprise on the other side. Sadly, he was the one surprised, and it was his last surprise. The tiny noise they had heard was the hit man placing a land mine against the door in such a way that anyone who opened the door, presumably the early rising Ivan Welland, would release the detonator spring and be blown up.

Young Charlie Berrigan, an agent for only two years, was the recipient of the present that was meant for Ivan Welland, and he was instantly killed. His buddy sprang from behind the couch where he was hiding and ran to the doorway to help his friend.

As soon as he reached Charlie's already dead body, there was another explosion, and he too was killed, his body falling against the corpse of the first. The killer had decided not to take any chances that the mine wouldn't work, and he had rigged a hand grenade to the door handle in such a way that the pin was pulled when the door opened. The time delay between the first explosion and the grenade was just enough to kill the second man as he came to help his buddy.

The killer had left the scene immediately after placing his lethal devices. He heard the explosions in the distance as he sped away, and presumed he had done his job and earned his money. Lights came on all over the neighborhood as people in the neighboring side-by-side townhouses were blasted out of their sleep.

The damage to Ivan's house was surprisingly small. The door, the exterior brick wall into which the door was set, and the simulated torchlight that lit the doorway was hanging from its wires, the beautiful painted wood front door with its brass hardware was nearly unrecognizable, but the inside of the house was untouched.

Blood from the victims was liberally spattered around, and smoldering wisps of detritus were spread over the path to the door. A block and a half away, Ivan's light and restless sleep was disturbed by the thump of the explosions. He immediately jumped out of bed when he heard the sirens screech into his consciousness.

"What is wrong?" Marina mumbled, peering at the clock on the bedside table.

"I don't know," Ivan said, propping himself on his elbow. "Just listen to those sirens. Something has happened nearby. I'm going to see what's going on." He sat on the side of the bed, his feet searching the floor for his slippers.

He nearly bumped into Julia outside the bedroom door. She was struggling to put on her robe as they walked hurriedly toward the staircase.

"What do think that noise was?" Julia asked him.

"I don't know, but I'll bet it has something to do with the reason we're staying with you tonight. I'll check with the Secret Service at once."

He had remembered to transfer his cell phone into his bathrobe pocket when he left the bedroom, so he took it out and pushed the number three. In a minute he heard the familiar voice of the White House Security Chief.

"This is Ivan Welland. Can you tell me what's going on in Georgetown right now?"

"Dr. Welland, are you all right?"

"Yes, why wouldn't I be all right?"

"Your house was bombed, and there have been casualties, at least two of my agents are dead. We did the right thing to move you and your family out of your house last night. Please stay where you are. I'll send more security to the Secretary's house. The perpetrator has not been caught yet. I repeat, the perpetrator has not been caught, and he might still be in the area. We don't want you out on the street. As a target, you are too recognizable. I'm still gathering facts. I'll call you back with all the details soon."

"I'm very sorry about your men. I guess they saved my life. I'll try my best to make it worth their sacrifice. I'll stay put until I hear back from you, Chief."

Ivan repeated what he had been told to Julia, who had by that time been joined by all the adults in the household. They moved around the kitchen, discussing the situation while Julia made coffee. Ivan pulled his cell phone out again, and this time dialed two, and then call.

"Good morning, boss," came Brooklyn's husky voice.

"I'm sorry if I woke you."

"You didn't wake me."

"It's only 4:30 in the morning, and I didn't wake you?"

"No, I have to get up super early in order to make myself look as good as I always do. Besides, our work day starts at six, as I recall."

Brooklyn was her usual self, even at that hour. She was a no-nonsense person who resorted to no tricks of dress or make-up to make herself look good. Everyone who ever met her knew that about her. They were also familiar with her sarcastic brand of wit, so it came as no surprise to Ivan when she said, "So, besides checking to see if I was asleep, why did you call?"

Ivan informed her that his house had been bombed, and that two Secret Servicemen had died. He told her that he was in Secret Service lock-down for the moment, and would probably go to work late that morning. He asked her to get the personal details of the men who had died, as he wanted to send flowers and visit the widows or nearest kin.

He also asked her to call Senator Carlson, the man Ivan rented his house from, to tell him about the damage so he could call his insurance company. The Senator had lost his last election and had moved back to Minnesota, but the real estate market was unfavorable at the time, so he had rented his house until he could sell it for a profit. Ivan suspected the three-term senator optimistically planned to run again in the next election. He hoped to win and move back in again at that time, an unlikely prospect in Ivan's judgment. Ivan reeled off a few more things that his assistant could do for him, and was about to hang up.

"Take care of yourself, boss. These guys are really after your hide, and they seem to have all kinds of weapons, too."

"Now you know why I'm so deeply interested in weapons control issues. It's just self-defense, that's all. My head is swelling with pride, though, at the thought that somebody wants me dead this much, and all the time I thought nobody cared. Please tell the others to keep working hard. We must be closing in on someone who doesn't approve of our plan for a no gun world. We want to smoke these guys out into the open, so tell the team to keep the pressure on."

CHAPTER EIGHT

B radley Burke planned to be frank in his attempt to get the Saudi royal family's reaction to Ivan's plan. Every member of the family was involved in the oil business, but only a few had the clout to influence policy.

Brad was in his element when he was dealing with Arabs. Perhaps he was one of the best negotiators in the business, but the Arabs were not far behind. Lately the senior Saudi family members had begun to realize that they had been making a mistake in constantly pushing the price of oil higher than the market wanted to bear. What's more, it didn't endear them to the West when they offered nominal sanctuary for terrorists within their country and financial support for radical Islamists outside the country. This policy was resulting in a feeling of anger and resentment in Western industrialized nations, which in turn was driving the push for finding alternatives to fossil-fueled vehicles, power plants, and factories.

There was a large number of influential people in the U.S. who were already clamoring for the Americans to put on a full-scale effort to replace fossil fuel vehicles with ethanol, electric, hybrids, or hydrogen. The Arabs, who still had enough oil reserves to last a hundred years, were eager to sell every drop before the international markets deserted petroleum energy and moved to other fuels.

Even though the burgeoning market for oil in China and India would take up the slack if petroleum sales to Western countries slowed down, there was every reason to suspect that if given a choice, these emerging economies would shift to any viable non-fossil fuel if it would improve the quality of their polluted air while still enabling their industries to keep booming along.

It is, perhaps, a stereotypical opinion that the Arabs are an ultra suspicious people by nature, but there are often good reasons for stereotypes to develop. Brad subtly used the research that was being done in the U.S. on alternate fuel development as a lever in his dealings with the Arabs. There was no need to tell them how close the scientists were to finding the solution. Brad used the fear of the impending loss of their markets to help keep crude oil prices down.

The irony of the situation was that the funds that supported the terrorists also came from oil profits. In spite of efforts to diversify the Arab economies, petroleum was still the chief generator of dollars in the Middle East. It was seepage from the petroleum business that found its way into myriad hidden rivulets that streamed down into the wells of Islam's secret treasuries. These siphoned-off petrodollars paid for the expenses of the so-called freedom fighters, along with the cost of their weapons. Gunrunners insisted on payment in American dollars. The dollars came from the oil business, ergo it was U.S. money that was funding the terrorist fight against America.

The Saudi royal family was well aware of the strained situation that existed between the oil-rich Arabs in the Middle East and their biggest customers, the industrialized nations of the world. Without coming out and saying it, the Saudi royal house was between a well and a hard place. If they angered the Americans, one of their best customers would move to a new fuel as quickly as possible and leave the Arabs holding the still half-full hydrocarbon bag. If they appeared to be too chummy with the Americans, the radical Islamic factions in their own country might take it into their heads to popularize the old belief that a caliphate was the appropriate body to rule the country, and not a monarchy that endorsed the present ancestral Hashemite line of kings.

There were elements in the nation, and indeed within their own family, that perceived the current rulers to have lost their warrior natures by indulging in sins made available to them by their access to the national oil coffers. The royals were well aware of the presence of the Great Satan who lurked behind the scenes, offering irresistible temptations to anyone who would listen to him. In order to keep their kingdom, and their heads, they had to walk a fine line between the Islamic clerics, the Al Qaeda sympathizers, and the principal sources of those petrodollars, the Americans. They were doing a balancing act that had kept them in power and made them, and a lot of their Arab friends, very rich.

Bradley Burke knew all this very well, and he'd helped his company thrive in the midst of the economic boom for a long time. He had made his fortune out of luring, tempting, bribing, and sharp trading with men for whom ideals were not even small considerations in the negotiations. But now he was being asked to use his silver tongue to persuade these same men that everything they regarded as weakness was really strength. If he could succeed in this task, it would be the triumph of his life. If he failed, as was much more likely, his business career would be at an end.

Fortunately he had only been asked to get a reading on how the oil sheikhs would react to Ivan's proposal that the world be compulsorily pacified. He had no idea how the Saudi royals and their OPEC brothers would receive this plan. He would soon find out if a calling to the higher goals of humanity had any resonance with the leaders of the oil rich countries.

From his previous discussions with princes, emirs, and sheikhs, Brad had learned that they all wanted to extend the shelf life of the petroleum economy for as long as possible in the rest of the world. They fully realized that cleaner energy sources would eventually be developed to replace petroleum, but they wanted the takeover to be slow and gradual. They understood that if they kept the price of oil low enough to make it the clear economical choice, they could slow the changeover to more expensive, and not yet widely available, cleaner energy sources. In the meantime they could use the profits to give their own economies a leg up on the rest of the world. They liked Ivan's idea that the guns were to be taken away from the violent dissenting sects, because it helped them to remain in power. Their idea was to allow the Americans to remove the weapons from the terrorists and all other violent revolutionaries in exchange for a policy of developing alternate energy possibilities very slowly. This is what Bradley Burke would relate to Ivan Welland and to the American government when he returned to Washington.

As Brad sat in his homeward-bound private jet, he found himself having a quiet epiphany. In spite of the immaculate, wealthy surroundings in which he had been immersed in Riyadh, he now felt unexplainably dirty. He imagined that he was standing on his tiptoes in filthy water that reached up to his mouth. His voice wanted to cry out, "Don't make any waves." His imagination pictured Ivan Welland in the water with him, but because of his great height Ivan was not having as much trouble keeping his head up to breathe. He interpreted this imagery to mean that Ivan's idealistic plan to douse the firepower of the world's arsenals was morally on a higher plane than his own usual compromises and trade-offs. Brad realized that all his life he had been dealing with basically flawed ideals, but he had convinced himself that in the real world moral compromises were inevitable.

It was not surprising that the oil business had attracted him. The early history of the petroleum business was rife with attempts by the oil barons to create a monopoly through stock manipulations and alliances with other industrialists, all of which was in restraint of trade. Although more regulated now, the industry was no further ahead morally. It was still controlled by power-lusting men who, hiding behind corporate legalisms, were determined to control the resources of the planet and the welfare of mankind.

Brad recalled how Thomas Edison's and Henry Ford's plan to make green electric cars in the early 1900s had been beaten back by false advertising, bribery, and the eventual outbreak of World War I. That had been a close call for supporters of the internal combustion engine and the petroleum producers. If visionaries like Edison had been allowed to develop a non-polluting vehicle, which they were well on their way to doing, we would now have a totally different ecological world.

All this made Brad turn his thoughts to the up-and-coming environmental conference that he was planning to attend in Washington. Perhaps in his position he could play a part in doing something good for mankind. He would make his report to Welland, then head over to the plenary meeting. He could not possibly know how much his life was about to change.

Bradley arrived back at Dulles International Airport, ducked into a waiting limousine, and was taken to the White House, where he was to meet Dr. Welland and give him his report stating that the Arab leaders were not against the concept of removing the illegal weapons from the Middle East.

"Hey, welcome back," Ivan said. "Have a seat. I can't wait to hear what the Saudis thought of my idea. Could you give me a summary of their responses?"

"I sure can. You realize, I trust, that the people I spoke with were members of the royal family, which in Saudi Arabia is the same thing as the government."

"I do."

Ivan had liked Brad Burke instantly. He struck him as frank and honest. They felt comfortable with each other as they sat in Ivan's office, but they were nonetheless forced to deal with uneasy issues.

"I had a pretty good round of talks," Brad began, after the initial niceties were put to rest. "I spoke frankly with my Arabs connections, and I asked them their opinion about your suggested solution to the violence problem. They all thought it was a very interesting idea. They would, of course, want to see the final program in written form, signed by the President, and ready for presentation to the U.N. Sheikh Hamid particularly thought that, although the U.S. didn't need, nor was it likely to get, unanimous authorization from the United Nations, transparency and public relations issues required that the announcement and explanation of the policy had to be made in the world media, and what better platform for that is there than the U.N.?"

"I believe the Sheikh is right," said Ivan, "and it's our intention, if approved, to present the plan in a way that the Saudi royal house can support. As with any progressive action in the Middle East, Pan-Arab states must be 100% on board or failure is assured. But getting militant Islam on board is another matter. They'll have to come around sooner or later when they run out of ammunition, but for the time being they still have masses of destructive weapons out there to raise hell with, I'm afraid."

"The immediate concern of the House of Saud," Brad said, "is to make sure that the monarchy isn't replaced by a caliphate. U.S. support is critical in upholding the regime. Philosophically they have little in common with us, but they need us for political, economic, and military reasons. The religious right in their country is very strong, and they have to be kept mollified. So even though you can't expect any overt joy about your plan to silence the weapons of the extremists, any weakening of them is in the royals' best interest as well as ours. So I'd expect them to support your idea if the plan seems to be broad and includes other Islamic states as well as non-Islamic nations.

"I was disappointed, though, that I was unable to meet with Prince Umar al Quraish. He's a very influential man, since he's one of the king's sons as well as being the former Minister of Natural Resources. I've always felt he was a schemer, and at best only a fair weather friend of the U.S., but his words have to be taken into account. So that sums up the Arab position at this point, I think. On their behalf, I'd give it a qualified green light.

"But the theoretical end to violence and the actual cessation of terrorist acts are two different things," Brad continued. "The Arabs themselves must do away with violent jihad as a solution to the problems of the Middle East. The extremists will never submit to anything other than what they believe is the will of Allah. Therefore I think we have to work on the philosophy of Islam, and to do that the minds of the clerics will have to be turned toward peace. So that's pretty much it in a nutshell."

Ivan looked thoughtful for a while.

"We'll have a follow-up to the disarmament portion of the plan that calls for an ongoing conference of the religious leaders of the world," Ivan said at last. "It seems to me that each of the great religions has gone so far out on its own limb that they no longer realize they're part of the same tree. But if we lock these guys up together with no weapons, eventually they'll begin to talk."

"How do you think that would work in practical terms?" Brad asked him.

"As I see it, we'd begin a new seminary of religious thought. It would operate as a university, and each of the great religions would be a school. No pronouncements or statements would be allowed to proceed from the university communities that were not approved by all the schools, and by the board of governors. There'd be debates, conferences, and individual discussions, but they'd always have to be peaceful and non-violent.

"In the short term," Ivan continued, "I'd see various declarations emerging that found common ground in all faith-bound thinking. In fact, the university could do nothing at all until the basics were sorted out, but eventually I can see things like a world bill of rights for man, including a separation of church and state policy, coming out of the deliberations. Everything that goes on would be covered live by a C-Span derivative. I could go on and on about this concept, but I don't want to bore you."

"You're not boring me at all," Brad assured him. "It's just about the first worthy philosophical approach to peace that I've ever heard originating from a government official. Most of the good ideas start elsewhere, and later, when the rightness of the ideas become inescapably obvious, only then do politicians adopt them. So I congratulate you for the thoughts," Brad said, heartily and with feeling.

"I'm glad you find it interesting," said Ivan, with a grateful smile. "I judge from your last comment that you think I'll get some opposition from politicians along the way. If I'm allowed to proceed with these ideas I'll need all the support I can get from important personages in every field. A believer from the much maligned oil industry would be most welcome to help in the cause."

"I'd be happy to help with your proposal in any way I can. We must talk further. I'd like to see what you have in writing so I can put some more time into studying it."

"I'm very glad you're willing to help, but you may want to reconsider your position when I tell you I've been shot three times, and I've had the front of my house blown off already, and supposedly nobody except the President, my staff, and you have even heard my proposal so far. I think you can see why I'm personally anxious to do away with the ammo that these maniacs are using. I'd love to invite you to dinner at my house to discuss this further, but unfortunately it's being reconstructed at the moment."

"Well, if you'd like, I'd be happy to have you and your wife join me for dinner at my suite in town."

"That would be great, Brad. When, where, and what time shall we show up? Will your wife be there, too?"

"I've never managed to subdue a woman long enough to get one to marry me. But I think I can find someone to make up a fourth. How about next Thursday, at seven o'clock? My company keeps a penthouse suite in the Marriott Hotel on Pennsylvania Avenue. Do you know it?"

Ivan knew it well. He and his wife, Marina, had spent many weekends thrashing around in beds in that same hotel in the early days of their marriage. The two congenial men shook hands, both looking forward to their next meeting.

"We've been working hard on this plan," Ivan said, "and I think it's beginning to evolve into something fairly concrete. Look, I value your opinion and I'd like to try the final version out on you before I go to the President with it."

"Let me know if there's anything else I can do."

"I will," Ivan said, giving him a warm handshake. He had already decided just how Bradley Burke could help.

Now that his informal report was completed, Brad made his escape, explaining that he was due at the conference to see if the environmentalists had devised any new plans to pillory him and his fellow oil executives.

Laura Murphy was worried that the extremist elements in the environmentalist camp would take over the movement, and it would be seen by middle Americans as just another noisy dissent from the left-leaning ultra radical wing of the protest-prone supporters of the movement. It was obvious to her that Jane Player was intending to make this happen.

Laura felt that she understood the motivations of people who, like Jane, were deeply resentful about having been estranged by society for reasons of sexual or ethnic discrimination. She sympathized with them, but the crazies among them had clearly gone too far. Average people had grown tired of their strident voices, and they were now beginning to react with a vituperative backlash. Mixing all these issues into the valid concerns of the environmentalists would prevent rational people from finding an intelligent answer to the pollution problem. Laura wanted to knit America together. These other groups, however, seemed to want protest more than progress.

Laura Murphy decided to find out if the animal rights wing of the conference had aligned itself with the moderates or with the extremists. Raoul des Anges was the most outspoken person in America on the subject of animal rights, and Laura knew he was attending the conference. She decided to invite him to lunch and discuss with him his perceptions of how things were going. She didn't really know Raoul, having only been introduced to him once at a previous gathering, but after hearing his creative, heartfelt, address in which he convincingly defended animals and their place on the planet, she was left with the distinct impression that he preferred animals to human beings. His suggestion that rifles be given to deer so they could defend themselves against armed hunters was worth a giggle.

"Don't you think," Laura asked him at lunch, "that Jane Player's approach is a little too combative, and therefore not likely to result in any real progress?"

"You don't like Jane, do you?" Raoul responded.

"Well, as I was saying, I do think she has a way of putting people off with her aggressive approach."

"But do you agree with what she says, or don't you?"

"I agree with her position in general, but I disagree with her way of doing things. It seems to me that her attitude is counterproductive."

"Don't you see what you're doing? Your rejection of Jane's position is a rejection of Jane herself," he stated with certainty.

"I didn't reject Jane. I only reject her strident style."

"She may be a bit strident, but the real enemy is the vast, sleep-walking public, and they need someone like Jane to wake them up and call them to defend the world and the creatures in it, before it's too late"

"Well, it would be nice if she'd get her facts straight, then. She made a number of errors in her presentation."

"Just like a professor. You can't see the forest for the trees. You're all caught up with the details. I listened to your speech, and I've read your articles too, and I can see that academia is a great place for a person to be if she wants to play with children. But when it comes to dealing with adult leaders in the world of globalization, I'll stick with people like Jane."

"But she loses credibility when she doesn't present her case accurately."

"Well, if you're so eager to contribute something to the cause, why don't you be Jane's fact checker, then?"

Raoul congratulated himself on putting down the hot-shot professor while at the same time he pretended to be suggesting a helpful proposal for her to put her piddling, uptight, puritanical interest in perfect accuracy to a practical use. But as far as he was concerned, Jane was much too good to get bogged down in the details. She could see the big picture, and that was what the movement needed. Yes, let Laura be the fact checker.

"Thank you, Raoul, for that insight," said Laura. "I'll keep it in mind."

"You know, in this world we're all part of one group or another," Raoul observed, enjoying this opportunity to talk down to the elitist professor. "So when the sharp knives come out, a person turns to his own kind for protection. If you're in a minority group you'll suffer persecution, and that's why we stick to our own kind of underdog – blacks with blacks, Latinos with Latinos, Muslims with Islam, workers in unions, and so on. *You*, though, you're alone. Who sticks with *you*? You have only bloodless reason to offer, and no one with any passion wants *that*."

"You must be crazy. You want to throw reason out in favor of passion? What kind of world would it be if we did that?"

"It would be the world as it is. The real world. The one you haven't even realized is out there. You've been cooped up in your ivory tower all your life while the rest of us are out here in the trenches fighting the good fight. If you really want to help us, you'll have to grow up and get a taste of the real world. If you want to get anywhere you'll have to start by getting a hard edge, like Jane. You should use her as your mentor."

Laura shook her head in disbelief after she parted company with the self-righteous Raoul des Anges. What an unsatisfactory conference on the environment this had been! The majority of those present were either so narrow that they considered only one aspect of the problem, or else they were so prejudiced in favor of their own group of adherents that it was impossible to negotiate any kind of a settlement with them.

As she settled back into her chair in the lecture hall, Laura wondered if the conference was going to turn out to be nothing more than a royal waste of time.

CHAPTER NINE

The Arab press treated Mansurallah's raid on the Red Sea resort as if it were a heroic victory over the Israeli army, when actually it was just an attack on some helpless tourists. This kind of glaring misuse of the press was typical for the Arab language media, whose clientele were only interested in hearing about great historic victories for Islam. Pro-Western coverage was virtually non-existent, and any semblance of a search for truth was anathema to the Islamic-controlled press.

When Mansurallah came across an Israeli newspaper with an account of the raid he had led, he was incensed to see that the journalists referred to his achievement as "a cowardly attack on innocent, sleeping non-combatants." The Israeli article made it look as though he and his brave men were disgusting scorpions that had crawled out of the desert just to kill peace-loving, unarmed vacationers in their beds.

Mansurallah was livid when he put down the paper, and he resolved to make his next raid on a military target, just to show them how wrong they had been in assuming that he and his men were cowards. His Wahabist training had caused him to believe that the only good infidels were dead infidels, and the way they died didn't matter as long as they did die. Senior jihadists who preceded him had always put fear-inspiring terror ahead of moral values in their priorities of desired results. He was sure that in his world, where every infidel was a combatant, he would clearly be received as a conquering hero.

The men in leadership positions in all the various jihadist groups had long ago come to the conclusion that any attack that killed infidels was a worthy one. The effect of terror on the enemy was as great, and perhaps greater, than a battleground victory, for it was less likely to succeed against an enemy who was militarily strong. So Mansurallah was proud, not ashamed, of what he had accomplished. Even so, if the Israeli Defense Force wanted to have its ears boxed, he would be happy to comply with them in his next mission.

For some time Hezbollah had been offering rewards to the faithful who brought them the uniforms gathered from dead enemy soldiers. A class of scavengers had arisen that followed those engaged in military actions against Israeli, American, and British troops. Whenever an opportunity presented itself, they would fall on a wounded or dead man and strip the body. The collection of such uniforms was assembled and kept safely in the basement of a neighborhood mosque.

Whenever Mansurallah had a reason to disguise his men, he would tap into the supply. The lethal scheme he was presently hatching called for a squad of his men to be dressed up in the uniforms of American Marines. At that moment he was acting as the quartermaster and divvying up the uniforms among the members of his informal army of jihadists. When his men were dressed in the enemy uniform and had successfully passed his inspection, he would outline his plans for the next attack.

Mansurallah's plan called for his men to infiltrate Israel one by one, and then reassemble as a squad later at a location and time of his own choosing. He would not reveal this information to them, however, until they were ensconced in safe houses inside Israel.

Infiltration was a touchy business. Border inspections were meticulously done at Israeli checkpoints, and all Arabs wishing to enter were searched and screened. But Israel's neighboring Palestinians had been crossing the borders for over sixty years to work, trade, and do business with the

Jews, and they were smart enough to occasionally smuggle a terrorist across the line.

Once inside Israel, there were relatives and sympathizers galore to billet the heroes of the jihad. But the real problem involved the uniforms. It would be almost as hard to smuggle the American Army uniforms across the border as it would be to gain admittance from the Israeli border patrol for the men who would later wear them. Mansurallah would need help from his brothers in Hamas to make the arrangements.

Fortunately the Prophet had seen fit to unite all Muslims into a brotherhood to fight the infidels, and rapprochements of this kind were often made between the jihadists of one nation and those of another Muslim country. Thanks to his growing reputation as a prominent leader among the warriors of Allah, Mansurallah would have no difficulty gaining the support of his Muslim brothers, especially when they were told about the juicy next target he had selected.

In Washington D.C. the staff members of the Security Advisor to the President of the United States were looking forward to meeting with their boss. They had been working tirelessly to dig up the facts that Ivan needed in order to piece together a workable policy that could be presented to POTUS. They were overjoyed that Ivan had survived yet another attempt on his life, but with the second attack following so closely on the first, they were frantically trying to discover who was behind the efforts to eliminate their chief.

Theories concerning the identity of the perpetrators had proliferated wildly, and each member of Ivan's trusted inner circle had a different suggestion as to who might have done it. Ivan was personally much more interested in the ongoing work they were doing to safeguard the world than he was in securing his own safety. Naturally he was concerned about his life, and he couldn't just ignore the effect that his death would have on his wife, Marina, and their little daughter,

Julia. Politically, too, he was concerned about the effect it would have on the nation if someone as close to the President as his Security Advisor were to be assassinated. What real security was there for anyone in America if someone in his position could be murdered on the street or in his home?

On the basis of this concern, Ivan allowed the first part of the meeting to deal with the attempts on his life. He asked each of the team members to speak about who they thought were the probable assailants. Damian Rutledge led off.

"I think the smart money would be on Al Qaeda. They have the kind of weapons that were used in the attack. As clever as they are, they've probably seen Ivan's fingerprints on the recent interruptions of their lethal schemes. They're not a bit shy about issuing fatwas, and bloody revenge is within their capability, as well as being high on their priority list."

"Okay," Ivan said. "And what's your opinion about this, David?"

"I believe it's someone with a personal grudge who's hired a hit man," said David Feingold.

"Abdul, what do you say to that?"

"It's easy to blame the Arabs. "The sad thing is that most of the time you'd be right. This time, though, I don't think it was the Arabs. But it might have been someone who wanted to make it *look* as though the Arabs were responsible. I've spoken to many of my Arab contacts, and most of them have no idea who Ivan is or what he does. It's not that jihadist terrorists wouldn't be glad to kill him, since he's a big target as the Security Advisor. But if they had better intelligence they'd know that Dr. Welland is their *most* dangerous adversary, and I'd have known about this, since I'm in close contact with the Arab community here. But I've never heard Dr. Welland's name mentioned in Arab circles."

"Well that's a relief," said Ivan. "It does say something, though, about my inability to accomplish anything worthy of making me known to them."

"I hope you can keep it that way," Abdul said.

"How about you, Brooklyn?" Ivan smiled, turning to his assistant. "Who do you believe is trying to kill me? You can remain silent if you think your answer might incriminate you. I wouldn't blame you for wanting to get rid of me, considering all the work I unload on you. But tell me, if I let you off the hook as a suspect, who do you recommend to take your place?"

"Since I'm not going to confess, you're asking me to find a fall guy, is that it?"

"Yup."

"In that case my vote goes to the 'shadowy figure' in all the mystery novels I like to read. Generally speaking the shadowy figure isn't revealed until the end of the book, though," she added, pleased with the way she had fudged her answer. Fudge number two came when she asked, "And who does the victim think is the villain?"

"The almost victim," Ivan corrected her. "He thinks he understands the motive of the villain, but he's not ready to lay charges yet. I believe this is an onion case."

"Okay, I give up. What's an onion case?" David asked.

"You know, one with layer upon layer upon layer. An onion that has to be unpeeled, in other words."

"Oh."

"I think each of you has a piece of the puzzle," Ivan went on. "Damian's suggestion that Islamic terrorists are to blame is in this case not the most likely scenario, in my opinion. They're more probably just the fall guys."

"I didn't think they were the only possibility," Damian said defensively.

"Even so, you might be partially right. We have to look at all sides of the question. So David, you think it's someone who has hired a hit man. I agree with you on that, but I doubt that their motive is a personal grudge against me. I don't think I'm that important, or that iconic. It has to have more to do with the work that we've been doing recently.

What have we been doing lately that some clever, important person would like to see us discontinue?"

"We're working on a plan to shut down the ammunition makers," Damian said, "so maybe it could be someone in the chemical explosives industry."

"Or illegal weapons traffickers," said Abdul. "Guys in that business would have access to the weapons that were used when they tried to do you in."

"Maybe someone in the Defense Department doesn't want his budget used for buying a whole bunch of crappy weapons to quiet the crazies down," Brooklyn suggested.

"Any or all of those could be right," said Ivan. "Now you see why I said it was an onion case. Anyhow, I'm going to suggest that we put the matter of my personal skin on hold for the moment. You don't need to worry about me. I'm in close contact with the Secret Service on this investigation. I thank you all for your concern about my tenure in this job, but I think we should get on with our work, and let the T men do their jobs. I'm going to call the meeting to order now, so we can get on with the really important work that's critical to the well being of our nation and the world we live in. I need to know exactly where each of you stands with regard to your piece of the project. Who wants to go first? Damian?"

"Well as you know, Abdul and I have been collaborating with each other to find out the identities, methods, and routes used by the weapons smugglers supplying the Middle East. Interestingly enough, we've found out that the people at the top of this business are the same ones who operate the drug running businesses. So we think that since drug producers and distributors use plenty of guns, it's not at all surprising that they become closely involved with the sources of their weaponry. They seem to have taken over the distribution of weapons as an adjunct to their normal drug smuggling activities."

"That's an interesting observation," Ivan remarked. "Can you identify these individuals?"

"We've identified the big three. The first has the most obvious and direct connection to drug trafficking. His name is Rafael Alvarez, and he's the head honcho of the Cali Colombia cartel. He's known in the business as *La Víbora*, which means *the Viper*."

"Good work, boys," said Ivan. "And the second one?"

"The second one is the Basque separatist ETA leader. His name is Beneficio Ybarra. He runs a paramilitary gang dedicated to carving an independent Basque state out of France and Spain, and he finances most of his political movement with drug and weapons smuggling revenues."

"Interesting," Ivan said. "I've had my eye on the Basque separatists for a long time now. And the third one?"

"The third one is an Israeli thug called Shlomo Sussman, who's moved up the ranks of his organization and is now the most important gangster in weapons trading in the Middle East. Although drug smuggling is only a small part of his business, his weapon supply services are invaluable to the jihadists. It's ironic that he's a Jew."

"Excellent work," said Ivan, sitting forward in his chair. "So in your opinion, what percentage of the weapons traded can be accounted for by the labors of these three men?"

"These guys are not just three individual men," Damian pointed out. "Each one operates a network of criminals that number in their thousands. Many of them don't even realize that they're part of a big organization. They see themselves as individual operators, and sometimes they've got large numbers of henchmen working directly for them."

"True enough," Ivan agreed. "But it's hard to believe they really have no clue about who they're working for."

"Well, it works more or less like an ordinary franchise. Whether they're dealing with drugs or weapons or some other illegal product, the merchandise comes from various centralized factory wholesale warehouse locations. The sellers, distributors, and the mules or transporters buy their goods from these wholesalers, who in turn buy them from the producers. These people are important, because without merchandise from the producers, the whole organization is out of business."

"So we cut off the head of the snake," Ivan said, "and the body squirms for a little while and then dies."

"Exactly," said Abdul. "It dies whether it was a Muslim snake or any other kind."

Ivan asked them to put their findings into a report that he could use in his upcoming presentation to the Cabinet.

"Now let's hear from David about his progress."

"Brooklyn and I have been working on an exercise in econometrics. We've been extracting the cost of explosive ingredients from foreign transactions moving through the World Bank. This has required the building of an algorithm to analyze all the transactions in order to isolate the relevant ones. With Brooklyn's invaluable assistance, particularly on the domestic side, we've determined the costs to the U.S. of the Defense Department's equivalent purchases of explosive chemicals. This has yielded some quite astounding results."

"Well, what are they?" Ivan asked.

"Our figures show that the production of chemicals used to make explosives in the U.S. vastly exceeds that of the rest of the world, expressed in U.S. dollar equivalents," David said. "I'm embarrassed to say that a lot of these chemicals are escaping into the rest of the world in one way or another. Some legal, and some not."

"How can that be?" Ivan said, looking alarmed.

"It seems that many of the chemicals being exported are registered as raw materials, and not as explosives. Often harmless chemical ingredients can be combined with other substances which make them lethal. So although it's safer to ship them separately, this doesn't preclude their being mixed together at the destination in order to make bomb materials. But for purposes of declaring the nature of the shipment they're listed as fertilizer, or some such false end product."

"So you're telling me the guns and the bombs that are killing us are being made from our own ingredients?"

"It looks that way. Huge quantities of these materials are being shipped out of the U.S. I'm sorry to have to point this out, but some greedy American corporate citizens are responsible for a great deal of the violence in the world, and it's not going to be easy to persuade them to give up this profitable business."

Ivan frowned. "That's a hateful thing for an American company to be doing."

"Yes sir, it's a disgrace, but a very profitable one."

"Well, we'll have to face up to the facts, accept the blame, and correct this abysmal situation. Can you prepare me a report with numbers to support your allegations, and in a form that I can take to the Cabinet?"

"I'm working on that right now."

Ivan's beeper began vibrating on his belt. It was his hot line, and was never used except in emergencies.

"I've got to go," Ivan said abruptly. "Keep up the good work, all of you. We'll get together again soon to finalize our policy discussion paper."

On several of the many trips that Brad had made to Saudi Arabia, Peter Dunbar and his wife DeeDee had accompanied him. For some reason the only important person on the Arabian oil scene who didn't like Brad was Prince Umar al Quraish. The Prince, however, did seem to like Peter, or maybe it was DeeDee he liked. Brad just dismissed it as being one of those *you can't win 'em all* type of things.

The Prince was one of the wealthiest men in the world, a fact that DeeDee didn't fail to notice. The Prince's interest in women was well known to Brad from previous encounters in Hollywood and elsewhere. Umar's consuming hobby was attested to by the size of his stable of concubines. DeeDee's fantasy romance was that a desert sheikh would one day sweep her onto his gleaming white stallion and carry her off to his tent in a distant oasis.

Brad suspected that some sort of modern day version of her fantasy had occurred when she had met Prince Umar, but he never mentioned it to Peter. He kept his observations to himself, mostly because he was not interested in either of these people, and also because he felt that what DeeDee and Umar did together was none of his business. He could only hope that they would return the favor and keep their own noses out of his business at Paramount Petroleum.

DeeDee, for her part, was by no means swept away by her dreams of being carried off by the Prince to his oasis in the desert. She was clearly able to differentiate between fantasy and reality. For DeeDee the Prince was the male counterpart to her own conniving soul. The man who might be king, and who if not selected for that role, could at least help her to coronate her husband at Paramount Petroleum, was a man with the heart of a lonely hunter just like her own.

What would transpire between them was something that, if not worthy of a "Sheikhsperian" tragedy, was certainly something that approximated it.

For others who found themselves close to the action, it would be equally dramatic in its effect.

CHAPTER TEN

The phone rang in Laura Murphy's hotel room just as she was about to enjoy the eggs Benedict that she had ordered from the room service menu.

"Hello?" she said, replacing the silver lid over the eggs.

"Is this Dr. Laura Murphy?" said a male voice.

"Yes," Laura said hesitantly. "Who's calling?"

"This is Brad Burke of Paramount Petroleum. I heard your speech at the conference today. I just wanted to let you know that I thought your ideas were interesting, and the only rational ones offered by any of the speakers."

"Even though we're on opposite sides of the issues?"

"That's why I called. I'm not sure we *are* on opposite sides. I'd like to discuss some things with you in private, if that's okay. Could we meet some time?"

"Sure. What do you have in mind for a place and time?"

"How about the hotel penthouse in, say, three hours?"

"Sounds good to me."

"We'll have dinner then, shall we?"

"Okay," Laura replied, thinking that the penthouse was the upscale restaurant belonging to the hotel.

"Just take the elevator up to the top floor. I'll be there."

"Very well. See you at seven."

At the appointed time the elevator ground to a stop at the top floor of the hotel. Laura was as gussied up as she ever got – make-up, hairdo, basic black dress, heels, and tasteful jewelry. She looked for the bell, but she could only find a door knocker in the shape of an eagle's talon holding a ball.

She rapped with the authority suited to her position as a full professor. She had no intention of giving an inch in her position on the oil industry's immense responsibility for the state of the world's environment, so even her rapping on the door had to be firm.

Laura had Googled Bradley Burke's background, and found his biography to be pretty much what she would have expected of the Chairman of a major petroleum company. There had been no indication that he was married. She expected that he'd be in his early fifties, judging from the dates when he had graduated from Yale and Harvard. Laura pictured him as a conservative Ivy League Republican, handsome enough to look the part of the chairman of the board of a major corporation.

Bradley had the advantage of having seen Laura and heard her deliver her lecture. He too had some idea of her background from reading the short bio on the bottom of the handout he received when he attended her talk. He liked the pert, intelligent way she looked.

Brad had been a woman liker, not a woman lover. He had had more experience with women in a sexual way than he could remember. His success with women was not due to his being an irresistibly handsome, wealthy, available man. He was not overwhelmingly handsome, but most women found him attractive. His financial status was not visible to the casual eye, as he didn't flaunt his wealth or position. His availability was also invisible. Most women assumed that at his age he was married, separated, or divorced – none would have guessed he had never been married.

Brad thought that females had a difficult time imagining a single, heterosexual man never wanting to be married, because most women, he observed, were unable to believe that someone of their gender hadn't successfully used her wiles to land him. Wiles never worked on Brad, however, because he was one man who actually listened to women, and he could easily discern which ones were works-oriented, and which were grace-based.

He'd had nothing to do with dumb, foolish, girlish, arm candy women for many years. The women with whom he'd had relationships were successful in their own right, and didn't need him as a permanent adjunct to their lives, just as he didn't need them to be trophies for his ego. Intellectually accomplished women were just simply more interesting.

His talent for listening had benefited him in two ways – first, he learned a lot, and second, smart women appreciated him. He was capable of being friends with women, with or without the sexual element. He pictured Laura Murphy as another of these women with whom he could be a friend. He was eager to see if this was true in light of the fact that they were coming from diametrically opposed points of view.

Laura pushed back a wisp of her brown hair as she waited for the door to be opened. She could never decide if her hair was blondish brown, or brownish blond. Had she had it colored either way it might have looked better, but being natural was part of her persona. She wore contact lenses so she wouldn't always look like a timid intellectual professor fumbling around for her eyeglasses. Her optometrist had once suggested that she could brighten her blue eyes by wearing tinted blue lenses. She had taken his advice, but that was as far as she was willing to go in the artificial bodily enhancement department.

Brad opened the door. "Welcome, Professor. I'm so glad you accepted my invitation. Please come in."

Laura smiled and stepped into the palatial suite that had hosted notables from all over the world during its history. She quickly noticed the panoramic view from the picture windows that spread across the far wall of the large sitting area. The predominant color in the room was blue, and it accentuated the tint of her contacts. She walked over to the windows and gazed down at the city streets.

"What a beautiful view. It makes one think that great things must inevitably happen here."

"Yes, a lot of important things have taken place here in Washington, and I'm sure they'll continue to do so. I've always thought of DC as one huge, magnificent conference center where the real issues of the world are decided."

Laura thought his comment was a bit too nationalistic, but she didn't want to get into a political diatribe over issues of international relations. She was there to see what environmental policy changes she could get from this senior representative of the oil industry, not to provide him with a platform to espouse his ultra-conservative opinions.

"Aren't you going to offer a thirsty girl a drink, before you beat her plowshares into swords?" Laura asked.

"I'm sorry, Dr. Murphy. What may I offer you?"

"Irish whiskey would be nice." She had been introduced to it by her father soon after reaching the age of eighteen, and she had grown to like it. "Neat, with no ice, please."

Brad liked her choice. It indicated a loyalty to her ethnic roots. He pressed a buzzer, and a liveried man came in and took their order. In a few minutes he returned with two bottles on a tray – Bushmill's 21 Year Irish whiskey and Glenrothes 1989 scotch whisky. The tray also had on it a liter of Glenlivet spring water and two crystal nosing glasses. Brad dismissed the waiter and poured the drinks himself.

"As you can see," he smiled, handing Laura her drink, "I'm not loyal to my Irish ancestors. I prefer scotch."

He raised his glass and repeated the famous Humphrey Bogart toast from the film *Casablanca*. "Here's looking at you, kid." After the words slipped out he wondered if Laura was old enough to have seen the black-and-white movie.

"Why, thank you Rick," she said, with a wide smile. Brad was delighted by her reference to Bogart's character.

They sat across from each other in two light blue easy chairs that must have been put there by someone who expected a serious conversation to take place. Brad decided to plunge right in.

"I guess you're wondering why I invited you for dinner, so I'll start by saying that the oil companies aren't nefarious organizations out to poison the world's environment. The folks working in the petroleum industry have families, they enjoy the beauty around them, and they'd never knowingly do anything to destroy or devastate the earth."

"Then why do you do it so often?" Laura felt she might as well start off by being tough to see how he'd react.

Brad, experienced negotiator that he was, had seen this ploy many times before. In addition to being a good listener, he was calm and infinitely patient.

"Well, I can assure you that we don't do it on purpose. Our industry spends more on pollution prevention in one year than all the specialized protest groups will spend in a hundred years. Our money goes into counteracting spills, accidents, and explosions. We don't just put out press releases about the environment – we actually *do* something about it."

He took a sip of his whisky and paused for a moment to look at the attractive woman who sat quietly listening to him. He could see that she was concentrating on what he said.

"There was a time when wildcatters and drillers could have made a mess in their enthusiasm," he said finally, "but those times are long gone. Nowadays if a spill occurs, we clean it up. Cleaning up the spill in Valdez, Alaska, cost one of my competitors over a billion dollars. We've learned from our bad experiences, and now oil tankers are built with double hulls. We've made great progress, and some of the credit goes to environmentalists like you. You've raised our consciousness and made us better corporate citizens."

"Thank you for recognizing our contribution," Laura said. "However, the big problem today is with air pollution. The automobile exhausts and industrial smokestacks are fouling our atmosphere and giving our people respiratory illnesses that are often fatal. What are you going to do about that?" she asked, hoping to get him into a corner.

"Well, we don't make automobiles, you know. Sure, we supply the gasoline to meet the demand of the public, but we aren't responsible for the popularity of the car as the principle mode of transportation. I must say, too, in defense of the car manufacturers, that they've vastly improved the mileage that we're getting from a gallon of gas, and the latest exhaust systems have reduced emissions a great deal. We've made improvements as well. We've purified our products, removed the lead additives, and done a huge amount of research that has resulted in cleaner emissions."

"That's something, but the basic problem remains the same. Fossil fuels pollute the air we breathe and we've got to get away from using them."

"I agree totally. We consider ourselves to be in the energy business now, you know, not the oil business. We've invested huge amounts of money to discover and process natural gas, and to manufacture gasses like propane that burn cleaner than oil."

"I've heard all those arguments before, Brad, and I'm not convinced that the oil companies don't want to use up every last drop of oil before they and the auto makers switch to electric or hydrogen fueled cars. The OPEC monopoly gouges everyone with its ever increasing prices, and even finances the terrorists who want to kill us. As far as I'm concerned, progress is just too slow. Period. Mankind will be gasping its last breath at about the same time as the energy producers finally get around to solving the problem."

"There's something in what you say. But unfortunately it takes a lot of time and huge amounts of money to implement the solutions you're looking for. Furthermore, we have to keep things moving *while* we make these changes. The organizations that you support have a certain role to play, but all their good intentions can't accomplish the conversion to hydrogen-fueled vehicles without many years of focused work on the part of everyone concerned."

"I don't know about that. Just look what happened with the computer revolution. It didn't take long for it to change our way of working."

"I don't think that's a very apt comparison, Laura, because you're forgetting about the difference in scale. Computers are small compared to cars. We can miniaturize a computer, but we can't miniaturize people so they'll fit into vehicles the size of a laptop. When we talk about the massive amount of material needed to produce new vehicles for everyone on the planet who wants one, we're into another scale altogether. You might also consider how much energy it's going to take to manufacture all these hydrogen-fueled vehicles. Obviously the power to fuel the changeover must come from fossil fuels, too. This is going to take a lot of time, and you may be right about mankind expiring from lack of oxygen before we wipe out air pollution. Anyway, we've still got plenty to talk about, but let's do it over dinner. What do you say?"

"That suits me fine. A good argument always stimulates my appetite."

They moved to the table that had been elegantly set for two diners. The server was the same man who had brought their drinks. He poured a fruity young white wine, and then dipped a chilled gazpacho first into Laura's bowl, then into Brad's. He passed them a basket of salt encrusted hard roles, along with a dish of sweet cultured butter.

The two were silent for a while. Laura was wondering why such an urbane man as Brad was so short-sighted and lacking in erudition. It seemed to her that he had little concern for future generations. Brad, for his part, was thinking that Laura's views on pollution, ecology, and the environment were praiseworthy but impractical. He also felt that she was too quick to create a hullabaloo over actions that had been taken in the past, and over which the current and future crop of leaders had no control.

"How have you liked being a professor?" he asked her. Does it satisfy you?" Brad thought that taking a rest from the discussion of the serious items that divided them might make their dining experience more enjoyable.

"I really like teaching," Laura told him. "The contact with young minds keeps me sharp, and I have to admit it's a bit of a power trip. Some of the other aspects of the job don't interest me so much, though. Grading papers, administrative work, and the competitiveness of small-minded colleagues – those things wear on my patience. But I like writing, so when I get into a topic that I personally relate to, I enjoy it very much. The status that goes with being a professor gives me a platform for voicing my research findings. The pay is adequate for my needs, so all in all, I'd say that yes, I'm satisfied with my job. And how about you, Brad?"

"I haven't really thought about it, but I'd say I'm very satisfied. I have a large staff, so I'm not personally tied down by administrative details. I attend meetings, I synthesize the summaries of my department heads for the annual report, and the next thing you know another year has gone by."

Laura smiled and scrutinized his handsome features. She was taken by the color of his eyes, which were a dark shade of violet. She also noticed that his ears had no lobes. She associated lobelessness with young, highly energetic yuppie types, but she had no idea what this conclusion was based on. It must have been her observation of hundreds of student ears listening to her lectures over the years.

"I guess I'm a bit of an oddball in the oil business," Brad was saying. "I'm not involved in the engineering or in the mining side of the company. But I've been to every rig, refinery, and subsidiary in the company, so I believe I've picked up a certain amount of knowledge that enables me to muddle through. My best friend since the early days of our employment is my chief geologist, and he has kept me in touch with exploratory matters. Every now and then I get involved in a large-scale negotiation, and I enjoy that very much. So to sum up a long story, Laura, I'd say that I'm very satisfied with my job."

"I think I was really asking if you were satisfied with your life," Laura smiled.

These soft womanly questions were the hardest for Brad to answer because they dealt with subtleties, comparisons, and touchy, emotional things like feelings. For a man, Brad was good in the area of understanding other people's desires, but he was not so good when it came to his own. He knew that Laura would probably attempt to lead him into a discussion involving unquantifiable personal details from which she would evolve an estimation of his sensitivities.

He was beginning to like this woman, but he wasn't about to open up to her yet. He decided to try to shift the conversation back into her court to see how open she was prepared to be with him, before he did any off-loading of his own.

"My job has been the principal occupation of my life," he told her. "I've traveled widely, done a bit of offshore sailing, met many of the great people of our time, and generally have been happily married to my work. Aside from job satisfaction, how pleased are you with *your* life?"

Laura was not surprised that Brad punted, rather than plunging into the defensive line of his soul's desires. She had decided that all men were impaired when it came to revealing who they were. She had come to the conclusion that they had a certain universal emptiness inside them that they fought hard to keep hidden. She also thought that what they were hiding was best obscured anyway, as it was most probably a spiritual vacuum. Why was even this man, whom life had conferred with every honor except kingship, unable to honestly reveal his inner self? What had he to fear from her? She decided to probe a little further.

"I've noticed that men seem reluctant to be totally honest with women," she said. "I'm not sure if it's genetic, but it does seem to be generic. I want to know what a man has in his soul. What does he believe? How does he feel about religion, the meaning of life, the destiny of mankind, the relationship of the sexes, his attitude toward child rearing, and his definition of marriage, among other things?"

Brad just looked at her, thinking that it would take him a long time, or perhaps forever, to come up with answers to her many questions.

"But you prefer to tell me about business, traveling, and sailing, as though this were the essence of your life," Laura said, deciding that her best option was to move slowly. "Look, we're here to discuss something we can't agree on, and we both know it. The best we can hope for is the fairest compromise. I want a clean world, and you probably do, too. But I want it right now. That's impossible – I know it, and you know it. If it were immediately possible, you'd probably help me all you could. But you have to return profitable results to your shareholders, and I want that too. For all I know the pension plan at my university is loaded with Paramount Petroleum stock, and if it doesn't do well I may be facing life as a bag lady in my old age."

Brad chuckled at that idea.

"Anyway," Laura went on, "I believe we can work together in a practical way to make this a better world, but I can't do it if I don't know what's in your heart. So all that's left to say is, come out, come out Brad, wherever you are."

In all his negotiations Brad Burke had never been asked to bare his heart. He found it exciting to be dealing with someone who could provide him with something new to deal with. But at his age he felt it wouldn't be seemly to spill his guts to a woman.

"We haven't even had our dessert yet, and already I'm being given indigestion," he said.

Laura laughed at that, but she realized, a bit too late, that her approach had probably upset him. Perhaps it had been inappropriate for her to ask him such personal questions so soon after the first course of their dinner. She had never before tried the full frontal honesty approach in tackling a potentially dangerous enemy. After all, how often do the opposing sides of philosophical arguments end up co-operating with each other?

Were her issues with Brad a question of life and death? In a sense they were, as all life on the planet was threatened with extinction if things continued as they were going. Many species of life had already become extinct, and many more were endangered, so the problem carried its own time bomb. She owed it to her cause to do everything in her power to shorten the time frame for agreement on what was satisfactory environmental progress.

"Wouldn't it be wonderful," she said, "if we two could work out some sort of plan whereby our two political, social, and economic viewpoints could be brought together?"

"T'would indeed," Brad replied.

While the waiter cleaned the plates away, poured the last of the wine, and offered them fresh coffee, Laura and Brad had a moment to consider what they accomplished so far. Brad's opinion of Laura had blossomed into a distinct attraction to her. She was bright, honest, brave, and the best date he had ever had that wouldn't end in bed.

Laura, for her part, liked Brad as well. She felt he was sophisticated, gentle, patient, and a good listener. She did wonder whether he would ever be able to open up enough so she could have a look at the man within. She reckoned it was far too optimistic of her to expect that to happen in such a short time, but she liked him well enough to give him a second date, if he asked.

The dessert was a steaming hot, freshly made mousse au chocolat, served with a dollop of whipped cream. The coffee was strong, but without a hint of bitterness.

"The meal was perfect. Thank you, Brad. It was almost as though you'd researched what my favorite choices of food would be. You didn't do that, did you?"

"No, of course not. How would I have done that?"

"Well, you certainly hit my appetite's G spot. A friend who knows me well claims that except for a Blue Whale, I eat more shrimp than any living creature on earth."

"That's not a very flattering comment. You'd better stick with my brand of flattering."

"Is that an option?"

"Of course. We haven't even begun to reach a meeting of the minds."

"Can we argue again some time?"

"I'm going on a trip tomorrow. If you give me your number I'll call you when I return in a couple of days. Will you still be in DC until then?"

She wrote her cell phone number on the back of one of her business cards, and handed it to him.

"I'll be here for several more days after the conference. Where will you be going? No serious trouble spots, I hope."

"No, I've just visited the Emirates, Kuwait, and Saudi Arabia, and now I'm bound for Venezuela. There's a definite shortage of Irish whiskey in those places, or I'd have been tempted to take you along," he joked.

"I'd be thrilled to go to those countries some day, with or without the booze."

"I'm not sure I could convince my Board of Directors that my taking one of the foremost protestors of their policies to the Middle East would qualify as a deductible expense. Perhaps if I promised to place you in the King's harem and not bring you back, they might buy into it."

Laura laughed. She liked his male sense of humor.

"I'd offer you a cigar and a cognac," he said, "but I have to get up in a couple of hours. We're seven hours behind them here, you know."

"You guys have already done enough damage with the automobile exhaust fumes, so let's not start with the cigars," Laura said, getting up from her chair. "I'll make a list of the practical things the oil industry can do to make me, and my environmentalist friends, happy for the time being. Cigar smoking won't be on the list. I'll have it ready to present to you when we see each other again."

"I'll list the things you can do to make me happy too," he said, as he walked her to the door of the suite.

"Thank you so much for the wonderful meal and the honest conversation," she replied, as they approached the door. "For a capitalist robber baron and a polluting ogre, you're pretty cute."

On a spontaneous whim she kissed him on the cheek, and he watched her disappear into the elevator. He didn't have time to say what was on his mind. If he'd had time it would have been, "you're not bad for a whiny do-gooder of a tree hugger."

He really did wish he could take her with him on his trip.

CHAPTER ELEVEN

Mansurallah had decided to give the Israelis a heart attack. He was going to attack them in the very heart of their country. He was going to give Israel, and her infidel patron, America, a cardiac arrest. He would show the Jews, and their debauched Western allies, what Allah could accomplish even in the most heavily protected part of this land that rightfully belonged to the Palestinian people, but which now housed the American Consulate and the Knesset of Israel.

The American Embassy remained in Tel Aviv when Israel moved its capital to Jerusalem. This had displeased the Israeli politicians, who had made the switch to the historic capital in order to counter the claims of Islam that Jerusalem was their holy city because the Al Aqsa Mosque was located there. This always infuriated the Jews, since the Al Aqsa Mosque (also known as the Dome of the Rock) had been built right on top of the ruins of Solomon's temple, the most holy site in the history of the Jews. The Israelis wanted the support of the Americans for this move, but they didn't get it from them or from anyone else, for that matter. The position of the Jews was that since Jerusalem had been *their* holy city long before Islam came along, it was a natural thing for them to have their capital there. The Arabs saw this action as inflammatory. The Americans pussy-footed around the issue by locating their Consulate in Jerusalem while leaving their Embassy in Tel Aviv.

Palestinian Arabs had watched the American Consulate building for years. Nobody went in or out without the knowledge of the neighborhood residents. To Mansurallah's Arab eyes, and to most Muslims, the presence of the Jews in Israel was a continuous source of irritation, and the presence of the American Consulate in Jerusalem was regarded as rubbing sand in their wounds. As far as Mansurallah was concerned, they might just as well have built it on the Dome of the Rock itself. Many wars had taken place, but no Islamic force was able to dislodge the Jews from Jerusalem or the Americans from their Consulate. If Mansurallah's plan succeeded this would no longer be the case, at least as far as the American's diplomatic building was concerned.

Seven of his men had already taken up residence inside Israel. The uniforms had been collected, and alterations had been made so that they fit the new owners. Brightly painted plastic buttons had been substituted for the brass buttons normally found on Marine dress uniforms, so that they would pass through the metal detection scanners at the border. The uniforms had been packed in with a shipment of Egyptian-made prayer rugs for sale to the tourist trade. Mansurallah was to be notified by e-mail when his men in Israel received the uniforms. Three more men with false documents would arrive in Israel momentarily.

Mansurallah would not be going on this mission because he was so widely known by the Israelis that it would be too risky for him. He would much rather have gone himself, as waiting and watching were not his style. Nevertheless he had to restrain himself and be content to plan the maneuver, supervise the logistics, and trust the men he had trained for this operation.

The Consulate General of the United States in Jerusalem is as close to being an embassy as it is possible to be. The unprepossessing stone building was intended to blend in with its surroundings. The show Embassy in Tel Aviv was far grander in its appearance, but high walls topped with barbed wire surrounded both buildings, and armed U.S. Marines in dress uniforms guarded the entrances.

The Ambassador in Tel Aviv performed the ostentatious ceremonial duties of the office, but the Consul General in Jerusalem had other responsibilities that held more sway with those who knew the true function of diplomacy in Israel. The Consul, a former CIA executive in the Middle East section of the Agency, was the man in charge of negotiating all security, military, and political matters with the Israeli government.

The Consul General in Jerusalem regularly received his instructions from Washington in the diplomatic pouch that was delivered by messenger every morning. The two couriers rotated in bringing the daily pouch from Tel Aviv. One or the other would drive up from the southern coastal city in an armored car that was used for such errands. The daily drive wasn't risky because the pouch contained no top secret documents. Even so, the usual security measures pertained. The drivers used different vehicles, departed and arrived at varying times, and made no stops along the route.

Mansurallah's lieutenant in Israel was interested in this daily delivery, not because of the contents of the pouch, but because of the regularity of its transfer procedures. He knew that any action that is frequently performed becomes routine. Enemies often let down their guard during times like these. Casual surveillance revealed that the car arrived at the gate of the Consulate, showed some ID to the Marines on guard, was recognized, and then the car was admitted to the inner courtyard through swinging wrought iron gates.

The pouch, which was attached to the driver's wrist by a chain, was delivered to the reception desk in the front lobby of the building, where it was signed for. The chain was unlocked so the pouch could be left with the Marine on duty at the desk. As a rule the large wrought iron gate opened to allow the courier's car inside before the ID check was done, since the Marines were so familiar with the procedure.

The plan that developed in the terrorist's sly mind called for him to know the route taken by the courier. By following the courier, Mansurallah's men were able to find out that the drivers were used to their job and followed a routine path to the Consulate. Mansurallah had been trained in the Saudi desert by his friend Ali "the Detonator" to think minimally. He did his best to get the most out of the fewest men at the lowest cost, while causing the heaviest blow possible to the infidels. He followed the Detonator's advice when planning his attacks, and this operation was to be no different.

He told his followers to pack as many men into a car as possible. At first it looked to them like one of the acts in a circus, when an incredible number of clowns would burst out of a Volkswagen bug. Mansurallah had to disabuse them of this idea. Their purpose was not to pack the ultimate number of men into a car, but to put seven men with weapons in a car in such a way that they could exit quickly and be ready to shoot immediately. It was not until the men got to Israel that they understood what the exercise was all about.

The members of Mansurallah's terrorist team made their way across the border to the safe house where their comrades were holed up. An Arab pushing a handcart through the streets had delivered a bale of prayer rugs to the house. This was a common sight in Jerusalem near the tourist shops on the Via Dolorosa. The men waiting in the safe house had already distributed the uniforms among themselves, tried them on, and made the necessary adjustments.

When the new recruits first entered the safe house the men inside thought a squad of Marines had captured them, but they soon recognized their comrades. They understood then that the fake uniforms would have the same effect on the Marines and the Israeli Defense Forces. That moment of faulty recognition would give the disguised terrorists just enough time to attack and kill their unsuspecting enemies.

Mansurallah waited impatiently for news of the attack on the American Consulate in Jerusalem. He had approved the date of the operation, and now all that remained was for him to get the news that everything had gone as planned. He always felt better when he was personally involved in the attacks that he was in charge of. His wrinkled forehead and the way he tapped his index finger against his tea cup were signs of the concern he had for his fighters. He took his anxiety out on his wives, giving them orders and finding things around the house to complain about. While he fretted and fussed, Allah's work was being done without him

The courier's car was proceeding along its usual route to the Consulate building. He had to brake all of a sudden, for a school bus full of children had stopped to discharge some of its passengers. There was no way for the car to get around the bus in the narrow Jerusalem street. As he waited behind the bus, the courier saw three U.S. Marines come out of a shop and approach his car. He assumed they knew him, for he frequently delivered the diplomatic pouch and there were always Marines at the gate. One of the Marines came up to his window and gestured for him to roll it down. He did, and the Marine thrust a pistol in his face.

"Open the doors or die," the Marine barked.

The courier did as he was told. The passenger door opened immediately, and one of the false Marines climbed in. He held an AK-47 across his lap and pointed the weapon at the courier. The two other men dressed as Marines got in the back seat. Then another vehicle pulled up close behind the courier's car. In it were seven men dressed in Marine uniforms – five in the seats, and two in the trunk.

The school bus closed its doors and trundled up the street. The two cars followed it until it turned, then they went straight ahead until they arrived at the Marine guard post in front of the Consulate building. Instead of showing their ID, the false Marines in the first car shot the real Marines at the guard post, using pistols tipped with silencers.

Two false Marines in the first car got out and pulled the dead Marines out of the way, jammed the gates open, and let two cars drive inside the compound. The false Marine in the back seat shot the courier as soon as the car stopped.

Two men took over the posts held by the real Marines and readied themselves for any eventuality. The other eight men walked into the lobby of the Consulate and began shooting everyone in sight. The Marine uniforms had provided them just enough cover to permit them the element of surprise, and they got the drop on the other American Marines inside the building. Six terrorists ran from office to office shooting anyone they could. The other two jihadists placed plastic explosive charges against the load bearing columns and supports.

In two minutes the mission was accomplished.

Mansurallah's men ran out of the Consulate, pulled the body of the courier out from behind the wheel of the car, and five men jumped into the seats. The other five got into the other car. The two cars drove off in opposite directions.

From the upper window of one of the buildings across the street, a man was watching the Consulate. Minutes later, Israeli police cars came screaming into the compound. Several officers ran into the building with their guns drawn. When they were all safely inside, the man across the street casually depressed the red electronic detonator button.

The explosion was heard all over Jerusalem. The building collapsed as if it had been demolished by an atomic bomb. The terrorists managed to add a few Israeli policemen to the death toll as well. The man who set off the charges mingled with the crowd that had begun to collect, then disappeared from the scene.

Mansurallah was beside himself with joy when he saw the news on Al Arabiya's broadcast. CNN and the other Western news agencies were scooped so badly by the Arab reporters that Western media executives concluded that they had been tipped off that the attack was to take place. The details in the Arab media were so precise and had come out so quickly that it was a fair assumption that they had had an accurate foreknowledge of the event.

The mood in Mansurallah's house changed instantly to one of celebration. His critical barbs at his wives ended abruptly, and he began to think about how he would visit them that night. He would treat every one of his wives to something especially memorable on this occasion. What better reason to celebrate? What better way to commemorate a victory, and who better to emulate than the beloved Prophet? He informed his wives that he felt it showed that he cared for them equally, and that the women with whom he shared sexual relations were brought personally closer to one another other because of this practice. He never thought to ask his wives how they felt about it.

The news reports couldn't tell the story as accurately and in such detail as the heroes who had accomplished this victory. Mansurallah could hardly wait to hear the personal stories that his men would tell him when they returned. It would be some time before he heard them all, however, as the men had to slip out of Israel one by one, as unhurriedly and as carefully as they had slipped in.

Mansurallah called his spiritual comrade, Maulana al-Mutanabbi, to tell him about the glorious triumph. He knew that the cleric would want to include it in his Friday sermon.

Maulana was thrilled by the news.

"This is an honor and a splendid victory for our Prophet Muhammad, praise be unto him," he said, sucking in his breath and letting it out with deep satisfaction. "You must be sure to come to the mosque to hear what I will say."

The cleric knew that the successful result of this raid would be an encouragement to Islam, and would increase the flow of volunteers for the cause of jihad.

Mansurallah loved the home life prescribed in the Koran. How could the infidel monogamists seriously expect to convert the world to their system of marriage? It was so much more efficient for a man to have more than one wife. Perhaps this was the cause of so much of the immorality in the West. How did the Jews and Christians expect one woman to suffice for a man's needs? Of course, he thought, men in the West must be nearly impotent anyway, as the population of the so-called advanced nations had declined to the point where they are not even replacing themselves. He believed this was another reason that the future belonged to Islam. He had read somewhere that the sperm count of

Western men was consistently decreasing. Mansurallah had ten children, and he was sure that nothing was wrong with his sperm count. Large families had all sorts of advantages – blood loyalties, more hands to perform the work, and the accumulation of property among close relatives.

With the success of the bombing raid on the U.S. Consulate in Jerusalem, the name of Sheikh Mansurallah had become legendary among the secret supporters of violent jihad. Outside Islam he was only one of many anonymous terrorist leaders that were always sought but never found. Within the inner sanctum of Islam's religious hierarchy, however, Mansurallah was a heroic figure and a much-feared leader whom no one wished to oppose.

Mansuralla had succeeded in turning countless jihadist terrorists into freedom fighters respected throughout Islam. His supporters thirsted for victories, and he had given them several memorable ones. But a terrorist leader is only as good as his last successful attack, and he must constantly be planning ever more impressive raids.

The idea for his next assault on the infidels came to him in a creative flash that he attributed directly to Allah.

The news of the terrorist attack on the American Consulate in Jerusalem was the reason Ivan's beeper had vibrated. He had to credit the attackers with having had a tremendous amount of audacity, and no little organizational ability. The description of the way the attack had been carried out prompted him to think it had to have been planned and executed by none other than the terrorist leader known as *The Detonator*. That was impossible of course, because he had been severely wounded during the attempted hijacking of the ocean liner, *The Controller of the Oceans*. Ivan knew he had survived, and when he recovered he was held as a prisoner in the facility at Guantanamo. Why, then, did this latest attack have his fingerprints all over it?

CHAPTER TWELVE

Brad Burke arrived back at Dulles International Airport and got off the corporate jet belonging to Paramount Oil. He then stepped into a waiting limousine and was whisked back to his hotel. He stopped at the desk on his way in. The concierge recognized him, handed over his keys, and arranged to have his luggage sent up. Brad took the elevator to the top floor and let himself into his suite. He took off his jacket, reached into the pocket, withdrew Laura Murphy's card, and called her on his cell phone. He was surprised at how hard his heart was beating.

"Hello?"

"Hi Laura, this is Brad Burke. How are you?"

"I'm fine, and you?"

"I'm well. Say, would you care to join me for dinner again tonight?"

"That would be nice. Yes, I'd be happy to have dinner with you. Will it be Burke's choice of menu again?"

"But of course, Mademoiselle."

"Oh good. I want to see if you can choose my favorite things a second time."

"Ah, ze shallenge. I adore ze shallenge. I'll expect you then – same time, same place."

"Fine. See you later, Brad."

His heart was still beating hard when he snapped down the lid of his cell phone.

When seven o'clock rolled around, Laura knocked at the familiar door. Brad had showered, changed his clothes, and dabbed on some expensive cologne. When he opened the door he intentionally blocked her from entering, offering his cheek to be kissed just as she had kissed it when she had left him the last time they had met.

"Sorry, lately I've been spending so much time kissing and being kissed by Arab men, I thought it would be really nice to be kissed by a woman for a change."

Laura gave him a quick peck and brushed by him, gently compressing her breasts across his chest as she passed into the suite. She wondered if she had been a little too forward in doing that, but he had started the friendly stuff. It was a bit out of character for her to behave in a kittenish fashion, but she liked this man for some reason. She felt a bit puzzled, nonetheless, by her strange attraction to him. It was like fraternizing with the enemy, since he represented the opposing side in the environmental polemic.

Yet it had been a long time since she had felt this kind of chemistry with a man. She had enjoyed the companionship of many men before, but had never felt strongly enough about them to even consider marriage. She had always laid it down to her being justifiably choosy. She felt that the available men she knew were simply not good enough. It wasn't that they weren't socially good enough – it was that they weren't morally *good* enough. Back in her student days she had tried the "if it feels good, do it" philosophy, and had nothing but heartache to show for it. "Give me a man with high moral character to love, and I will show the world what true love can do," she thought.

Brad, for his part, had been through the same trials with women – partly his fault he would readily admit – but he had more or less concluded that his life would have to be lived in a state of permanent bachelorhood. Lately he had simply been uninterested in the women he'd met, but indifference wasn't something he wanted on a permanent basis.

Laura, however, was undeniably stimulating to him. Her arguments, although the opposite of his own, were rational and thought-provoking. He could deal with her on an intellectual level. Whether she could be more than just a debating partner would have to wait until he knew her better. He had to admit that he was attracted to her, and that alone was more than he had felt in some time. Patience and careful listening, the tools of his negotiating skills, would in time reveal more about her. He was willing to put the time in to see how things turned out, and he hoped she would reciprocate.

He guided her to the same seat she had occupied the last time they had spoken. Two bottles stood on the table nearby, one single malt scotch, the other Irish whiskey. Brad poured the drinks, handed Laura hers, and took a seat.

"Now tell me how the conference went," he said.

"I made the mistake of trying to unify the forces. I had private conversations with Jane Player and Raoul des Anges, hoping to bring them to the point where we could all present a single platform for progress. They would have none of it, though, and I felt like a complete failure."

"They're the failures, not you," Brad assured her.

"Thanks for your vote of confidence, but I find it strange that I feel closer to the position you voiced than I do to theirs. How weird is that? All these years I've been anti-globalization, against the massive pollution caused by industrial corporations, and outspoken about the failure of big business to put morality before profits in order to make the world livable for all people, and now my own colleagues and supporters are opting for strident confrontations that will create chaos and solve nothing."

"That's strange. I've been feeling more sympathetic to your position since we had our last discussion. So much so that I've been thinking of resigning the task that Lesley Studdard and his Oil Producers Association assigned to me, which was to fight back the efforts of the environmentalists trying to rush our industry into anti-pollution measures that we supposedly can't afford."

"Oh, don't do that, Brad! I don't want to have to break in someone else just when we we're making some progress."

"All right, I'll promise to stick it out, if you'll promise to be gentle with me."

"I promise. So tell me about your trip to the Middle East. How did that go?"

"Well, it was mostly a balloon-floating, attitude-testing, observing, and reporting mission. In general, I think it went as well as could be expected. At least they didn't shoot down my balloon. I was able to interest the Saudis in buying Paramount's plastics business. If the deal goes through it'll be for several billion dollars."

"What was this balloon?" Laura asked.

Brad thought for a minute about his conversation with Ivan Welland. He had been sworn to secrecy, so he couldn't explain his mission in detail to Laura, but he could try to generalize it a bit. "Can I trust you to keep it to yourself?"

"Yes, of course. If you ask me to, I will."

"There's a U.S. government initiative floating around the executive branch. I was asked to try it out on some high-ranking Arab officials, to get their reaction to the idea."

"What is this idea, then?" Laura inquired.

"Well, it's still in the development stage, but it's meant to reduce the violence in unsettled regions by removing ammunition from the hands of those who seem unable to refrain from using weapons. The idea is that the United States should stop producing chemically explosive materials. They'll invite all international manufacturers of such chemicals to do likewise. Any producers that volunteer to go along with the program will be paid for an entire year's production by the U.S. government so they'll have time to find other materials to manufacture. That way the plants don't have to be idled. If they don't agree to and comply with these terms, the U.S. military will blow up their plants."

"Good heavens! Does it have to be so violent?"

"I hope it doesn't have to go that far, but it would be a whole lot less violent than what we're seeing in Darfur and all the other trouble spots in the world. And blowing up the plants wouldn't involve any loss of lives, of course, so there's really no comparison, when you think about it."

"And how is the government supposed to pay for the purchase of all these chemicals?"

"Apparently U.S. expenditures for the purchase of such materials exceed the amount expended by the rest of the world, so it won't raise the Defense Department's budget. As it was explained to me, the idea is based on some neighborhood mothers in Dallas who got together to agree not to allow their children to play with dangerous toys. After a short time the removal of the explosives will result in guns and bombs being rendered totally useless. And once the violence is ended we can get on with substantive discussions. The point was made that it's cheaper and less dangerous to have a defense policy that removes the shooting option *before* the guns go off, than to run around trying to pacify a world that's already embattled."

"It sounds interesting to me, but can it be done? Is it really possible?" Laura asked.

"I believe we can pull it off. I'm sure there are some who will oppose the idea for reasons of their own, but the majority will like it, I suspect. But those who think they can get power easier at gunpoint will hate it. The illegal weapons dealers won't approve, as they'll go out of business when the people with the weapons no longer have ammunition."

"Who thought this up?"

"The President will get credit for it I'm sure, but Ivan Welland, his Security Advisor, is the real author of the plan. Shall we eat now?"

"Well kudos to Mr. Welland. Yes, let's eat. I'm starving, and I want to see what's on the menu."

"It's *Dr.* Welland, actually. He's one of your academics, you know. I'm not sure how they persuaded him to work for the government, but I think it was a coup for the American people. I've invited him and his wife to dinner on Thursday. I'd love you to meet them and round out a foursome. Will you come and be my co-host?"

"That sounds delightful. I'd love to meet them."

Brad pushed the server's button, and the same waiter as before appeared from the next room and served them each a cup of lobster bisque. Then he poured them a glass of Chablis, and passed the kosher salt encrusted crescent hard rolls and butter. Laura tasted a spoonful of the rich lobster, sherry and cream infused soup.

"Oh, oh, oh," she moaned. "This is superb. It's the best soup I've ever tasted, and these rolls are perfect, too!"

Brad was pleased that she was enjoying his selections. He hoped the rest of the meal would be as popular as the soup. The next course was a Caesar salad made in a wooden bowl rubbed with garlic and tossed with a dressing that included olive oil, lemon juice, salt, a raw egg, crumbled Gorgonzola cheese, and anchovies.

The pièce de résistance was Brad's humorous nod to their Gaelic heritage – the entrée he had selected turned out to be Irish corned beef and cabbage with boiled potatoes. The sudden change from the effete Continental cooking to the traditional peasant fare was a success with Laura. He had evidently given some thought to the menu, and it was a sign to her that he cared enough to take her preferences into consideration.

The dessert was a magnificent crème brulée. Fresh brewed coffee followed. The waiter brought a bottle of Bailey's Irish Cream and left it on the table with the scotch and Irish whiskey. Laura saw that as another of Brad's thoughtful touches.

The couple moved back to their easy chairs for coffee. Brad asked Laura if she would like anything else, and if not he would release Edward the waiter so he could clean up and go home.

Another good sign, Laura thought. She appreciated Brad's concern for the waiter, who otherwise might have stood around for no good reason instead of being at home with his family for the rest of the evening. She found Brad to be a cultivated man, and she didn't mind admitting to herself that she thought he was very good company. Sitting and talking to him had a naturalness about it, almost a domestic quality, that made her feel relaxed and happy.

Her recent experiences with academic men had influenced her to always keep her guard up, and she wondered if Brad's sending the waiter home was a ruse to get her alone. It was awful to be so suspicious, as Brad had done nothing to suggest that he had ulterior motives. In the present case her distrust was based on an ambivalence totally of her own making. On the one hand was the unfair expectation that either he or she would do something embarrassing, while on the other hand she liked this man, and found his aura of confident control to be interesting. No, it was more than that, she told herself. He was downright sexy. The sudden electricity she felt was baffling, a little frightening, but very desirable to her.

Brad's mind was also running along on two levels. On the business side he wanted to accomplish his mission, which was to organize a breakthrough effort to solve the practical problem of greenhouse gasses and global warming, while on the personal side he was increasingly feeling a warming of another kind. He wondered to what extent the two of them could work together if they became lovers.

Since he obviously cared for Laura he was being far more reticent about employing his accustomed matter-of-fact direct approach to women, which when he delivered it with wit and wisdom, was usually successful. Brad was learning that having a lot of experience with superficial women didn't necessarily help when the subject of his ardor was an intelligent, mature woman not given to flirtations or short-lived affairs.

"Wouldn't it be wonderful if we could come up with an environmental initiative to match Dr. Welland's ammunition proposal?" Laura said.

"It would certainly be a worthy objective," said Brad.

"Shall we try and see if we can come together and get something going in this direction?"

Neither of them said a word about her unintentional *double entendre*, but they both recognized it and felt the zing. Laura cleared her throat.

"Did you have time to make up the list of environmental items that we might successfully tackle in the coming year?" she asked.

"I did. And how about your list? Do you have yours?"

Laura opened her purse and pulled out a piece of paper. "Here's mine."

Brad reached into his shirt pocket and fished out his list, "And here's mine."

"Okay. Let's swap."

They were seated on opposite sides of the coffee table, facing each other.

"Is something wrong? You're staring at me," she said.

"Nothing's wrong. I was just looking at you, that's all."

"Well, let's look at the lists, shall we?"

She passed hers to Brad, and he passed his to her. Their hands touched during the exchange, and each wondered if it was accidental.

Brad had had to stand and move closer to her in order to give her his list. He stayed put and read her list, as she read his. The lists were identical, not in the order of the items, but in their overall content. It was an absurd moment of recognition of the fact that their minds were very close in the way they thought.

The steadily growing spark of attraction that they felt for each other ever since they had first met was immediately fanned into flames. Instant mutual self-awareness struck them like a bolt of lightning. The inadequate relationships with the opposite sex that they each had had in their pasts were exposed to a revelatory bright light, and they knew from that moment on that they belonged with each other.

Laura suddenly stood up and they embraced. Brad kissed her, and she kissed back with all the intense feeling that she had been controlling for so long. There was no ferocious tearing at each other's clothing, no impetuous wild behavior, but there was between them a heat and a mutual desire that was deep and undeniable. Laura had been with too few men, and Brad had been with too many women, but now the playing field was level and they were equal partners. Just as they had understood each other with their minds right from the beginning, so now their bodies sought unity one with the other.

They felt like a husband and wife that had been separated by a long war. Although it was their first time, to Laura and Brad it seemed like a glorious homecoming that had been much anticipated for a long, long time. And then, after the hunger was satisfied, they talked for most of the night. In the morning, separating was the hardest thing either of them had ever done, but Laura had to return to Madison, Wisconsin and her job at the university, and Brad had meetings scheduled in Calgary.

It occurred to him that he could probably drop Laura off on his way to Alberta. He would have to call his pilot to make a new flight plan, but if she wished, he would do it.

Of course she was pleased that they could stay together a little longer, but she needed to go down to her room to shower, pack her things, and check out. It was agreed that Brad would pick her up in his limo in front of the hotel in one hour. He walked her to the door of the suite, and opened it. They kissed impulsively. Even an hour of separation now seemed onerous to them.

Prince Umar, the Arab Sheikh, and DeeDee Dunbar, the wife of Brad's friend Peter, were scarred and hardened warriors in the battle of the sexes. Her natural red hair and full-figured, statuesque body were an enticing change for him, since the majority of the women in his harem were dark-eyed, dark-skinned beauties of a different background and temperament. His wives were submissive and obedient, dedicated only to fulfilling his every whim in the bedroom and wherever else he happened to be when they were around.

DeeDee Dunbar, on the other hand, was dangerous and demanding, and played an entirely different game with him. He found her self-indulgent, egotistic nature to be so utterly repulsive that it turned him on in ways he had never experienced before. He allowed her to go as far as she wished down the primrose path, for he knew it was also her path to destruction. Prince Umar enjoyed dreaming about the day when her destruction would lie completely in his power.

As far as DeeDee was concerned, she was attracted by this exotic Arab potentate for completely different reasons. His willingness to use the power of his wealth and princely position overtly to gain his own ends was like catnip to DeeDee's feline nature. She hated weak men who wouldn't pursue their desires. Conscience, loyalty, decorum, morality, fidelity – all these were anathema to DeeDee.

Prince Umar, for his part, only had scruples with regard to matters of Islam and his family, and in this way he believed he was morally superior to her. He had to laugh when he finally heard what it was she wanted from him besides wild sex. It amused him to discover the secret of her most cherished desire, because arranging for the removal of human obstacles was what he believed he did best.

CHAPTER THIRTEEN

Ivan Welland was rehearsing the things he would say at the Cabinet meeting that afternoon. He had received the data that his able staff had provided. He had drawn what he was certain were inescapable conclusions. He couldn't imagine, in the face of the evidence he was going to present, how anyone could remain in opposition to his plan.

Ivan's devotion to job and country was unconditional, and he had no patience for those whose commitment was less than total. He was perhaps a bit naïve to think that at the Cabinet level of government petty items such as jealousy, cowardice, self-promotion, and personality defects wouldn't play a part in the most important decisions of the nation. In this Ivan was mistaken. People take themselves with them wherever they go, so sins and deficiencies continue to exist even at the top.

As National Security Advisor, Ivan was a notch below the Cabinet members in rank, and the members of the Cabinet were administrators as well as advisors. In order to get anything done in the government, the civil service department heads had to cooperate fully with their Cabinet Secretary. The President appointed, and the Senate approved, all Cabinet nominees.

The fact that bureaucracy moves slowly, or not at all, can't always be blamed on the politicians. Often it's the civil servants who, like grains of sand in the gears of government, create the sludge that grinds things to a halt. Convincing hundreds of thousands of managers, workers, union leaders, and ordinary employees to do more work, better work, or different work has generally proven to be beyond the best abilities of the most skilled politicians in our democracy.

Ivan knew this, and had personally experienced it many times in dealing with matters of intergovernmental affairs. Welland had a plan to counteract what author Sonia Jones referred to as the *rampant mediocrity factor*, or the RMF. Ivan had been greatly entertained and edified by her book called *It All Began With Daisy*, in which she described the affairs of a small company lost in the clutches of governmental red tape. Welland felt inspired by her book to think deeply about the inefficiencies involved in governing a democracy, and the challenges of making improvements without turning the country into a dictatorship.

The problem now wasn't a question of when, but rather if the U.S. should tackle Ivan's weapon solution. First he had to get people to stop shooting each other, and the first step in that direction had to be to convince the Cabinet of the United States that the country should take this problem on.

If it became possible for him to work on a restructuring arrangement for the deployment of government workers and resources, Ivan knew he would put Brooklyn in charge. She might not have been the only fully charged battery on the government payroll, but she was the only one he knew. He asked his loyal assistant to come in and chat with him for a while.

"What do you think it will take to convince the Cabinet that they should adopt our plan for worldwide ammunition control?"

"You only have to convince one man – the President. It's his decision, and all the others are only advisors. It could be that he's already made his decision and he just wants to be reassured. Perhaps the President wants to keep an open mind and hear what his closest supporters have to say. Maybe he doesn't have the strength of character to go it alone, even when he thinks he's right. In the end, though, actions such as the ones you are proposing are his to take, and his alone. Whatever the purpose of the Cabinet meeting is, I know you'll do a first class selling job of what I believe is an excellent idea that will benefit mankind tremendously if it's carried out."

"Thank you for the kind words," Ivan said.

"One more thing. If you fail to gain approval from the Cabinet to go ahead with your plan, I'd like you to remember something my father told me when I was a teenager. He said, *When everyone around you agrees with you, you know you're wrong.* I realize that this kind of contrarian view is probably not as omniscient as it sounds, but it doesn't take away from the fact that you can still be right and not be popular."

"I like what your father said. Most of the time it does seem as if good, new ideas are opposed or rejected by the majority, but often wise ideas prevail over the long run. That's when the opposition comes forward to help claim credit for the idea. It's difficult to be patient in these circumstances, and even harder not to become cynical."

"Well, remember that you serve at the pleasure of the President. He was the one who gave you your job, and not the Cabinet members. He never would have scheduled a Cabinet meeting to discuss your plan if he didn't have some confidence in it," Brooklyn reminded him.

"The plan might not cure all the world's problems, but if it can prevent us from killing one another, it will solve the first problem. After that it's up to the Department of State, not the Security Advisor, to solve the rest of the problems," Ivan said. "Anyway, thanks again for bucking me up. I'll let you know how we made out as soon as I can."

Ivan always referred to the proposal as though he were not the author of it, but Brooklyn and the team all knew who should be getting the credit.

Ivan got up, put on his jacket, straightened up his tie, and said, "How do I look?"

Brooklyn stood back and gave him an appraising look, considering carefully before answering.

"You look fine. A bit too tall perhaps, but otherwise fine. Try to make that tall thing work for you. Stand near the shortest guy, so that by comparison you'll look as tall as possible. Maybe you can scare them into doing the right thing, in case logic fails."

Ivan pretended to be a rapper. "Six foot seven, and goin' to heaven, usin' an advantage biological to win an argument illogical," he chanted to an imaginary beat. "Take it to 'em with an attitude, but don't give 'em no latitude."

He cool cruised it out of his office door to giggles and a dismissive wave of the hand from his assistant.

In the austere, windowless, wood-paneled Cabinet Room with its huge, oblate table, the President of the United States was just finishing his opening remarks and introducing the subject that his Security Advisor had brought to the fore.

"Dr. Welland has evolved a plan designed to put an end to the murder, mayhem and destruction that Islamist terrorists have been causing throughout the world. I would like you to listen carefully to what he has to say, and then give me your opinions relevant to the implementation of his plan. Dr. Welland, you have the floor."

Ivan got up and faced the people sitting around the table.

"Great men of the past have said," he began, "that it's men, not weapons, that win wars. But I say that those men were still fighting with weapons, which is essentially what war is all about. Yet without arms and weapons there is no war, so we've tried for countless years to limit the possibility of war by controlling the proliferation of arms and weapons, but these efforts have not put an end to war. To win real peace, we must do something to make weapons ineffective. We should make them completely useless, in fact. The plan I'm about to lay before you deals with how this might be accomplished. It has two parts – the theoretical, and the practical. I'll start now with the theoretical.

"The history of humankind is essentially the story of the development of weapons. From stones, clubs, spears, knives, swords, guns, canons, and bombs to nuclear missiles, we've made great strides in the mechanics of killing. The history of civilized men only recently began when we became so good at building nuclear weapons that we reached a stalemate after we achieved a way to kill everybody. So, not by choice but by necessity, we agreed not to use these weapons, and we created a nuclear proliferation agreement. This treaty brought an end to the cold war and began a period of economic growth unlike any we've seen before. The prior efforts of the League of Nations to establish a poison gas protocol, and the subsequent chemical weapons conventions put forward at the U.N. have made the use of massive scale lethal poisonous compounds against humans unthinkable, except for madmen such as the late Saddam Hussein. The point is that although weapon suppression agreements haven't led to perfectly satisfactory outcomes, in the main the results have been beneficial for humankind.

"Ladies and gentlemen, I'm asking you to consider a cautious shift in attitude. I'd like you to consider something that the founders of the City of Brotherly Love said to King Charles the Second of England in 1660: *We utterly deny all outward wars and strife, and fighting with outward weapons, for any end, or under any pretence whatsoever.* This is our testimony to the whole world. What I'm recommending is the very first teetering step toward a time when all nations will make that same testimony.

"My proposal owes its origin to that nuclear treaty, to the Geneva Convention, and to my mother's powerful insistence that children not be permitted to play with dangerous toys. She was always running out of the house to stop her children, and the neighbor's children, from poking each other in the eyes with makeshift stick swords, or clobbering each other with anything else that came to hand.

"We children refused to understand the consequences, and I confess, I was the guiltiest of all because I was the biggest kid with the longest reach, and I thought I could win all the mock duels. Of course, my mother didn't listen to the protests of her son and his friends. She just kept the peace until we grew up. This story is a parable for peace. The idea is to stop dangerous, immature behavior – at least that's the theory – until all the leaders grow up.

"Now for the practical part of my proposal. At the moment, the weapons being used in the Middle East and in other places where terrorists operate, are weapons that function on the basis of manufactured chemical explosives. Gunpowder, dynamite, TNT, or plastic, they're all made in factories somewhere. My plan is to put an end to the manufacture of explosive ingredients found in the weapons now being used.

"The first part of the proposal is to announce the plan in the United Nations, and solicit the cooperation of all peace-loving countries. The second part of the plan is to enforce the embargo on explosives. Some of these chemicals are being produced in places where the U.S. is not popular. Fortunately, at least for the moment, we're feared in those places. It will be instructive if you'll allow me to show you some of the visuals I've brought along to illustrate my points."

Ivan had the big screen pulled down from the ceiling, and projected the first of his charts and graphs on it. The first chart showed the countries known to be manufacturing chemicals used in explosives.

"You'll notice that our country," he said, "is by far and away the largest producer, both in tonnage and dollar volume. The second chart shows the funding in the Defense Department budget that was allocated to the purchase of these explosive materials. You will see immediately that the amount we spend on these items exceeds the amount spent on them by the rest of the world. My plan calls for us to redirect these defense funds and purchase the entire production of the rest of the world's explosives for one year."

He paused for a moment while the members of the Cabinet murmured among themselves. Then he put up his hand to ask for silence.

"The factory owners," he continued, "can then use the year to develop other products. After that, any factories that don't conform to the terms of this offer will receive a missile via airmail from the U.S. Defense Department. One or two properly aimed missiles should suffice to persuade any recalcitrant arms dealers to change their minds. I suspect there'll be very few workers willing to punch a clock in an illegal chemical factory that's expecting an ICBM attack at any moment.

"I'm hoping that the Department of Defense will agree that if our enemies have no gunpowder or chemicals related to the function of weapons that are designed to kill, it will be a good thing for all of us. I think this approach makes sense in that there are many fewer chemical explosives producers than gun manufacturers. We've been chasing guns too long. In my opinion, we should have been looking for ways all along to shut down the ammunition makers.

"I've had my staff work working on the practical aspects of implementing such a plan, and we have a great many supporting details such as the location, size, and ownership of an estimated 95% of the facilities that manufacture ammunition or produce the chemicals necessary to operate arms and weapons. As I'm sure you can appreciate, this information is highly sensitive and, of course, it's classified. I've shown it to the President, and he's decided that it be kept on a need-to-know basis for the time being. So for now this is just a general Q and A session. I'll be glad to answer any questions of an unclassified nature that you have now."

The first question came from a sour and antagonistic Secretary of Defense.

"Dr. Welland, you've evidently decided that this country can be the military police department for the world, but our allies, and every self-respecting independent nation in the world, will be opposed to this cuckoo idea of yours, on the basis of the fact that it will interfere with their internal affairs and threaten their sovereignty as independent nations. Won't your proposal enrage every enemy we have, and at the same time turn off every friendly ally?"

"Good question, Mr. Secretary. But I believe that our allies already see us as the policemen of the world. Many of our friends have taken the position that they can let Uncle Sam take on this thankless job. Many countries are buying huge quantities of munitions and weapons from us, and I'd be willing to bet they'd prefer to do something else with their money if the world were disarmed and pacified. If we succeeded in terminating the manufacture of ammunition and arms-related chemicals, we would also be putting an end to our lucrative weapons sales. But a good question for this country to ask would be, *Can we get along without this huge export business?* I, for one, happen to think that we would be able to find some alternative products to sell, ones that are less destructive and more life-affirming than weapons."

"A follow-up question, Dr. Welland," said the Secretary of Defense. "What about countries such as Russia, India, Pakistan, Indonesia, China, and Brazil – what about them? Do you think these large and powerful nations are going to trust us to have all the weapons and not use them?"

"We already have the majority of the advanced weapon systems now, and we don't use them. What would change if we made all ammunition and arms-related chemicals illegal? I venture to say nothing would change. We'd still disagree on lots of things, but the difference would be that we'd be forced to do it non-violently. We learned to deal with Russia on nukes, so I don't see why we couldn't learn to get along with everyone in a weaponless world."

Ivan nodded at a woman on the other side of the table.

"Yes, Madame Secretary."

"There are countless numbers of weapons out there already. How would your plan deal with those?"

"Thank you. That's a fair question. This is going to take time to accomplish. I suspect we'll be destroying caches of explosives for years. But the immediate and future effects of this plan for peace will be very powerful. Those nations or groups that have loaded guns and rocket launchers will tend not to use them if they think there's no more ammunition to be had. Much of the materials of war are degradable over time, so the longer they're not used, the more likely it is that they'll fail if they *are* used.

"Look, it's a question of removing violence as a way to deal with problems. To return to my mother for a second, she used to cheer whenever a child would say, *sticks and stones will hurt my bones, but words will never hurt me.* So I say, let's bury each other with words, if necessary, but let's never again kill anyone with bullets. Let's bury the bullets. That should be our battle cry. Bury the bullets."

"What kind of Pollyanna crap is that, Mr. President?" the Secretary of Defense burst out.

"Take it easy, Roger. We'll just discuss this matter in a civilized manner. Then I'll decide what to do."

"If I tell my generals that all they're going to do from now on is find, condemn, and destroy all the gunpowder in the world, they'll laugh me right out of the Pentagon. I might as well start carrying a purse."

"What do you say to that, Welland?" the President asked.

"I'd say it would be better if we all carried purses rather than AK-47s. I'd also say that we should study the Swiss military system to see what we can learn from them. They have an all-volunteer reserve system, no missiles or nukes, and they haven't had a war in 800 years. And I'd say that the generals are *your* generals, not the Secretary's."

Ivan distributed a file to the Secretary of Defense and the other members of the Cabinet.

"In these folders you'll find details of a comprehensive media campaign that will convince any naysayer at home, as well as abroad, that supporting the President's program is in their best interest. My staff has produced a computer-enhanced sample DVD of the damage that would be done to an actual existing ammunition dump in Hezbollah-controlled Lebanon if a nuclear sub fired a missile into their weapons storehouse. The DVD, with its recognizably accurate site location just outside of Beirut, proves that the U.S. knows where the munitions are kept, and it gives an accurate but hypothetical portrayal of what could be expected if the President ordered a missile strike on this site.

"The DVD is a purely graphic concoction like a scene in a war movie. No one is hurt by this theatrical rendition, but the message is clear. A similar film will be sent to any head of state who opposes the President's War on Explosives. A recognizable local site in every dissenting country will receive the simulated virtual missile attack. A voice-over in the local language will advise all the would-be foot-draggers that an intercontinental ballistic missile has been aimed at the target illustrated in the film, and that if complete and immediate compliance to the President's request is not met, the resulting damage would be as portrayed in the film."

"Do you actually believe, Dr. Welland, that this slick piece of electronic theatricality is going to deter one single committed terrorist?" asked the Secretary of Defense.

"I do, especially after your boys unload an ICBM on one or two deserving rogue government headquarters. I suspect this action will have an amazing deterrent effect on any other non-compliant nations. They'll comply for two reasons – first because the President will insist on it, and secondly to avoid being closed down for supporting terrorists and giving comfort and assistance to enemies of the United States."

"What the hell are you talking about?" the Secretary shouted. "Are you advocating that we start using nukes?"

"Certainly not. This program is about *not* using weapons, and especially not nukes. It's targeted at those countries that have, or would like to have, nuclear weapons. By putting a stop to the ability to use conventional weapons now, we're pre-empting the development of nukes later on. The time to put an end to the arms race is now, before it gets out of hand, and while we have unquestioned superiority. I only hope it's not already too late."

"I've never heard of anything more idiotic…" the Secretary of Defense began.

The President interrupted. "Mr. Secretary, let's hear Dr. Welland out."

"For many years now the Hollywood film producers have been making fictional stories that have influenced the world's opinions of our country, much to our detriment. It's about time they did something to assist the nation that has given them the freedom to get rich while they disparaged and exaggerated our faults. They have done this because their most liberal legal interpretation of the freedom of speech laws permits them to do it. This behavior has had dire effects on our own country. Our citizens no longer have confidence in our government. This nation's morals have been shockingly perverted in the eyes of the world for the purposes of titillating and marginalizing the intelligence of our citizens. Why do it, you may ask? I believe it's because keeping the people in a stressed condition benefits certain segments of our economy."

"Which segments, and how are they benefiting?" shot back the Defense Secretary.

"Your segment, for one," Ivan said. "Nothing produces budgetary generosity for your department like a good war scare, and similarly nothing is as financially beneficial to energy stocks as a healthy boost in the price of oil."

"So you're saying that propagandists have been creating conditions that suited their purposes without regard to the truth, because conflicts have a salubrious effect on the economy?"

"That's exactly right, Mr. Secretary. And if a person in a high position such as yours isn't conscious of it, how can an ordinary voter know what to do? At last we have a President who is willing to buck the powers that be, and give peace a chance. So let's take this opportunity to do something glorious that benefits mankind. We may never get another chance like this to tackle the issues of peace and pollution head on."

"Thank you, Dr. Welland," said the President. "Have you anything else to add?"

"Yes, sir. This exercise is a form of political parenting. Just as a parent has to lay down the rules and discipline a headstrong child who fails to behave in a socially acceptable manner, so the President must also require obedience from the childish nations of the world. And like the parents of wayward, protesting children, the President must expect to be hated and misunderstood by those under his control until the children mature, at which time they undoubtedly will come to see how wise their parents were, and come to love them for it. Like the exasperated parents, the proponents of the President's plan for peace must be willing to enforce their authority when all else fails. It is a given that the parents, like the President, will be saddened by having to *enforce* what were perfectly legitimate requests.

"At the outset we intend not to fire any missiles, but we should do all we can to convince any and all delinquent national leaders that we'll most definitely launch them against the enemies of this world disarmament initiative. Subsequently, if we're challenged by any egotistic leaders too full of themselves to see the risks to their nation and to their people, we must be steely-nerved enough to see the threat through.

"The point that the U.S. has no business messing in the internal affairs of other sovereign nations was strongly made by the Secretaries of State and Defense. I counter these arguments by making the analogy that compares rogue states with children addicted to drugs. The first step has to be to remove the illegal substances before taking on the larger issues that caused the children to use them in the first place. Whatever changes of heart are necessary to cure the addiction, it has to begin with halting the taking of mind-altering opiates.

"The weapons are the drugs in my analogy. Whether the motives for the use of weapons is a hunger for power, religious orthodoxy, acquisition of territory, or subjection of populations by their leaders, the tools for pursuing these objectives have to be withdrawn as the first step to modifying this behavior. The irony of the situation is that in those violent parts of the world where societies protest the immorality of democratic peoples, they see no contradiction in using the wealth they get from selling oil to pay for weapons with which to kill their own best customers."

The debate raged on for over an hour. The President finally adjourned the Cabinet meeting. He thanked everyone present for their ideas and thoughts, and deferred any decisions until he had a chance to study the proposal further.

Ivan went back to his office, where Brooklyn advised him that the Director of the Secret Service had called, and requested a return call. Ivan punched in his number.

"It's Ivan Welland calling you back, Director."

"Ivan, we've been trying to determine the identity of the man who shot you, and although we don't know all the details, we've found out that the shooter was in the country illegally, that he's a Colombian with a criminal record there, and most likely connected to the drug trafficker Rafael Alvarez, known as *La Víbora*, alias the Viper. Do you have any idea why these Colombians wanted you dead?"

"No, none whatsoever. My department is working on stuff that might make some nasty people angry, but it has little or nothing to do with Colombia, or drugs. If I worked at DEA or ATF, I could understand it. I don't approve of illegal addictive drug making, using, selling, or distributing, but I don't think I'd be on the top of any drug lord's hit list. Maybe someone in another business just hired a hit man from the drug business to do me in."

"Possibly. I'll stay on top of the investigation, and let you know when I get more information."

"Thanks Director, I appreciate that. Needless to say, I wish you luck."

After amusing the Prince with several indescribable and even unmentionable sex acts, DeeDee was finally working Umar around to giving her something else that she wanted very badly. Luckily, as usual, her desires weren't too far removed from his. The labyrinthine workings of their devious minds were almost enough to span the differences in their cultural backgrounds, and assassinations were well within the realm of possibility for both of them.

When they exchanged the names of those they would have be victims, they found themselves to be as close in mind as they had been in body. Arrangements such as they were making with each other needed to be hidden from the light. Third parties who were able to carry out their missions without bringing attention to the real perpetrators needed to be located.

"I will find some infidels who are unconnected to us to do the job," Umar said.

"When it is done I will give you a son," DeeDee replied. She had learned that there is no real sex with women for an Arab unless a son may result, and she tantalized her Prince with the idea.

CHAPTER FOURTEEN

Sheikh Mansurallah's youngest wife, Samarra, had been a disappointment to him. She was beautiful and he loved her body, but her mind was another matter. His mistake had been in marrying an educated woman. She had studied journalism in the U.S. and was fluent in English. She had chosen a career as a reporter, and for a short time she had worked for the Arabic news agency, *Al Arabiya*.

It was then that she had met Sheikh Mansurallah. He had been captivated by her and simply had to have her. During her studies she had picked up some annoying ideas about women's rights, monogamy, and political freedom. Mansurallah knew that he could never have this woman without spinning what for him would be a fantastic web of philosophical nonsense. Samarra was fooled by his powerful position in Islam and by his inspiring words concerning the new peaceful Arab world that he was helping to build. Her judgment was clouded by his rhetoric, and she eventually consented to marry him.

Mansurallah had been a persistent lover, but his virility was overshadowed by his disdain for her desires, so she was left unfulfilled. After the honeymoon in Damascus, she went with her new husband to visit his family in their village. She was introduced to his first three wives, of whom she had previously been told nothing. These uneducated provincial women had found her to be unsatisfactory on all counts of domesticity, but according to Sharia law, she had no choice but to live in her husband's house and be submissive.

The entire equilibrium of the household was disturbed by the domestic tribulations that her arrival had provoked, and Mansurallah was furious. Samarra thought perhaps he would divorce her, which was the only way she could get away from him. Her idea was to withhold herself from him, thinking that he would give up on her and gladly divorce her. That turned out to be a severe miscalculation on her part.

When she turned down his almost nightly advances, he began arriving with the other wives in tow, and they would hold her down while he raped her. She was chained to the wall of her room and given a chamber pot to use. The wives would bring her meals, jeer at her, and occasionally give her a bucket of water to wash herself with. He promised her that she would learn to properly submit to her husband according to the Koran, or she would get this treatment indefinitely.

As time went on Mansurallah grew doubly disappointed in Samarra, for she had failed to bear him a son. After giving the problem much thought, he developed a plan that would serve two objectives – the political as well as the domestic. He cannily began to treat Samarra better. He told her he thought she had learned her lesson now, and as long as she was an obedient wife he would find some more interesting things for her to do. He told her how he now realized that she wasn't just a simple village woman, and that she needed some intellectually stimulating work. She agreed with that, as she would have agreed to anything in order to change her life of slavery and submission. Mansurallah forced his other three wives to ease up on Samarra. When they protested, he just shooed them away and assured them that things would soon return to normal.

As part of his plan Mansurallah arranged a meeting with his mentor *the Detonator,* so called because of his great aptitude in developing new and unique explosive devices. Mansurallah told him about the special challenges involved in his next mission, and asked him to work on a solution for his problem. The Detonator roared with laughter when he heard his friend's plan. He told him he was a genius to have invented such a creative scheme, and he promised he would go straight to work on his part of the project.

"What is the smallest plastic explosive device that we could use to slaughter a room full of people at a press conference in Washington?" Mansurallah had asked him.

"Something the size of a can of soda could do it."

"Could the charge explode in a forward direction?"

"Yes, that would pose no problem."

"Could the bomb be detonated from a distance? And what if the bomb were inside the body of a suicide bomber, could it be detonated from, let's say, a hundred feet away?"

"Inside a suicide bomber?"

"Yes, I have seen the idea used by drug smugglers on TV. People they call mules swallow several condoms filled with drugs, then they clear through the metal detectors at the customs check points. Later the drugs are passed in the mule's bowel movement. But we wouldn't have to worry about retrieving the cargo," Mansurallah added with a smirk.

"I see. Clever boy, why should it matter to a martyr if the bomb is located inside or outside his body? It would be a whole lot less detectable inside, as compared to wearing one of those clumsy suicide bomber vests. I assume your bomb is going to be surgically inserted."

"It will be surgically implanted in the womb of the mule, or should I say in this case, the camel?"

The detonator chuckled. "Do you want the detonation to be controlled remotely, or do you want the bomb carrier to set it off himself?"

"It would be best if it were remote controlled."

"Okay, I'm going to need to do some experimenting before I can answer those questions. Do you need to locate a camel to transport the bomb?" asked the Detonator.

"No, thanks. I already have one in mind."

Next Mansurallah went to speak to Samarra's former boss at the *Al Arabiya* head office. He and his exploits were well known to the editor. There was clearly no question of refusing Mansurallah's request, as non compliance might have carried some heavy penalties, not only for himself but for his family as well. When Mansurallah left the office he carried with him an open invitation for Samarra to rejoin the staff at *Al Arabiya* as a correspondent in Washington, D.C.

Bradley Burke's Learjet taxied up to the private aircraft section of the Madison, Wisconsin airport. Laura and Brad embraced, and he kissed her tenderly.

"It's only for two days," he reminded her.

"I know," she said, "but I'll miss you a lot."

"I'll be thinking of you, too. You just make reservations at the best restaurant in town, pick me up here at six PM, and we'll have a lovely meal. Then you can take me home and have your way with me. Okay?"

"More than okay, it's sublime," Laura said softly.

A plan was developing in her head, and she was not as sad about their separation as she might otherwise have been. Her pace became more confident as she thought about it.

She found her car in the parking lot and drove directly home. She used the bathroom, washed, and combed her hair. Then she got into her car and headed for the University.

She parked in the spot marked "Dr. Murphy." The private parking spot was a perquisite that came along with her last promotion. She dodged into the building and went to the office of the Chair of the Department of Environmental Studies. She found him seated behind a stack of files and papers that looked exactly as they had the last time she had seen him in his office the week before. Obviously nothing much had gotten done since she had left. Laura believed the pile of papers would look the same until the day Chet retired.

"Dr. Wainright, how are you?" she asked him, knowing how much he enjoyed being called by his title.

"You're looking well, Miss Murphy." He gazed at her a bit too appreciatively. "Have you been working out?"

Chet Wainright and his professorial colleagues were the reason Brad seemed so perfect by comparison. She noted how he called her Miss Murphy, when after all she was a doctor, too. His personal comment about her fitness was equally annoying. She supposed she should have told him she had been doing her exercises in the nude every morning. He had commented on her home gym once before, when he had attended a get-together in her apartment. His prurient imagination could then have dealt with that imagery for the rest of his unproductive day.

"If you have a minute I'd like to discuss something with you, Dr. Wainright."

"How could any man refuse you?" he answered.

"I'd like to take my sabbatical leave. It's overdue, and I've come across a very worthwhile project that I'm anxious to begin working on."

"What is this project?" he asked, looking approvingly at her décolleté, and then to her crossed legs.

"I have a chance to work on producing a cooperative solution to industrial air pollution in conjunction with a representative of the Petroleum Producers Association."

"That doesn't sound very academic to me, but I suppose if this is how you wish to use your sabbatical time, I'll allow you to seduce me into approving it."

How typical of university life, she thought. From the time she had first started university she had been sought out by her professors either to do research for them or to be their mistress. What about women's liberation? Women had traded the altar and the pedestal for a job and a couch – big improvement. Even when she became a professor she found herself being treated as prey all over again. So much for equal opportunity for women.

Nevertheless, she had accomplished her mission. She had a good, secure job that gave her status, decent pay, lots of time off, and independence to do projects that she liked. She hadn't had to compromise her moral standards, either. But Laura was not deluded. She believed that a person didn't become wise by doing foolish things.

By taking her sabbatical she would have the equivalent of fifteen months to concentrate on her project with Brad. And working with him would be heaven in more ways than one. It would be such a relief to work with someone like

Brad, a man that was an accomplisher, not an academic theorist. He was a brilliant, powerful, mature man with a sophisticated knowledge of the world. Together they would both be able to design an environmental program that would be beneficial to everyone.

She could just picture it. She would, of course, have to do the actual writing, as men seldom wrote as prolifically or as well as Laura did. Brad could supply ideas, guidance, criticism, and the wisdom he had gained from his experience in the business world. They would both have to keep their jobs, of course, as his clout came from his position in the corporate industrial arena, and her authenticity came from her position as a professor. But being on sabbatical meant that she could remain in the University's employ, do a project that excited her, and be paid while doing it. The big bonus was that she could be free to let her relationship blossom. As long as she had her laptop with her she could go anywhere with Brad.

Laura decided to channel some of the excited energy that she was experiencing into cleaning the apartment so it would be nice when Brad returned. She called and made dinner reservations as he had asked. Then she decided to create a format for their project into which they could drop modules once they had written and formalized them. She hoped he'd be pleased and proud of her. She had never felt motivated to make a man proud of her since she was a little girl and wanted to please her father by doing well in school. Now Brad was the one she wanted to please, and she wished with all her heart that he felt the same way about her.

Laura felt her life had been renewed since Brad had come into it. On the day he was to return she went to the hairdresser, a chore she usually tried to avoid, but this time she treated herself to the works – wash, cut, styling, manicure, and pedicure. Then she went shopping and bought a new dress, shoes, and a supply of skimpy underclothes of the type she would have made fun of in former times.

She was sure the women in Brad's circle were elegantly dressed in order to be alluring to alpha males, and Laura didn't want Brad to be disappointed in her. She actually had had fun shopping, primping, and pampering herself. As the time for her to go to the airport approached, she looked at herself naked in the full-length mirror, and then she checked her reflection as she put each new garment on. She stepped into her new heels, did a slow 360 degree turn in front of the mirror, thought she looked much better than usual, picked up the keys to her Saturn sedan, and went to the airport.

Over dinner, Laura told Brad about her plan to take her sabbatical leave so they could work together on their project. He had been touched to learn that the woman he loved had voluntarily arranged her life to accommodate his for the next fifteen months. She had grasped the essentials of his job with its heavy travel schedule. She had realized also that his value to their mutual project was tied up in his having the connections that came along with his job. Best of all, she had seen to it that they could spend a lot of time together. He admired her wisdom in providing a way for them to evaluate their relationship and to give it time to develop. As she lay naked in bed with him Brad knew that she had withheld nothing, but in return she expected much from him. He hoped that his constricted emotions could be freed so that he could give this woman all she needed from a husband. He was still breathing heavily from exertion when she spoke.

"What are you thinking about, Brad?" Laura whispered.

"I was hoping you were as happy and as satisfied with me as I am with you. How was it for you?"

"Oh, my God!" she said, and went silent.

"Well, tell me. Go ahead."

"I just did. It was *oh, my God!*" Laura raised her voice to punctuate her opinion. "So, how was it for you?"

"If it gets any better my old heart will give out."

"We'll have do exercises to strengthen our hearts."

"Will a trip to Washington on Friday count as exercise? Will you come with me?"

"I'd be delighted to go anywhere with you Brad, but what's the occasion?"

"I've invited my friend Ivan Welland, the Security Advisor to the President, and his wife Marina to dinner, and you've already agreed to be my date. Do you remember?"

"Yes, of course I remember, but being like this with you tends to make me forget about everything else. Where are we going?"

"I thought we'd eat in the suite at the Marriott."

"The same one where we first met?"

"The very same," he said.

"That will bring back memories."

"Yes, the best ones of my entire life."

"It's the same for me," Laura said, laying her cheek happily on his chest.

Prince Umar was furious. The assassination for which he had paid big money in advance had been botched. DeeDee had informed him that it was Dr. Ivan Welland who was behind the plan to put a stop to worldwide explosives manufacturing. This plan, if carried to fruition, would result in Prince Umar's being demoted in the hierarchy of the royal family. Furthermore, it would cut into his personal fortune because his part in the national petroleum legacy was the production and distribution of chemical explosives, which of course enabled him to supply funds and materials to certain fundamentalist elements within Islam. His connections with extremists were the source of his feared political power. The contract to remove Welland was handled in typical Arab fashion – it was surreptitious, cold-blooded, and transacted in a way that was difficult to trace.

Assassinating a high level American government figure must not be attributable to any Islamic entity, or the trouble that could occur as a result might dethrone the monarchy. Umar had gone to much trouble to source out a hit man with no ties to the Middle East. His associates in the illegal arms trade had recommended the Colombian drug lord, Rafael

Alvarez, as the best man for the job. The Prince had personally called the head of the Cali Cartel and arranged for the hit on Ivan Welland. The price, timing, and method of payment were negotiated as a simple business deal. After the first failure, when the victim had been saved by virtue of his having worn a bulletproof vest, Prince Umar had been assured that a second hit would not fail. Buoyed up by the fact that the dead assassin was an Hispanic man and totally untraceable to any Arab cause, the Prince was persuaded to agree to a second attempt.

Prince Umar was beside himself after the second attempt had resulted in the death of two men, neither of which was the intended victim. He called Alvarez personally and raked him over the coals.

"Our contract called for removal of the garbage, but the pile is still standing tall. What are you going to do about it?"

"You never informed me that the garbage was wrapped in protective packaging."

"Couldn't you have anticipated that? I was told you had experience with this type of disposal. If your merchandise is of the same quality as your services, I can't imagine how you ever succeeded in your business."

Alvarez, known as the *the Viper* in his neck of the woods, was not used to being talked down to in this manner. But he might need the support of this rich Arab Prince some day, so he held his temper in check.

"I'll take care of the disposal problem, don't sweat it."

"You've had two chances. You're not going to get a third chance to mess up. You aren't dealing with Americans now. Two strikes are all you get. I should have had my friends at Al Qaeda do this little job. They actually know something about bombs. Damn it, even you murderers are mediocre these days. Your contract is cancelled. I expect you to return the advance payment I made to you."

Prince Umar slammed the phone down. He was almost as angry with himself as with the infidel snake. The words had slipped out before the he could stop them. He hadn't meant to say anything over the phone that could be used as evidence to connect him with the events in Washington. He hoped that the CIA electronic spies hadn't overheard his conversation.

Far away in his jungle hideaway in the mountains of Colombia, the Viper indulged in a stream of invective that had his acolytes trembling. They tried to stay well out of sight, lest his fury become focused on them.

CHAPTER FIFTEEN

Ivan Welland knocked on the door of the penthouse suite, with his wife Marina at his side. The door opened and Brad asked them to come in. Ivan presented Marina to Brad, and then Laura was introduced to the Wellands.

An instantaneous congeniality sprang up between the couples. As sometimes happens, the group fell into a pattern of peer recognition. Small differences having to do with social position, religion, financial standing and ethnicity immediately disappeared.

"I'd just like to inform all you doctors that you are not to look down your respective philosophical noses at me, as I too am a doctor twice over," Brad said with a smile. "Furthermore, my doctorates are honorary, which is a source of great pride, whereas yours are merely earned, so they're dishonorable by default."

"The Book of Proverbs teaches us that *before honor is humility*. I suggest you take that to heart, Dr. Burke," Ivan chuckled.

Laura and Marina went to the balcony to look at the view and get acquainted. The two men, taking advantage of their time alone, saw to the distribution of beverages and then sat down to discuss the status of Ivan's ammunition initiative.

"The idea you floated for me in the Middle East went all the way to the Cabinet," Ivan said. "I don't know whether it's going to take off or not, but I'm optimistic by nature, so I live in hope. I'm waiting for a presidential decision on the plan as we speak. Now, on a different topic, Laura seems like a terrific woman. As we say in Texas, you should rope this one in."

"She is, Ivan. I'd hate it if anything happened to spoil our relationship. Some folks are saying that because we've fallen for each other we can't work together. But I don't believe that."

Just then the women came back into the room from the balcony with their empty glasses.

"Marina is fantastic," Laura said. "She knows more about U.S. history than most American-born professors!"

The four young people sat down at the dining room table, looking forward to enjoying good food and good company.

Mansurallah scrutinized Samarra thoughtfully. "We don't seem to be having any luck making you pregnant," he observed. "I'd like you to see a gynecologist."

"We haven't been married long enough for you to worry about that," Samarra replied demurely.

"My other wives got pregnant almost immediately after the weddings. I'd like to have the assurance that you are fertile. I'll make an appointment and we will go together."

He seemed to have his mind made up, so Samarra knew better than to argue with him. In a few days they traveled to Damascus and went to the offices of Dr. Hamed Husseini, a young Palestinian gynecologist who had been educated in Texas. He was one of the brighter students in the refugee camp where his family lived. Payment for his education was provided by money that ostensibly came from the treasury of the PLO. He, his family, and a representative of the Hamas group, had concocted a dramatic refugee story for the boy to use in order for him to obtain a student visa to the U.S. He was instructed to join one of the many large Baptist churches in the Dallas area and pretend to convert to Christianity. If he was convincing, he would be adopted by church members who were always anxious to convert Muslims.

It worked like a charm. The young man was welcomed, coddled, and helped to obtain scholarships with Protestant sponsorship. A committee of church people gladly supported his claims for refugee status, and he was eventually granted a green card. After his preparatory work he took the MCAT exam, did well, and was admitted to medical school. In the end, he did his residency in Ob/Gyn, and took a particular interest in surgery. In time he became eligible for permanent residency, and eventually he applied for U.S. citizenship, but his secret Hamas sponsors in Palestine had also arranged for him to keep his Palestinian nationality.

He felt a certain gratitude for their sponsorship, as well as a humanitarian desire to help his people, so he returned to the country of his birth. Now he could come and go as ordered by the leaders of Hamas, who didn't hesitate to remind him who had made him a doctor. Nor did he miss the suggestion that the health of his parents in Palestine should be his first priority as a health care worker.

Through the network of interconnected radical Islamists, Mansurallah had been referred to this particular physician. He had prearranged with his counterparts in Palestine that the doctor be told to do anything that he asked of him.

Dr. Husseini had been expecting and dreading the arrival of his patient and her husband. He was reticent to do what Mansurallah had discussed with him, but when the screws were tightened, he had reluctantly agreed. His instructions were to do a pelvic exam, claim to detect a uterine cancer, then await further instructions from Mansurallah. The woman was his wife, so Mansurallah had the right to sign any permission that was required for the treatment she was to receive. It would be handled as a typical medical procedure, except that Samarra didn't have cancer or the right to choose her own treatment.

Mansurallah and Samarra were escorted to an examining room, and she was asked to undress and put on a gown. The tall, dark, bearded doctor came into the room, took a history of the patient, and prepared to examine her. He snapped on a pair of rubber gloves and had Samarra get up on the table.

Mansurallah pretended to be caring, but he was actually ill at ease because another man was being familiar with his wife. It didn't matter to him that the man was a physician, or that his plans for his wife's future didn't include anniversary parties.

When Dr. Husseini finished the examination, he took off his gloves, told Samarra to dress, and asked Mansurallah to accompany him into the next room.

"How do you wish me to present the information to your wife?" asked Dr. Husseini.

"Just use your common sense," snapped Mansurallah, with undisguised irritation. "Say what you'd normally say to any woman who has cancer and needs surgery."

"I'll do my best, but this won't be easy for me. I'm not in the habit of breaking the Hippocratic oath."

"You have no choice, my friend. Either you break your oath, or you'll end up in the care of one of your colleagues, or maybe even in the morgue, right next to the rest of your family members."

"I'll arrange for the procedure at once," said the doctor, in a trembling voice.

"I knew you'd understand. By the way, how much time will be required for her recuperation?"

"She should stay off her feet for a few days. In a couple of weeks she'll be able to do whatever you wish."

"If you speak of this to anyone, or fail to successfully do your part in this affair, you will suffer the consequences that I have already described."

The doctor fearfully nodded his assent, and wondered how he had ever gotten himself into this mess. Perhaps he never should have left the U.S.

Dr. Ivan Welland was sitting at his desk pondering a report he had received from his respected subordinate, Damian

Rutledge. The report was an attempt to attribute the terrorist attacks in Eilat and Jerusalem to the same individual.

Damian's evidence was convincing to Ivan. The weapons used were similar, the raids had been meticulously planned, and they had been precisely executed. The scale of the operations, the number of men involved, and the military tactics employed were too similar to ignore. The fact that the two events used no suicide bombers or IEDs, the two most lethal weapons in the jihadist armory, was another linkage. Ivan was inclined to concur with Damian's opinion, but what could the U.S. do to help the Israelis catch this clever killer and his capable team?

The phone rang and interrupted his thoughts. It was the President.

"Dr. Welland, I've decided to go with your plan."

"Very well, sir. I've drawn up a timeline and a detailed step-by-step action plan. Would you like to see them before we proceed any further?"

"Yes. I'll need to sign off on it. Bring everything you have in writing and we'll go over the plan with key staff members. Be in the Situation Room at 0900 tomorrow, and you may bring any of your staff that you feel would be helpful."

"Yes sir. Thank you, Mr. President."

As soon as he was off the phone, he asked Brooklyn to step into his office.

"I've just received the go ahead on our project to stop the manufacture of explosives and ammunition world wide. We shall be going to the Situation Room at 0900 tomorrow for a planning session. Please call David, Damian and Abdul and have them come right over. We'll want to be highly organized and prepared for this meeting."

An hour later the team had assembled in Ivan's office. Ivan took Damian aside and said, "I've read your notes on the attacks in Israel, and I think you've drawn the right conclusions. Even though the attack in Jerusalem was on the U.S. Consulate, the site is in Israel, and the Israeli security establishment will be the point men in the investigation. I'll offer them the assistance of our department, and I'll begin by sending them your analysis. However, in my experience the Israelis prefer to handle these matters in their own way. Although they'll appreciate our offer to help them, they'll pursue the conspirator and his band of perpetrators and dole out justice deftly in the Israeli style. Right now we've got to focus on the plan we're going to present to the President."

When everyone was seated, Ivan led off with his outline of the plan. Each section was headed up by a stated result to be achieved. Under each desired result was a list of activities that needed to be accomplished in order to attain the objectives. They busied themselves listing the tasks that had to be done, determining who would be in charge of seeing to it that it got done, and the timelines for each task. They all agreed on a conservative estimate of the schedule to complete all the tasks. The work went on throughout the day, but by evening Ivan felt confident that the plan was well formulated, and that he could present it, along with the step-by-step implementation program, to the President.

CHAPTER SIXTEEN

The Detonator had finished his preparations and had called Mansurallah to let him know. They agreed to meet at the bomb maker's shop. At the appointed time Mansurallah showed up, careful to make sure he wasn't being followed.

"Allah Akbar, I'm happy to see you," Mansurallah said.

"I, too, am glad to see my brother in the cause of Allah's justice," the Detonator replied.

"What do you have to show me?"

"A camcorder video," the Detonator said, gesturing to Mansurallah to have a seat. He slapped a DVD into the player, and turned on the TV. "Watch this carefully."

An Arab man was walking with a boy, presumably his son. The father was leading a camel mare, and the boy led the camel's calf. As they approached an Israeli checkpoint the father went first. The man submitted to a thorough search of himself and the camel. After he was waved on, the boy with the calf approached the soldiers doing the search. It was a newborn calf and it was bawling for its mother. The father dropped the bridle rope and let the camel mare turn back to her calf. The boy let go of the calf's rope, ostensibly so the animal could nurse the calf. Both the father and the boy wandered off while the animals circled in the road among the Israeli soldiers.

The father turned around to look at the camels, which was a signal to a man nearby to depress the button on a small hand-held device about the size of a cell phone. There was an enormous explosion, and the checkpoint vaporized, along with the camels and the soldiers. The father and son walked away.

"Where was the bomb?" asked Mansurallah excitedly.

"It was in the camel, of course," said the explosives expert. "After the calf was born, I planted some plastic explosives in the cavity. Neither the metal detectors nor the Israeli guards at the checkpoint detected anything suspicious. I think now you see the relevance of this demonstration."

"You are a genius!" Mansurallah declared loudly. "And how large was the charge?"

The Detonator formed a semi-circle with his hands to indicate the size of the plastic explosive.

"All the glory goes to Allah," said Mansurallah.

"Yes. Now let me give you what you came for, and teach you to use it," said the Detonator, leading Mansurallah to a fancy wooden box that stood on the workbench.

The Detonator suggested that a sterile bag could be used to contain the bomb at the time of insertion. He also thought that the surgeon should stitch the bag with the IED in it inside the human camel's womb to secure the charge and keep it from moving around in the uterine cavity.

"I have marked my creation with an X which is to face outward when implanted," he said to Mansurallah. "This is important in order to shape the explosion as you directed."

The Detonator reached into the box and pulled out a woman's belt. It had a large circular buckle made of copper.

"The martyr is to wear this belt," the Detonator said. "The copper will melt and form a projectile at the instant of detonation. If the martyr is facing the target it will have the same effect as a direct hit by an armor-piercing shell, and the explosion will kill many people. It is a variation of an idea I saw on American TV on the Discovery Channel. They called it the 'Krakatoa' after the huge volcanic explosion that happened on that island in the nineteenth century. The program was called *Future Weapons*. I thought it was nice of the American infidels to help me make this discovery. Do they think we are too stupid to copy their weapons and use them ourselves? Maybe they intend to sell their weapons to us? Or sue us for patent infringement if we copy theirs?"

"Thank you, my friend," said Mansurallah, chuckling. "I will deliver their idea back to them with your compliments."

Brad Burke and Laura Murphy had been having the time of their lives holed up in her apartment in Madison, Wisconsin. They worked all day and made love all night. Both activities had been extremely satisfying. They felt the work that they were co-authoring had come into a glowing cohesion, and they were anxious to test their recommendations out on some neutral but respected person. They both hit simultaneously on Ivan Welland as that person.

They had become almost inured to the way they so often seemed to arrive at similar ideas. Together they would go to Washington and show their program, which they had named *Ammunition Demolition*, to Ivan Welland. In their minds they were writing a declaration of independence not for the people who lived on the planet, so much as for the planet that had to tolerate the people who lived on it.

Brad called Ivan and made an appointment, and they flew to Washington on Brad's plane. They had their laptops and their files with them. They believed they had written a document that would stand up to scrutiny in Congress and the courts of America, and utilizing the auspices of the U.N., it would spread to the rest of the world. Burke had no idea how their project would be altered by his being assigned a mission that was more pressingly important even than the one that he and Laura had worked so hard to make into a practical compromise.

Soon after Ibn Mansurallah received the bomb from his friend the Detonator, he called Dr. Hamed Husseini and arranged an appointment for his wife to have emergency surgery the next day. He informed the doctor that he would be present during the operation, so the operating room staff should be told he was a visiting surgeon. He would need to be masked and gowned, scrubbed in, and he would bring the implant with him.

Next, Mansurallah found Samarra and told her that they would be going to the gynecologist again in the morning. He told her the doctor had identified a malignant mass, and it had to be removed surgically before it metastasized and killed her. He had carefully rehearsed what he would say in answer to her questions, and he acted the role of the concerned husband with the practiced skill of a master liar. Finally he convinced his wife that there was no choice. He optimistically predicted that after the surgery she would be able to have the child that they both wanted so badly.

Having a child with this husband was not high on *her* list of priorities, but in their culture not having a child reduced her to being a nonentity in the family hierarchy, so a baby would solve one problem of her status as a wife. It was bad enough that she was younger and prettier than the other three wives, which of course provoked their hostility, but on top of that she was educated, and this was something for which they couldn't forgive her. As long as she didn't bear a child, the three witches would hold that over her head, and if she didn't conceive, Mansurallah might well divorce her, which would bring shame on her parents. Either way her situation was not good, but staying alive was obviously a top priority. So she accompanied her husband to the hospital like a lamb being led to slaughter. Mansurallah seemed to be very supportive and understanding of her fears, but in reality he couldn't wait for the anesthetist to put her under.

Dr. Husseini looked at Mansurallah, hoping he would change his mind about the unnecessary, cruel surgery he was about to perform on the man's wife. When the only sign he got from Mansurallah was an encouraging nod to proceed, he was forced to pick up a scalpel and begin. The doctor wanted to follow standard procedures and make the entry cut as small as possible. It was then that Mansurallah showed him the bomb and pointed out that it was a great deal less flexible than the small opening that the doctor was about to make. The incision would have to be larger – perhaps half the size of the opening for a Caesarian section.

It was the first time in Dr. Husseini's training that he had to follow the instructions of a life taker, instead of a lifesaver. There was no other choice for him, however, as he had seen the pistol that Mansurallah had intended him to see in his belt. He hoped it would be the last time that he would be put in such a position, and to ensure that was the case he resolved to go back to the States as soon as possible. He was very much afraid that if the procedure he was doing to this woman was successful, he would be ordered to do more just like it. But if for some reason the surgery was unsuccessful, he might not live to do another. Either way, a hasty post-operative retreat might be the only solution for him.

When the incision was made and the bleeders sewn closed or cauterized, the explosives were put in a sterilized bladder bag and inserted into the woman's womb. The doctor deftly closed the opening, carefully stitching the various layers of dermis together, and leaving only a thin line of pink flesh. He fought back the mental image of what this lovely woman's abdomen would look like when the bomb within was detonated. He struggled with an imaginary picture of the carnage left behind by a suicide bomber. He had personally assisted in many surgeries caused by bombs, so no detail was omitted from his imagination. Mansurallah read the doctor's mind, and put his arm around his shoulder,

"In times of war, men must have the courage to do things they otherwise wouldn't even think of doing. I thank you, and Allah will bless you, for what you have done. You have turned your scalpel into a scimitar for Islam."

Dr. Husseini was pretty sure that was not why he had gone to medical school, but he wasn't about to protest the words that Mansurallah was putting into Allah's mouth. That was the problem with being a moderate Muslim. The choices were a stoic silence or, for those who voiced opposition to the jihad, a traitor's punishment that might include torture or violent death to the protester and family members. Under the threat of his own death he had helped build a living "Trojan Horse" that would result in many actual deaths. When confronted with the reality of terror, his earlier militancy was diminished. He no longer felt the debt he owed to his family should supplant the code of human decency. At least in America he was not forced to be silent in order to survive. At that moment he had his first glimmer of what "freedom of speech" was really all about.

When he parted company with Mansurallah he had already begun to devise a reason to make a trip to the U.S. He knew then that he would never go home again.

Mansurallah supervised Samarra's recovery period with tender care and solicitous concern. When he felt that she had finally let down her guard and warmed to him a little bit, he told her he had a surprise for her.

"I know you have felt useless here in the house this past year, so I have spoken to my friend at *Al Arabiya* about giving you a job, and he has agreed to take you back as a reporter for special assignments. He told me he was sad to have lost you as a correspondent for U.K. and American news, as your English was perfect and you had lived in the U.S. and England for a sufficient amount of time to pick up their idioms and their ways. Would you like to work again?"

Samarra had fallen for him when he was charming, and his recent kind behavior toward her had softened her again.

"Oh yes, Ibn, I'd love to work again, but only if it pleases you," she replied in her feigned, newly-learned compliant voice.

"It does please me," Mansurallah said in a soft, unctuous voice. "How would you like to work in America?"

"In America?" Samarra replied, not daring to believe her ears. "But you don't like America."

"This is true, but I'm not going with you."

"You trust me to go to America without you?"

"Of course! You are my wife, after all. I know when I am home in my village I am an old patriarchal husband, but I am turning over a new leaf, you will see."

"What does the editor in Dubai want me to cover in the U.S., do you know?"

"He wants you to cover the upcoming presidential press conference. He will give you the details later."

"That's great, Ibn. Thank you for being so sensitive to my need for work, and my desire to be intellectually useful," Samarra said gratefully.

"Go now and make the call to your editor," he said. "You must leave soon to be in Washington D.C. on time."

Samarra went to the phone to make the arrangements with the editor of *Al Arabiya*. Mansurallah smiled inwardly. He appreciated his perfect perfidy almost as much as a good plot against the infidels. He had called the editor earlier in the day to remind him that he would be getting a call from Samarra, and to review with him the details that were expected of him. He told the editor to submit a question that his wife was to ask the President during the question period. Lastly, Mansurallah told the journalist that he was sending a friend to watch the conference on TV with him. This friend would be instructed to make sure that everything that Mansurallah had requested was done, or the editor and his family would be sure to regret their failure to carry out his order to the letter. In appreciation for his cooperation in this matter, Mansurallah promised him exclusive pictures of a great historical event.

Mansurallah received the camera equipment by messenger. It had been sent by his contact at *Al Arabiya*, and was to be used to film the press conference. Mansurallah immediately took it to the Detonator.

"I need you to retrofit an emitter into this digital camera so that it will detonate the *Krakatoa* when the filming has begun. Can you do that?"

"Of course. I have done this type of installation several times before. It is very successful, as it begins filming at the moment of detonation, so the explosion and the photographic recording of the event are done simultaneously. We have made some incredible photos that we have analyzed, and the results have led to bigger and better bombs. Some of these pictures have also been used as a tool to recruit candidates for suicide bombings. When they can see that it is painless and over in an instant, their bravery is heightened."

"However you do it, it must not be detected by the scanners of the infidels. Is that possible?"

"Yes. I use the same button depressor mechanism that comes with the camera from the manufacturer. There is only one potential problem – the picture-taking button must be pressed at the right time. If the button is pressed prematurely it will fire the bomb wherever it happens to be at that moment. You understand that, don't you?"

"You provide the sound, but the visuals are up to me."

"Exactly. Together we are a team. "

"Yes, as always. We are Allah's A team, you and I."

Mansurallah left the Detonator to his work. He pulled out his cell phone and called one of his trustworthy lieutenants.

"Youssef, is that you?"

"Yes Sheikh, it is I."

"Youssef, I have an important mission for you. Please meet me in the café on Joffa Street. You know the one."

"I'll come at once."

"Good. I'll see you there in a few minutes."

Mansurallah could see Youssef's face as he received the call to action. He looked harmless enough. Most people would have thought him a nerd, but this nerd had nerves of steel. He had acquitted himself well on several attacks. Youssef had been educated in the U.S. until the age of fifteen, and his English was still very good. His parents had sent him home to receive proper Islamic religious training.

He soon fell into Maulana's network, and little by little he was found to be an excellent warrior for Allah. His hatred of Americans was based on the prejudicial treatment that he had received from his schoolmates. He was teased for being an Arab. Comments about his aquiline nose, his oily skin, and his religious beliefs had built up a hatred that had escalated until he had found an outlet for his fury in his membership in Mansurallah's group of fighters.

When they met in the café, Mansurallah told Youssef that he was sending him to the U.S. He was to pose as a cameraman working for *Al Arabiya*. He would be given all the necessary identity papers and credentials that would gain him admittance to the press conference he was to attend in Washington with Mansurallah's wife, who was a bona fide reporter for the Arab newspaper. He would probably be assigned a place in the back of the room since he was an Arab, and the many photographers from the more popular Western media services would be given the best places.

As long as he could see Mansurallah's wife clearly, it didn't matter if he was close to her or not, just as long as he could tell that Samarra was facing the podium. When she stood to ask her question he was to take her picture. That was all that was required of him. After the explosion he should slip out of the room as quickly and unobtrusively as possible and return home immediately. He was not to discuss the mission with anyone, especially Samarra. Under no circumstances was he to turn on the camcorder before Samarra rose to ask her question. When Mansurallah felt Youssef was totally clear about his mission, he dismissed him to go home and prepare for his trip.

The Detonator had had a metal craftsman friend of his make a beautiful large circular copper belt buckle with a verse from the Koran inscribed in cursive Arabic script. It was polished and varnished to a lovely sheen, and the bomb maker had it fitted to a genuine leather belt of tanned camel hide. He had placed it in a fancy box so that Mansurallah could give it to Samarra as a parting gift.

Mansurallah presented it to Samarra the night before he was to drive her and Youssef to the airport.

"This is a lucky token to protect your womb while we are apart," he told her. "I want you to wear it at the conference so I can see it on TV when you rise to ask your question."

"It is beautiful," Samarra said. "Thank you, Ibn. It was very sweet of you, and I promise to wear it."

She thought he might want to have sex with her before she left, and since he had been so nice of late she dared to ask him if he wanted to come to her bed.

"No," he said, patting her arm. "We will wait and give you time to heal completely from the surgery. When you return to me, we will try again to make a son."

It may have been one of the most flagrant betrayals in history. Mansurallah's wife would be an unwilling martyr to the cause, but she would never know it. Sheikh Mansurallah would go down in history, not only for being one of Allah's greatest warriors, but one who had inspired his wife to martyr herself in obedience to Allah's plan to assassinate the Great Satan of the West. It pleased Mansurallah's sense of irony that this very unsatisfactory wife should finally prove herself to have some worth, both as a weapon and as a woman who would enhance his reputation among his peers. At the same time he would be rid of her without the embarrassment of divorcing her. How deliciously ironic! It was perfect.

In the morning Mansurallah loaded Samarra's suitcase into the trunk of his car. When she was ready, he opened the passenger door for her and she slid onto the seat. He stopped to pick up Youssef on the way to the airport. Since they had never met, Mansurallah introduced his reporter wife to the counterfeit photographer. He saw them off at the gate of their flight and then drove home alone, well pleased with the way his nefarious plan was unfolding.

CHAPTER SEVENTEEN

Ivan and his team had confidently taken their seats in the Situation Room. The biggest part of their task was over when the President had indicated that he was willing to execute their plan to control the manufacture of explosives.

Each aspect of the implementation of the plan had been discussed and documented. All that was left was for the President's staff to understand the plan and cooperate in its implementation, and for the President to sign off on it. They hoped that by the time they left the meeting they would have reached an agreement about how their proposal would be announced to the country and to the rest of the world.

The State Department would no doubt be assigned the task of explaining the plan to the international community. Their skills in diplomacy would be expected to bring most of the powerful nations into compliance with the plan to halt the manufacture of ammunition and explosives. For the sake of the people in harm's way the team wanted to get a large majority of nations to agree to the terms of the plan, and to do it within two months. Those nations unwilling to comply would be given a final warning to do so, or their ammunition production facilities would be restrained by force.

Each one of the responsible government departments was given instructions to move the plan into a first priority position and get to work on it immediately. The Defense Department was given the task of developing the tactics necessary to enforce the terms of the plan. The military services were to be put into "ready mode" and instructed to take the intelligence data that Abdul had collected about illegal arms dealers, as well as the information that Damian had assembled about explosives manufacturing plants, and

be ready to eradicate those who were intentionally non-
compliant. It was a massive project that Ivan hoped would
fully occupy the nation's defense establishment, providing
them with a sense of military importance while he worked
the other side of the street.

The Treasury Department was to immediately prepare
the documents that each manufacturer of ammunition would
be required to complete in order to take advantage of the
U.S. government's offer to purchase the existing inventories
and the following year's production. Auditing, monitoring
of disbursements, proof of delivery, and all other financial
details would fall under the U.S. Treasury Department's
control. The Attorney General's department would pursue
any American violators legally, as quick compliance at home
was regarded as a must. If the world was to comply, the U.S.
had to be seen to lead by example.

The investigative and intelligence agencies were to pool
all information concerning the manufacture and distribution
of explosives and ammunition. As each complying nation
came on board, information about their manufacturing
capabilities would be assimilated into a database. Eventually
it would be compiled into a computerized system that could
be used by the defense forces charged with bringing the
entire world into compliance with the terms of the plan.

Ivan had gone so far as to write a sample announcement
speech for the President to use when he addressed the
nations. Naturally the President was free to change any part
that he wished, but Ivan thought he might appreciate having
a starting point in hand. He decided to read through the
speech once more before he had it delivered to POTUS.

"My fellow citizens of the world," the speech began.
"As President of the United States of America my
responsibilities are to uphold the Constitution and defend the
citizens of my country. I confess, however, that I've had an
increasingly hard time carrying out these particular duties.
My two primary functions, upholding and defending, seem
to have caused some consternation in various parts of the

world. I'm hoping that this little talk will clarify what the United States stands for and what it is trying to do.

"Upholding our Constitution doesn't mean we are trying to impose it on any other nation. Our Constitution doesn't have to be anyone else's, although it is a great document that we have used for over 200 years, and I would recommend it to students of government anywhere in the world. Through the years we have amended it twenty-seven times, so it wasn't a perfect document and it will probably continue to be a work in progress.

"The first ten amendments, or improvements, are what are known as the American Bill of Rights. I also humbly suggest that no country be without a similar document that clearly states what their government legally *can't* do to its citizens. I'm not going to take up any more time advocating our system of government, except to say that the United States has no desire to, or intention of, forcing any nation to do things our way, but with one proviso.

"This leads me to the second part of my responsibilities, which is defending the citizens of the United States. It is in this area that my presidency has encountered difficulties, and it is in this same area that I'm forced to act if I'm to do my job. Nearly everyone in the world knows that terrorists attacked the United States on September 11th, 2001. That heinous attack, along with some smaller prior ones, have resulted in many lethal conflicts, but they all have one thing in common: *weapons*. There is no absolute assurance that without weapons world conflicts would disappear, but there is certainly no doubt that the world can't solve its conflicts with the United States by using weapons. We have too many weapons ourselves, some too powerful to contemplate using, so weapons are not the way to solve a conflict with the world's most powerful country. There is also no way I can defend our citizens from attacks, small or large, as long as the world is crammed full of weapons. I'd now like to suggest a solution to this problem.

"The United States, I'm ashamed to say, purchases a dollar volume of weapons for its military and security use that is equal to that of the rest of the world combined. My country will now offer to buy all the chemical explosive materials produced in the world for a period of one year, as well as discontinue our own manufacturing of such items. Since guns, canons, rockets, grenades, missiles, and other weapons are of no use without the powder, plastics, Semtex, TNT, or dynamite that causes them to function, we need only halt the production of these chemical explosives to render the weapons useless.

"During that year the explosives manufacturers can devote themselves to finding another product to make. We will expect that all nations will volunteer to do this, since no compliant nation will have armed enemies, therefore none will have any need for weapons. During this first year of worldwide non-violence we'll make great efforts to resolve our differences in meetings, conferences, negotiations, and debates – whatever it takes to stop the genocide.

"At this time in history there is only one superpower, and it is the United States. But there is no benefit to being the only superpower if no *super* good comes of it. This country and this president are going to use our power to end violence and warfare among the tribes of man once and for all. Therefore any nations that are not willing to lay aside whatever weapons they may have stockpiled before I declared this embargo are warned that the full weight of the power of the United States will be brought to bear on them for any breach of the cease-fire that is to begin tomorrow.

"Every human being is a separate and distinct creation, and no man has the right to take the life of another man. This should be self-evident to every human being, but if there are any who believe that their credo, religion, nature, or system of government supersedes the commandment, "Thou shalt not murder," then my nation's power will be unleashed on them to the full extent of its range, so help me God.

"Tomorrow a fully detailed description of how this plan for victory over violence will operate will be on the front page of every newspaper in the world. It will be broadcast on every news program on the radio and TV. I promise that the United States is not interested in occupying the land of any nation. We are not going to overthrow governments, or conquer nations. Our only intention is to put an end to violence by removing the weapons we use on each other in those times when we are too angry to find a peaceful way to convince people that our cause is just.

"Dead people are not convinced. They are never going to be convinced – they are just dead. Therefore, the United States is going to do its best to remove the principal weapons of death. We invite every nation of good will to join with us in this task, but we warn those nations with evil intentions toward any other nation, be it for reasons of race, ethnicity, religion, territory, politics or any other reason, that we will meet any employment of weapons with an unremitting force designed to make such choices very painful. Those who live by the sword will die by the sword.

"You may be wondering why the United States is choosing this moment to announce such a unilateral plan of disarmament. Why is the American President being so naïve as to expect that countries that do not share his worldview will put down their weapons on his say so?

"These are good questions. The answer is that for the first time in the history of humankind a single nation has the power to enforce peace without exploiting other nations. My element of haste in announcing this plan is due to the fact that some countries are now working towards the acquisition of nuclear and other weapons of mass destruction.

"Once a country refuses to abandon the manufacture of weapons of mass destruction, we can no longer just sit back and wait until these weapons are used. Prevention is our purpose, and deterrence is our chosen method of retaliation. If this most powerful of nations is not willing to use its power to ensure peace, security, tranquility, and international fraternity, then it is either a hoax, a bluffer, or just plain impotent.

"The United States is none of these things. If we must live in a world full of hate then you may hate us, but you will do it peacefully or not at all. Therefore I proclaim that starting tomorrow the penalty for using a gun against another human, planting a bomb, mine, or IED, using any weapon to kill or maim any person shall be deemed unlawful under all circumstances and subject to capital punishment."

It was Ivan Welland's greatest hope that the President of the United States would announce that the new world order of non-violence was beginning, but whether he used what he had written or not, he hoped the President would be firm.

Ivan had the feeling, when he saw Brad Burke and Laura Murphy walk into his office from the waiting area outside, that he would be attending a wedding in the not-too-distant future. There was something about them that reminded him of the way things were with him and Marina just before they decided to get married. It was hard for him to put his finger on just what it was that made him jump to that conclusion, but he would have bet money that his intuition was correct. There was something that clearly indicated to him that they had reached an understanding on the deepest level.

"Please come in and have a seat." Ivan said, leading the way to the sitting area. "What can I do for you?"

Laura spoke first, not because Brad was reticent, but because the couple had decided that she should bait the hook and set it when Ivan bit on it. Brad was to prepare to reel in the fish, fighting its every maneuver to throw the hook and break free. Then at the end, if all went well, and with the fish alongside, Ivan would help them bring it aboard.

"Dr. Welland, we've come to you with some work that we've been collaborating on. We chose you to be the first to see it because you're a friend and a person in the government who is aware of the workings of the bureaucracy, and because we both thought of you simultaneously as the best person we knew to give us honest feedback on the viability of our plan. I feel quite certain you already know that our proposal concerns the environment. I'm sure that you're not too surprised that I'm involved in such a project, but you may wonder what Brad the Oil Ogre has to do with it."

"You realize I'm not involved in any way with this area. It's probably in the Secretary of the Interior's bailiwick."

"Yes, we do realize that, but we feel we need a neutral person, one with a keen intellect and some common sense, one who has no special professional or political stake in the issue. So we've chosen you, and there's little you can do to escape," Laura said.

"Very well then," Ivan replied, "I just wanted you to know that I don't have much clout outside this office. I only deal with the security interests of the nation and its President. I wasn't trying to avoid the issue or the pleasure it would give me to hear anything you have to say Dr. Murphy, and you too, Mr. Burke."

Laura then launched into the report that she and Brad had prepared. She covered all the main points in her summary, and then she made the observation that legislation would be needed to implement the recommendations.

"Your proposal is groundbreaking in its approach," Ivan said, when Laura had finished. "In my opinion, the idea of settling on a single non-polluting energy source to replace fossil fuels is terrific. But to get Congress enthusiastic about focusing on hydrogen as that fuel will take enormous amounts of arm-twisting among the naysayers whose efforts have been devoted to other fuels and technologies. There'd have to be a bill proposed by the President and a good deal of preliminary support for the concept in the Congress, but assuming you got over those roadblocks, I think it's the second best idea for U.S. policy changes that I've heard."

"Oh, and what's the first?" Laura asked.

"Brad already knows," Ivan said.

Laura looked inquiringly at Brad. "Do you know?"

"I think I can guess."

"Well, what is it?" Laura asked.

"Neither of us is allowed to speak of it yet," Brad said.

"But you won't have to wait long, Laura," Ivan assured her. "Just until the President's upcoming press conference."

"You boys wouldn't be in the old boy's club mode, would you now?" she said with an affected Irish accent.

"No darlin', it's not like that. It's something Ivan and I have been working on since before I met you."

"Now if you wouldn't mind, Laura, I'd like to borrow your man for a few minutes alone," Ivan said, and rang for Brooklyn to come in. "Brooklyn, this is Dr. Laura Murphy, the noted environmentalist."

"How do you do?" Brooklyn said.

"Please take Dr. Murphy to the cafeteria for a coffee so I can speak in private with Mr. Burke."

"Sure boss, I can do that."

The two women left, and both men could imagine that the women felt they had been excluded, but the Security Advisor had to work within certain parameters.

"I apologize for having done that little number on the women. I hope Laura will understand. I know Marina would have hated it if I'd done that to her. Anyway, I've spoken with the President, and he's going to ask you to head up the group that will negotiate with the chemical companies to shut down the manufacture of explosives, first in the U.S. and then worldwide. It will be a hard job, especially with the overseas manufacturers, who in some cases won't be persuaded without a little muscle being applied.

"The situation is critical," Ivan continued, "and the nation needs your expertise to help bring peace to this tired old world. I promise we'll let you get back to solving the important energy and environmental issues just as soon as possible. Please listen to the President's speech tomorrow, discuss it with Laura, and then think carefully about whether you can take this project on. We'll be waiting for your decision."

CHAPTER EIGHTEEN

The investigations in Israel into the murders in Eilat and the attack on the Consulate in Jerusalem had led the Mossad to a little arms dealer called Shlomo Sussman. Under heavy questioning the man admitted he'd sold arms to an Arab Sheikh. Serial numbers and ballistic tests had shown that these weapons were the ones used in both the attacks. Eventually the illegal arms dealer broke down completely. In exchange for a pledge that he would not be given the death penalty he turned state's evidence and confessed to having been involved in many deals in which guns and ammunition had been sold to jihadist terrorist factions operating in many countries around the world.

As a result of information gathered from Shlomo, the secret police had identified Sheikh Ibn Mansurallah as the leader of the cell responsible for the two unsolved attacks. In revenge the Mossad agents set up a daring assassination attack on the Arab terrorist. Their plan was to make it look as though the Sheikh had been involved in the preparation of an IED and that an accidental explosion had killed him. If it seemed to be an accident, then their counter intelligence operations could continue unexposed, and eventually the other members of his cell could be captured along with vital details concerning the supporters of the Sheikh.

That night Samarra and Youssef checked into their hotel in Washington. Mansurallah was sound asleep at home, after having visited his wives to demand his connubial rights. As he dreamed his dreams of fame and glory, a man dressed as an Arab silently affixed a magnetic bomb to the frame of his car just beneath the driver's seat. The bomb was made of parts often found in IEDs, and used in car bombings in the Middle East. Now that the bomb was planted, it could be detonated at any time. Agents of the Mossad would follow his car, and when he was in a location where innocent people would not be injured, they would detonate the explosives and consign another terrorist to the ministrations of his Allah.

Laura Murphy was listening carefully to what Bradley Burke had to say. He was explaining the critical role he was being asked to play in the affairs of the nations of the world. It was difficult for her to put aside the importance of her own life's work. There was little in the world that Laura valued more than the health of the world's environment, but she had to admit that an end to weapons and violence should take precedence in the short term over environmental problems. If the political and religious hatreds of the international community could not be brought under control, there might not be any humans around to enjoy the environment. She understood all this very well, but she could sense that after waiting so long for the right man to come along, she might not see much of him in the next few years if he accepted the President's assignment.

"I realize that if I take this job," Brad was saying, "we won't have the quiet, pleasant life we've been hoping for. No doubt I'll be away a lot. But how can I, in good conscience, not try to help the President to take the first really positive step in quelling the poisonous violence that's permeating the world? I promise that I'll come back as soon as possible and work full time with you on stopping people from poisoning the air, the water, and the food."

"Of course, Brad, you must accept it," Laura said, in the sad, sacrificial voice of the millions of women in history who have unwillingly sent their men off to war. "But what about your company? What's going to happen when you're away?"

"I've already found a number two man," he said with a smile. "I can accord myself an emeritus title like one of your academics, and move on to bigger and better things. My second in command is already President of the company, and he can run it just as well as I can. He would have succeeded me as CEO in due time, anyway."

"Well, I'm glad that you have your bases covered. I'm going to miss you, though."

"So why don't you come with me, then?"

"Right. Get serious, Brad."

"I *am* serious! Since you like traveling around in my plane so much, I was sort of hoping you'd come along."

Laura looked at him to see if he really meant it.

"What about *my* job?" she said. "When my sabbatical is up I'll have to go back to teaching my classes."

"I've been giving that prospect a lot of thought in the last thirty seconds, and I think you should be given another job," Brad said, half jokingly.

"Aha, the true chauvinist Mr. Burke is emerging from the dark places within. This Mr. Burke wants me to give up my job so he can pursue his own path to glory."

"That's not exactly what I had in mind."

"Well, what *did* you have in mind?"

"I was thinking of it more as a promotion for you. I'll make my acceptance of the President's offer conditional on two things. The first is that he accept your plan for the reduction, and eventual discontinuance, of fossil fuels, and the substitution of a program to develop hydrogen power. He can make it the lead plank in his platform for reelection. He'll certainly be reelected if his plan for compulsory weapon obsolescence succeeds, and with me heading it up, how could it fail?" Brad looked to see how she was reacting.

"Keep going," Laura said. "I want to hear about the second condition."

"The second condition is that you consent to become Mrs. Burke. I figure it will take a presidential order to get you to accept a proposal of marriage from a chauvinist ogre. You can get a leave of absence from the university to use as a hole card, and just in case you can't beat the chauvinist out of me in a reasonable length of time, you can get your old job back. While I'm busy with my project, you can be doing the myriad things necessary to get the support needed to put your plan into action. Once it becomes known that you're the author of the President's sweeping new environmental program, you'll be in such demand as a visiting professor that you'll be able to teach anywhere you choose. When that time comes I'll hold on tight to your apron strings and go with you wherever you go. That's my idea in a nutshell. "

"Why Mr. Burke, I do believe hidden in all that stuff about peace on earth and saving the environment, I heard a proposal of marriage. Did I hear you correctly?"

"Yes, Miss Murphy, you did. What's your answer?"

"Perhaps you should ask the President first if he accepts your conditions before you commit to such a serious step as marriage to a woman with so many underlying motivations and other priorities. If the President declines your first condition about the environmental clean-up, you may want to withdraw your second proposal, which is based on the first being accepted. How about *that?*"

"I'm glad I don't have to negotiate a peace accord with you. I'm sure you'd get the best of me. As far as marriage goes, however, we're dealing with a heart condition, and here I'm on firm ground. My heart is completely connected to yours, and this doesn't depend on the President, so I have to ask you something before I go into full cardiac arrest – Laura Murphy, will you do me the honor of being my wife?"

"Having carefully thought it over for thirty seconds, my answer is yes, definitely yes."

After tearful hugging and kissing, the couple retired to the bedroom where the negotiations continued.

Later Brad called Ivan to ask him to inform the President of his acceptance of his offer, subject to some conditions. He added another proviso, that the President should use his influence with the Chief Justice of the Supreme Court and get him to perform the marriage ceremony for them.

Ivan was happy and relieved to hear that Brad would accept the President's offer, and he was pleased to learn that his friends were soon to be married, but he was temporarily more concerned about another call he'd received right after Burke's call. The second call was from a Dr. Husseini, who told Brooklyn that he had information about terrorism that he would exchange for emergency refugee status and a flight to the U.S. for his parents and siblings. Ordinarily Ivan would not have spoken to the man himself, but would have had one of his staff interview him first. But Brooklyn had been so insistent that the doctor converse directly with him that Ivan had agreed to speak to him.

"Dr. Husseini, this is Ivan Welland. How may I help?"

"Dr. Welland, as I told your assistant, I have information about an upcoming terrorist bombing attack, but if I reveal it, not only my life but the lives of my family will be in jeopardy. I must have your absolute assurance that I can bring my family to the United States."

"I'll have to know the details before I can make a case for granting you and your family the immigration status you're requesting. I'm sure you can understand that until the accuracy of the information is established, my colleagues at the Immigration and Naturalization Service will not allow this kind of special entrance into the country."

"I can understand that, but it's a question of life and death. We lived in America before while I went to medical school, and I'm sure we were cleared to enter the country at that time. The government must have records."

Ivan didn't know that the efficient Brooklyn had already begun to check his story. As the men spoke on the phone she had printed out the information that had popped up on her screen. She pushed the paper in front of Ivan's eyes. Everything she had found out about Husseini's background led Ivan to believe the man's story.

"I'll tell you what I'll do," said Ivan. "You put your family on a plane and give us the flight information, and by the time they arrive we will have arranged some temporary status with the INS so you can meet them and bring them into the country. However, you must tell me the information that you have for me at once. Time can be of the essence in these matters."

The doctor explained to Ivan how he had been forced at gunpoint to perform an operation on a woman, and then been forced to place a plastic explosive charge inside her womb. The woman's husband, a well-known terrorist leader, had stood at his elbow during the surgical procedure to make sure the charge was put in place. Threats on the lives of his family had been uttered in the event he ever spoke to anyone about the surgery. He felt that he would be called upon to do the procedure on other women in the future, and the thought so revolted him that he got on a plane at once, determined to use the information to get his family out of the country.

"I realized that the woman was to be a suicide bomber."

"It certainly sounds that way," said Ivan. "I need to know the name of this terrorist so I can check him out."

"His name is Ibn Mansurallah, and his wife is Samarra. That's all I know, except that he comes from my home town, and everyone there is terrified of him."

After saying goodbye to Dr. Husseini, Ivan turned to his assistant.

"Brooklyn, please run a check on these people," he said, passing her the names of Ibn Mansurallah and his wife. "Be sure to check with the Israelis as well. Also, please see if the President will speak on the phone with me for a minute. Then call the INS and arrange with them to allow Husseini's family to get temporary refugee admittance status."

Ivan leaned back. He stared straight ahead, as though he were watching something so fascinating that he couldn't take his eyes off it, even to blink. Actually he was seeing nothing – he was just concentrating. Brooklyn had seen her boss go into his thinking mode before, and she knew not to disturb him until he came out of it. Besides, she had work to do.

Ivan couldn't get over Husseini's story about planting a bomb inside a woman's womb. Aside from the technical question of whether or not a suicide bomber with a bomb inside her body would be detectable by the standard scanner devices, there was the horror that such an event brought to mind. He decided to disregard the imagery and focus on preventing anything from happening. From the perpetrator's point of view, it probably didn't matter whether the bomb was carried internally or externally, but this way the internal bomb would be invisible to the naked eye. There'd be no need for a bomber's vest or any bulky clothing that could provoke suspicion. Ivan asked Brooklyn to check with a bomb squad expert to ascertain if this kind of bomb would be feasible, then he went back to his own thoughts.

Assuming that everything Dr. Husseini said was true, what would be the most probable target for such a bomber? Ivan reasoned that this type of bomb would be much more expensive to produce, since aside from the cost of materials, the special assembly problems, and the sacrifice of the suicide bomber's life, the cost of a surgeon to implant the bomb would have to be included. Since each level of fabrication carried the additional risk of detection, and since the first bomb would be a tip-off to the enemy of the existence of such a new procedure, the target would have to be of very high value to the terrorist group that evolved such a fiendish method of disposing of human life.

Ivan's continuing speculations led him to consider the upcoming events at which such a suicide bomber might appear. In many ways the internally implanted bomb had the same purpose as a bomb carried in the special jackets the terrorists had designed and manufactured for the past number of years, but the one major difference was that it was not subject to visual detection. Another difference between the new method of carrying a bomb and the traditional one was the limited quantity of explosives that could be carried. Ivan imagined that a person could only carry a small bomb internally, as compared with the large quantity of explosives that could be carried externally in a vest specially made for the occasion.

This line of reasoning led him to the question of the type of explosive that might be used. He would have to check with his experts as to whether any of the new, very powerful explosives had been discovered in terrorist hands. It seemed logical that a smaller bomb would have to be made of more volatile chemical ingredients that would create an even more powerful blast than those of the traditional suicide bombs.

More questions for his experts were popping into his mind by the minute. He forced himself to stop thinking about the technical properties and the construction of the bomb, in favor of considering the end uses of such a weapon. Like the majority of suicide bombs, this new invention was obviously designed to be used as an anti-personnel weapon. These weapons were usually detonated in places where large numbers of people were congregated. But people gather in all sorts of places, so that didn't narrow down the possible target areas very much. It was only when Ivan factored in the additional element of the high importance of the target itself that he began to realize that he was getting closer. If the target had to be someone of supreme importance, someone very visible to the public eye, who might that be? Ivan paused in his reflections and went out to see how Brooklyn was progressing with her assignments.

"How's it coming, Brooklyn? Have you come up with any information about those Arab names we were given?"

"Yes, I was just waiting for you to come back to earth so I could let you know what I've discovered. There's some interesting stuff here, but I'm not sure what it all means. For instance, Ibn Mansurallah was a suspected terrorist leader. He was on the Mossad's most wanted list."

"Was?"

"Yeah, he was killed in a car bombing incident just a few hours ago. Mossad is claiming no responsibility for the affair. They're trying to plant the idea that he was carrying an IED and it accidentally exploded. Personally, I don't buy that. I'd put my money on a planned assassination by the Israelis. So that ends any interest we may have had in him."

"Anything else?"

"The woman is Samarra Mansurallah, and she's his wife. She's an international news correspondent for the Arab press, and she's here in the U.S. now. Husseini checked out. He's legit – med school in Texas, residency in Philadelphia, good references all around. We're trying to get in contact with some of his classmates to see what we can learn about him personally. INS was cooperative and will grant a temporary visa to his family pending an investigation into the doctor's allegations. The President will call you back. I think that about covers it."

"Good work as usual, Brooklyn."

Ivan went back into his office to mull some more. He bent to sit down, but no sooner had his rump hit the chair than he bounced back up again and ran to the outer office.

"Brooklyn, where is Samarra Mansurallah right now?"

"Right now? I don't know, boss. All they said is that she's here in D.C."

"Damn! The President is the target. They're planning to assassinate the President! Mr. Mansurallah may be dead, but his wife is not. What time is the press conference?"

"It starts at 4:00 PM."

"That gives us two hours to find this woman. Call the Chief of the Whitehouse Secret Service and tell him not to admit the woman Samarra Mansurallah to the President's press conference. That goes for anyone who is with her. Tell him to hold them in isolation until I can question them. Do you know where Dr. Husseini is right now?"

"No, not exactly, but I have his cell phone number."

"Good enough. Call him for me, please."

Within in minutes, Brooklyn had him on the line.

"Dr. Husseini, it's Ivan Welland. I wanted to let you know that your parents are squared away. They'll be given temporary visas to enter the U.S. as soon as they land. Let my secretary know the flight as soon as you can."

"Thank you so much. I'm so relieved. Thank you!"

"No problem. But now I need you to identify the woman you operated on – Samarra Mansurallah."

"I'll be happy to do that, but can you arrange it so that my identity is kept secret? If her husband finds out that I was the one who fingered him, I'll be a dead man."

"Actually, Ibn Mansurallah *is* a dead man."

"What? What are you saying?"

"He was killed in a car bomb explosion."

There was silence on the other end as Dr. Husseini adjusted to this news. Then he let out a sigh of relief.

"We don't have any time to lose," Ivan said. "We'll still handle the ID without Mrs. Mansurallah seeing you."

"I'm at your disposal. One good turn deserves another."

"I'll send a Secret Service car to pick you up and bring you in. Where are you now?"

"The Columbia Hospital for Women. I'm not far from you. I'll wait for the driver at the main entrance."

"Good, then I'll see you when you get here," Ivan said.

In a few minutes Brooklyn announced that the head of the Secret Service was on the line.

Ivan picked up. "Chief, I'm sure there's going to be an attempt on the President's life during his press conference."

"What makes you think that?"

"It began with a tip from a gynecologist who claimed he implanted a bomb in the womb of a female suicide bomber. The woman, it turns out, was the wife of a suspected terrorist leader who was just killed by the Israelis in a car-bombing incident. She's a reporter for an Arab media service and will be covering the President's press conference. I've warned your people at the screening site to be on the lookout for this woman. I'm having the doctor brought in to identify the woman as the same one he did the surgery on."

"My God, Ivan, you're telling me that a bomb was implanted *inside* of her?"

"That seems to be the case," Ivan replied.

"I'll get on it right away."

CHAPTER NINETEEN

Ivan's desk seemed to him to be like a pond beset by a strong wind – the waves were springing up all over it. He was doing his best to stay focused on the big picture, even though he was well aware that he was now going to have to face immeasurable quantities of exasperating and wearisome details if he was to assist the President in his gallant effort to ban the manufacture of explosive materials all over the world.

But first and foremost the President, of course, had to be kept alive to make the plan clear to his fellow Americans. If he were assassinated during his speech, the news media would be focused entirely on the assassination and not on the content of the speech. For the sake of world peace and the President's life, Ivan had to concentrate all his attention on this problem and forget about his personal safety. However much the evil machinations of Ibn Mansurallah and his cohorts in the Middle East affected his own life, they were secondary in importance to the President's safety.

What was wrong with the world? Had everyone gone mad? Ivan questioned the sanity of those who thought the answers to the world's conflicts were to be found in the form of a bomb. Terrorists had bombed the Consulate in Jerusalem, they had bombed the resort in Eilat, they had bombed Ivan's front door, and a bomb had killed the husband of the woman who was carrying yet another bomb in her womb, which in turn was intended to kill the President of the United States.

How many maniacs were out there running around with deadly bombs? There wasn't a shadow of a doubt in Ivan's mind that the President must go ahead with the plan to remove the explosives from the equation. The U.N. had sponsored a nuclear proliferation treaty, and no one had died from a nuclear explosion in over sixty years. But in limiting the treaty to nuclear weapons the signatory nations had tacitly approved the use of conventional weapons of mass destruction, and it was these weapons that had killed millions of people since 1946.

At this moment Ivan would have welcomed another cold war, because the standoff between the Soviets and the Americans had killed no one in spite of the bombastic threats that had been fired off. If the plan to stop the manufacture of all other types of explosives was as successful as the nuclear stand down had been, the world could get a breather. If the U.S. and the Soviets could manage to stop the march to destruction, then Islam and the West could, too.

Maybe in time rational people would prevail, Ivan thought, and certainly the chances would be better in a world whose guns and bombs had been silenced. Just the act of opposing the President's plan would be enough to prove the evil intentions of such nations. In the atomic age the deterrent to using such weapons of mass destruction was the ability of the U.S. to respond with overwhelming force. Once again history was calling America to the task of providing the deterrent to those who would take over the world by force. Although the job of policing the world in order to excise the violent minority was not one America would have chosen, there simply was no other alternative offered by the other nations.

The hubbub created by the pre-presidential press conference was considerably greater than usual. The pressure was on the Secret Service to screen the attendees with extra care. Regular members of the White House Press Corps were well known to the agents doing the screening at the entrance to the press room. Journalists who had recently acquired press credentials were subjected to searches, careful questioning, and body pat downs. This was in addition to electronic scans like the ones at airport security checkpoints. The latest scanning equipment was said to reveal everything under a person's clothes. The reporters, especially the females, were very uncomfortable with this new assault on their privacy, but it was made mandatory by the Secret Service guards, and admittance was denied to anyone who refused to be scanned.

Margo Watson arrived early at the White House Press Center. Since this was her first presidential press conference, she wanted to make sure her credentials were in order and that she had been assigned a seat. As the others filed in, she saw the faces that had become familiar to her on TV. She was happy to have earned her way at last into the most august press circle in Washington D.C., and maybe even the world. Since she was a reporter who was unknown to the security force at the Press Center, the screeners carefully went over the contents of her purse, especially her cell phone and her small tape recorder. When the inspection was complete, she entered the conference hall and took her assigned seat in the back of the room.

The screeners had been warned to be on the lookout for one Samarra Mansurallah, but she had worked under her maiden name before her marriage, and her credentials were still in that name, not her husband's. In the U.S. she had been called Samantha Nasr, and the guards at the screening center made no connection with the woman they had been warned to watch for. The searches, both electronic and manual, had not uncovered anything suspicious, although her large copper belt buckle had come under close scrutiny.

Samarra's credentials were in order, so she was assigned to a seat in the back of the auditorium next to Wendy. Samarra was displeased with her seat assignment, for she felt that her position with the media was too important to allow her to be relegated to the back of the room. The Arab press was not highly regarded by the American government, however, as it was totally partial to Islam and editorially anti-American, but in deference to political correctness, the journalists couldn't be excluded from the conference.

Youssef, the terrorist and tyro photographer, was also searched and questioned at length. His camera was closely examined, but the Detonator's talents were such that nothing suspicious was detected during the inspection. He was shunted off to the dark little section of the room devoted to the photographers, where he placed himself behind the first rank of cameramen to await the moment when Samarra would rise to ask her question.

The President's Press Secretary went to the podium and began giving the reporters the rules that were to be in effect during the conference. Those who had previously submitted questions were to raise their hands at the appropriate time. The President would call on them one by one. They were to stand, state their name and press affiliation, and ask their question succinctly and politely.

The Press Secretary reminded them that they were not the paparazzi, and they should therefore behave like the cream of the journalistic world, which they were. A billion or more people were expected to be watching the President live on TV all over the globe.

He then told a few in-jokes to humor the reporters while they waited for the President. The reporters readied their pads, pens, and recorders, and the cameramen fiddled with their equipment. The air was full of expectation as everyone waited for the arrival of the leader of the free world.

Brooklyn announced that a Dr. Husseini had just arrived.

"Show him in please, Brooklyn," Ivan said.

"Ah, Dr. Husseini, thank you for coming. I'm just about to walk over to the President's Press Conference. Will you come along with me?"

The slender little doctor felt dwarfed by the 6'7" figure of Ivan Welland. Having been in the U.S. for many years, he was conscious of the White House and its importance to the nation and the world, so he found himself very much in awe of his surroundings.

When they arrived at the White House press conference room, Ivan led the doctor to the control room where the Secret Service monitored the security cameras. Ivan asked the agent in charge of electronic security to sweep his camera over the audience in the conference room.

"Let me know if you recognize anyone," Ivan said to Dr. Husseini, as the camera panned the faces of the reporters and cameramen in the room. When the camera moved along the last row, the doctor suddenly leaned forward.

"There," he said excitedly. "The two women seated next to each other. Do you see them? The dark one next to the aisle is Samarra Mansurallah."

Ivan sprang into action.

"Call the President's personal security detail," he said to the Secret Serviceman. "Tell them not to let POTUS into the conference room."

Then he turned to the doctor. "Dr. Husseini, please come with me. I must ask you to make the official identification of the suspect so that it will be legal, and also in case there are questions about the implantation of the bomb."

To a uniformed guard he said, "Take Dr. Husseini to the interrogation room and wait there with him on the staff side of the glass. While you are waiting, summon the on-call bomb expert and get him to join you at once."

Husseini and the guard left. Ivan hurried to the entrance of the conference room. Then he slowed down, and with great deliberation asked the Agent in charge of screening to tell him if anyone had accompanied the dark woman in the last row when she had checked in. When the agent told him she had come in with a cameraman, Ivan asked him to point the man out to him. They panned the camera over the faces of the photographers.

When the lens got to Youssef the agent said, "That's him! That's the guy who came along with her."

"All right then, we've got to take these two into custody for interrogation before the President comes in. I can escort the woman out, but you Secret Servicemen need to arrest the photographer quietly and simultaneously. Don't let him take any pictures. There should be no struggling, and no sudden moves. You must take his camera away from him. Don't let him snap the shutter or push any buttons, and the same goes for our men. I think he's a triggerman, and she's a human bomb. The camera may be the detonator. Ideally we should get this man out of the room quietly and without a fuss, but if he resists and you must use maximum force, you are authorized to do so."

The Special Agent studied the monitor for a few seconds, and then gave instructions to two other Secret Servicemen, and the three men moved off into the conference room. Ivan went in the other direction and entered the large room from the other side. He pretended he was going to slide into the aisle, as if he were going to take a seat. When he got directly in front of Samarra, he waited until she rose in deference to his size.

As soon as he was between her and the cameraman, Ivan took her arm and said, "Mrs. Mansurallah, please come with me." Ivan's size and the strength of his grip on her arm left her no choice but to obey. On the way out of the conference room Ivan kept his sizeable body between the woman and the cameraman. Samarra was hidden from Youssef by Ivan's body until he had marched her out of the auditorium.

Youssef, for his part, was busy being arrested by three burly Secret Servicemen, so he didn't notice that Samarra was no longer in her seat. Two men held his arms while the third gently removed the camera that was hung from a strap around his neck. He was marched out of the conference room rapidly, with hardly a protest, and taken to another interrogation room.

Welland began his interview with Mrs. Mansurallah by asking her if she was the wife of Ibn Mansurallah.

"Yes," she replied.

"Have you spoken to your husband lately?"

"No, not since I left home three days ago."

If this was true, Ivan understood that he would be the one delivering the news that she was a widow. He had no choice. He had to tell her the news, but he would watch her reactions closely as a way of gauging her character. He would also consult with Dr. Husseini, who was watching and listening on the other side of the observation glass.

"I'm sorry Ma'am, but I must tell you that your husband died a few days ago when a bomb exploded in his car."

At times like these Ivan's Texas manners sometimes took over and he returned to his boyhood vernacular, calling every man *sir*, and all women, *ma'am*.

Samarra just looked at him. She said nothing for a full minute while she tried to make sense of this news. Was this huge American official lying in order to get her to talk of her husband's affairs, about which she knew nothing but suspected much? Or had he pulled her out of the auditorium to indulge his hatred of Arabs by flexing his bureaucratic muscles? As for her husband's death, if it were true that he was dead, it would mean she was honorably released from a very bad marriage, and that was a good thing in many ways.

"How do you know this?" she asked at last.

"It was on the news. Apparently he was an important figure in your country, for Maulana al-Mutanabi himself lauded him in his funeral service. I can see from your expression that you don't know whether or not to believe me. Here's a cell phone. You may use it to call home if you'd like to. I'll leave you alone for a few minutes, if you wish."

"Yes," is all she said in reply, as she took the cell phone.

Ivan left the room and joined the translator and the others behind the glass wall to watch, record, and listen to her call. They had requested an Arab translator to be sent to the room, even though Dr. Husseini could have interpreted, but they honored his desire to remain unidentified in all circumstances, and sent for Abdul, Ivan's departmental employee. The men greeted each other with a nod and waited while Samarra's call went through.

"Hello," said a female voice that Samarra recognized at once as the voice of Mansurallah's first wife.

"This is Samarra. Is it true that Ibn is dead? I just heard this news from someone a minute ago."

"You just heard the news, and you conveniently couldn't get back for the funeral, but already you are calling to see what is to be your portion of the settlement?"

"That's not it at all," Samarra replied.

"Well I'll tell you anyway," the wife shot back in strident tones. "You are the fourth wife, and you have no children. I'm in charge now, and I tell you that after his first three wives and all the children have been taken care of there will be nothing left for you. You can come by for your clothes, but if you don't pick them up in a week, I will sell them, and the money will go into the estate. Don't call here again. We are grieving Ibn's loss, but not yours."

"Whew," Ivan said, "nice lady."

Ivan went back into the interrogation room feeling sorry for Samarra, but resigned to do his job and find out what she might know of Ibn Mansurallah's terrorist activities. He found her lack of emotional reaction to the news of her husband's death to be peculiar.

"Do you believe me now?" Ivan asked her.

"Yes, but I'm afraid you think I'm hard and callous in my attitude about the death of my husband. Ibn was a modern woman's nightmare of a husband. You have to believe me. He lied to me when we were courting. He never told me about his other wives, nor about his view of women and the institution of marriage, which were somewhere to the right of the Taliban's. So I'm not sorry that he's gone, and I don't care who knows it."

"I'm not here to judge your grief or lack of it," Ivan assured her. "But I would like to know everything you can tell me about his business and his friends. How did he feel about Americans, for instance?"

"He shared nothing of these things with me. I was a virtual prisoner in the house. I stood in line behind three harridans that hated me because I was educated. What he wanted from me was children – everything else was despicable. I know nothing about his business, and he never introduced me to a single friend, so I'm afraid I can be of no help with your questions on these topics. All I can tell you is that he hated Jews, Christians, and Americans."

"Your life must have been very depressing for you."

"It was. There were times when I just wanted to die, but at least that's over with now."

"It doesn't seem to me that your religion brought you much comfort."

"Not the way it was practiced in Ibn's village, anyway."

"You said you were suicidal. When did you decide to become a martyr?"

"Oh, so that's where you are going with these questions. You think since I was unhappy in my marriage I would consider becoming a martyr? That's total rubbish. I am not like those fanatics who think that Allah will reward them for killing infidels. No matter how sad my life was, I could never even consider taking any life but my own, and I never got to that point, either."

"So you deny that you are in America to be a suicide bomber?"

Ivan got the feeling that this woman was not a bomber, but he had to find out why a competent witness like the doctor would say such a thing about her.

"Of course I deny it, because it is not true."

"How then do you explain the bomb you are carrying?"

"What? I'm not carrying any bomb. See," and she held out her arms to indicate that they were empty.

Ivan was convinced that the woman didn't know she was a walking bomb. She would have had to be too good an actress to pretend innocence with such consummate skill. Her husband had rigged the bomb inside her without her knowing it. Dr. Husseini had been right all along.

"Please tell me, Mrs. Mansurallah, have you had a recent surgical procedure?"

"What business is that of yours?" Samarra said, with some indignation. "I don't see what my personal medical history has to do with the present situation."

"Well, normally it wouldn't be any of my business, but I have reason to believe that during a recent surgery a bomb was implanted inside you, and that makes it my business."

Suddenly it all became clear to Samarra why her husband had become so solicitous in the weeks after her surgery. He was caring for his bomb. Allowing her to go back to work was part of his plan, and the target was the President of the United States. Even friendly Youssef was an accomplice, although she thought he probably assumed she knew about the bomb and was a brave suicide bomber seeking martyrdom. Samarra knew that her abdomen felt different somehow after the surgery, but she assumed it was just tight internal stitches, and that in time it would all return to normal.

For a moment Samarra looked at Ivan with a totally blank expression as she processed what he had told her, then suddenly she burst into tears.

"Oh my God," she cried, looking down at her belly. "My God, what has my husband done to me?"

She was about to hold herself there, then she suddenly looked terrified and she spread her arms outward, as though she were afraid to set off the bomb inside her womb. She looked up at Ivan with a pitiful expression in her eyes.

"Help me! Sir, please help me. I don't want to die!"

The full weight of the revelation hit her all at once, and she fainted dead away in her chair. Ivan summoned help from the doctor, who had been watching from behind the glass. Soon the woman came around. She recognized Dr. Husseini as the man who had done the surgery on her.

"You," she said. "What are *you* doing here? You did this to me! Why did you do such a thing? Tell them I didn't know about the bomb inside me."

"Samarra, listen to me," he said, with pleading eyes. "I've already told them everything. I'm extremely sorry for what I did to you, but I only did it under threat of death. Your husband was holding a gun on me and looking over my shoulder during the whole procedure."

"What do I do now?" Samarra moaned.

"Perhaps the doctor can operate again," said Ivan. "If you trust him to do another operation, I'm sure he could remove the bomb."

"I would gladly do that," said Dr. Husseini, "but I need an operating room, and some assisting medical staff."

"Didn't you just come from the Columbia Hospital for Women?" Ivan asked him. "What were you doing there?"

"I was being interviewed for a post in the Department of Obstetrics and Gynecology."

"Perfect. What was the name of the doctor who interviewed you? I'll call him and make the arrangements," said Ivan.

When Husseini gave him the information, Ivan pulled out his cell phone and talked with the head of the Department of OB/GYN. It took a little arm-twisting to get the doctor consent to having this dangerous procedure take place in his operating room.

"Husseini put the bomb in," Ivan remarked, "so he can take it out, I suppose. Just don't use the ultra-sound machine on her. I'll send a Secret Service bomb expert along. He'll make sure that the operation is safe. Think of this as an opportunity to see what your applicant Husseini can do."

While Ivan was speaking with Samarra and Husseini, the bomb expert examined the camera they had confiscated from Youssef. He had taken the camera apart and discovered the cleverly hidden fine gauge wire that would send the signal to ignite the explosives in a remote location when the camera was activated.

Youssef was carted off to a holding cell where he would stay until he could be brought to trial. The Secret Service was about to order a cancellation of the President's press conference so that they could perform a total teardown and an electronic sweep of the rooms used by the press corps, since they didn't know where the bomb was hidden. Ivan was able to put a stop to that futile search when he explained that the explosives were surgically implanted inside the woman. It took him a while to convince the hardened Secret Servicemen that such an evil, unthinkable procedure had indeed been carried out.

As a result of the threat and the confusion caused by the assassination attempt, it was decided that the press conference should be canceled for that day and rescheduled to take place immediately after the President's speech to the United Nations General Assembly in New York on the following day.

CHAPTER TWENTY

The President's special agent in charge of his personal security advised POTUS that an attempt on his life had been thwarted. The news made the President's resolve to change things even stronger than it had been before. His professional political speechwriters had gone to work on Ivan's draft and polished it to the point where the President felt certain it was going to be an inspiring message that promised relief to a sick world. The change in venue of his speech to the United Nations would only serve to widen its audience. The political pundits, commentators, and his opponents would have something substantial to bandy about for a change. *Too idealistic, naïve, unenforceable,* and *over-ambitious* were the adjectives the President expected to hear from his critics.

POTUS ordered Ivan Welland to come along with him on his jaunt to the United Nations headquarters in New York City. He would give a monumental speech to the General Assembly, during which he would make the international announcement of his War on Ammunition program. The President had rescheduled his press conference to follow his address to the delegates, at which time he would answer questions from the international press. Since the ammunition ban was Ivan's idea, the President felt he should be at the United Nations with him. Besides, the Commander-in-Chief wanted his future Secretary of Defense to become involved in his job as quickly as possible.

Ivan climbed aboard Marine One, the large helicopter that usually transported the President from the White House lawn to connecting flights on Air Force One at Andrews Air

Base. As the Secret Service always did when protecting the President, they changed the procedure to keep any would-be assassin off his trail. As a result the President, the first lady, Welland, the Secretary of State, and a cadre of Secret Service bodyguards were slated to stay on Marine One all the way to the helipad at the United Nations.

The big, dark chopper came up from the south, turned over the East River, and the rotors whacked their way through the air to the landing site next to East River Drive. Had Ivan had telescopic vision he could have seen a figure ten blocks away on the roof of a Park Avenue building to the west. The man was picking the lock of the door that led down the stairs into the building from its roof. He was far enough away that, had he been seen, he wouldn't have been suspected of any conspiracy having to do with the President or the United Nations.

The chopper unloaded its human cargo as the thumping blades slowed down, and welcome silence replaced the noisy turbulence of the helicopter engine. To the degree that it is ever possible to move the President of the United States unobtrusively around the planet, the Secret Service officers covertly shepherded their charges into the building.

The President took a seat in the section reserved for the American delegation, and waited for his turn to be called to the podium. Ivan and the others took seats in the visitors' gallery, preparing to gauge the effect of the President's words on the international diplomats. The President had consulted with the friendliest of America's allies, so these representatives already knew what to expect, although they had been pledged to secrecy until the President could make the general announcement, which he was about to do.

The trouble with being the president of a democracy was that the leader was always both the villain and the victim of the piece. He was the villain of those who opposed change, and the victim of those who wished to supplant him. He was the target of more invective than the Devil himself, but this

President's motives were pure. As silence overtook the assembly, the President recited to himself the promise that the peacemakers would be considered children of God.

Then he drew himself up to his full height and began to speak with confidence to the delegates and press corps in the audience as well as to those who were watching their TV's at home. The pens of the press were poised to dispense criticism. The knives that dispatched Caesar in the senate of Rome were no sharper, nor their intentions less malevolent.

Nobody gets to be President of the United States of America without absorbing the advanced principles of public speaking. Candidates for the office of President are trained like actors to play a certain role. Public relations firms receive huge fees to prepare candidates for the campaigns. Coaches work with the contestants to improve their diction, pronunciation, and speaking styles. Usually the candidates are seen to have a certain set of appealing characteristics, and they are advised to adopt a presentation that reflects and emphasizes those traits. Whether the persona of the speaker is homespun, sophisticated, wise, educated, or just friendly, his stance has been rehearsed again and again before he steps up to any podium. The delivery of this President was manufactured to be witty, kindly, smart and honest. It was supposed to appeal to the masses as well as the intelligentsia.

The Secretary General welcomed the President to the dais, to the accompaniment of a moderate amount of clapping. When the applause died down, he began to speak.

"Ladies and gentlemen, I address myself to all the people of the world, and not merely to the delegates here present. I bring the wishes and hopes of the American people for a new permanent era of peace, security, and good will to all humanity. I will also put before you a sweeping plan that we believe will be the first step in realizing these desires for peace. Please listen carefully, as there are portions of this plan that require the support of all nations.

"In my life, in every place that I have gone, there has been a clamor for peace on the part of common men and women. We, and others who have come before us to this gathering of nations, have sadly failed so far to give people what they most desire with all their hearts. It is America's intention to rectify these failures by proposing a plan which addresses the very first problem on the road to peace. My government identifies this problem as being the spread of weapons throughout the world."

A big spontaneous buzz broke out among the delegates, and the President waited until it had died down before he continued. The audience was convinced they were hearing a well-balanced man of the world talking about a universal problem. The President gave a homily, which was the story of Cain and Abel. He pointed out that the story was just as true in our day as it was in bygone days. It was the story of man's disobedience to God, and the resulting first use of a weapon to commit the murder of an envied brother. At this point the President changed his style from educator to leader.

"There are two or three items of a confessional nature that I must acknowledge before going on. The first is that when it comes to weapons, the United States is the present reigning superpower. It goes without saying that the U.S. is responsible for manufacturing and selling more weapons than any other nation. The second point I'd like to make is that the use of these weapons, ours and everyone else's, breaks the bonds of peace between peoples and leads to wars. Third, the wealth of our country that is spent on weapons exceeds what is spent by all the other nations combined. What would happen if these funds were allocated to other items, like foreign and domestic relief, for example? What is stopping us from doing it? In a word, it is *defense.*"

The President paused and looked around the room.

"Whose defense? Why ours, of course. And whom are we defending ourselves against? Many of you, of course."

Uncomfortable chuckles broke out here and there, so the President delayed his next words for a moment.

"To achieve a cessation of war, murder, mayhem, and violence, as President of the United States I am hereby announcing a unilateral *Moratorium on Explosives*. If we can't get rid of weapons of mass destruction, we can control the production of ammunition, without which the weapons are useless. The emphasis is on conventional ammunition, as nuclear, chemical, and biological weapons are not presently the cause of many deaths. But guns, bombs, rockets, and missiles are the guilty devices. These weapons all depend on chemical explosives, so they must stop being used or produced. It is deeds, not words, that are needed if the killings are ever going to end. Righteousness, like charity, begins at home. So the *Moratorium on Explosives* will start with the United States. Beginning immediately, the United States will cease making the chemicals used in explosives."

The President took another sip of water, as the members of the audience murmured among themselves.

"With the money usually spent on explosives," he went on, "the United States will instead buy the entire production of these materials produced outside the U.S. for a period of one year, so the companies and workers that produced them can find other products to manufacture in their facilities, thus offering those companies a soft landing during the change-over period. To make the moratorium work, I have no choice but to request that all countries join the *Moratorium on Explosives* as our allies. The failure of governments to sign on and comply with the tenets of this declaration will be considered a hostile act, making those nations enemies of peace, and these enemies – hopefully there will be none – will be dealt with summarily by the allies of peace."

The murmurs in the audience grew louder and louder, until the President was forced to call for silence.

"Under the guise of defending ourselves we have, and you have, subscribed to a doctrine that allows any action, if it is done in self-defense. This position has been taken by nearly all nations, but there is a doctrine that precedes that one in time and importance. It is expressed best in the sixth commandment, *You shall not murder*.

"This means exactly what it says, that killing is *out*, under any and all circumstances, with the possible exception of self defense in the most extreme cases. In the twenty-first century murder, individual and mass, is most often done with guns or bombs. The nations of the world seem to have come to the position that this is permissible so long as weapons of mass destruction aren't used. Rejecting nuclear weapons resulted in the nuclear alternative being removed from the battlefields for over sixty years, during which time no one has died from an atomic bomb explosion. In fact the nations that have them have voluntarily disassembled many bombs, and we have an agency of this body, the IAEA, that does inspections to make sure that no devices are being built."

The President looked up and tried to engage as many sets of eyes as he could.

"Why don't we have an arms control treaty that includes conventional weapons, since these are the weapons that *are* doing the killing? I have heard many answers to that question such as, *weapons are too big a business to shut down*, or *we need weapons to protect ourselves with*, or *how can we be sure that others will give up their weapons if we agree to give up ours?* All these arguments are too pat and try too hard to get around the command not to murder. We simply must adhere to the commandment. If we can do it voluntarily, fine, but if we can't stop the violence willingly, then the tools of violence must be taken away."

The delegates could see that the most powerful man in the world was frustrated by the inability of the diplomats in the United Nations to bring about peace on earth.

"In this house of discussion and compromise, I propose that we begin at once to enter a new age of respect for one another. Killing is no longer an option. To insure that this moratorium succeeds, the United States of America, the last superpower, insists that the following three steps be put into effect: First, the manufacture of explosives is to end at once. Secondly, to encourage the nations to comply with the first item, the United States will buy the entire normal production of weapons grade explosive chemicals from any existing factories for one year, thus allowing manufacturers time to find other products to make in these plants. And third, it is mandatory for all nations to comply.

"The complete list of rules and regulations governing the procedures to be followed is being circulated now. With the Secretary General's permission, we shall break for a two-hour lunch period. During this time, please study the hand-out. You will notice that the last page of the rule sheets is a contract of agreement. Please sign the agreement and turn it in to the Secretary General. Failure to do so will put your country into non-compliance, the penalties for which are covered on the reverse side of the agreement.

"Finally, I have selected Mr. Bradley Burke to be my special Ambassador to the Nations."

The President went on to explain that Burke, as the Chairman of one of the largest corporate producers of explosive materials in the world, was in an excellent position to explain, negotiate, and judge the many problems that adherence to the Declaration's principles would incur.

"Burke will have a staff that will visit the manufacturing facilities affected, starting with the largest first, but eventually covering them all," the President said, and then he had Burke stand up so the world could see his face.

"I am issuing a press release so that the people of the world will be apprised of what is required of their leaders. When we reconvene in two hours, my Security Advisor, Dr. Ivan Welland, will answer any questions that delegates may have about defense, military, or weapons issues. My new Secretary of State, with whom many of you are familiar, as she formerly was America's Chief Delegate to this august body, will handle questions concerning diplomacy as well as issues dealing with international cooperation.

"I will hold a press conference to take questions from the press. Accredited press members are requested to go now to the Security Council room where I will meet you. Please sit in the assigned seats."

The President and his coterie of advisors moved to the Security Council room and took their seats at the large table. Members of the press sat in a semicircle before them.

"Each of you found written details of the *Moratorium* on your chairs," the President said, as he opened the meeting to questions from the press.

The protocol for asking the President a question was simple. The reporter raised his hand and the President called on him or her by name, using a seating chart that was on the podium. The reporter was to state his name and affiliation, and then ask his question. Many hands shot up. The President called on the first hand he saw by pointing to a man in the first row.

"Yes, Jim."

"Jim Bowers, CNN. Mr. President, isn't it naïve to think that all the nations are going to stop producing explosives at the same time, and what can we do about it if they don't?"

"That's two questions, Mr. Bowers," the President said jokingly, "but I'll answer them both anyway. It may be naïve, but we've tried everything and nothing else has worked, so I'm going to assume that if *all* the countries agree to stop the production of explosives, then none will be any worse off. I hope they will see it that way, but in the event that some leaders prefer to follow a violent path to power, I'm going to make the consequences so dire that they'll give up any such idea. Now, Mr. Bowers, I'm guessing that if you had a third question it would be *What are the dire consequences?* Am I right?"

"Yes, sir."

"We'll try to let the punishment fit the crime. Let's just say this would be where the naïve ends, and the realism begins. Next question. Yes, you there. John, isn't it?"

"Yes sir, John Poznicky, ABC World News. How much is your offer to buy the explosives for one year going to cost the taxpayers of this country?"

"Our research indicates that it will be less than the cost of present day expenditures for defense munitions, so we expect this program to save the taxpayers money. Next question."

"Ralph Bachman, Reuters. Mr. President, what will happen after a one year embargo? Won't the explosives manufacturers just go back at it the way they used to before your declaration of war on the production of explosives?"

"We have never had five minutes of worldwide cessation of fighting, let alone a whole year. I'm hoping the nations will like the change, and want to continue it. In a few minutes you will receive a press kit that will go into detail on the work that will take place during the year of the silent guns. We'll make massive efforts in diplomacy, public relations, and political pressures to counter resumption of weapons production, and most are covered in the handouts. Next."

"Marilyn Croft, BBC. Mr. President, what kinds of special efforts will you expect from the traditional allies of the U.S. in order to carry out your program?"

"If you're referring to the Europeans, Canadians, and Australians, they'll have to conform to the principles of the declaration just like all the other nations. But a little favorable press would be nice for a change."

The President was referring to the critical editorials of American policies that had become standard in Europe.

"A follow-on question please, Mr. President. What about the countries that are less likely to conform, like Iran, Syria, North Korea, and China?"

"I wouldn't like to be in their shoes, or in the shoes of any nation that depends on its munitions to keep power over its own people. For these countries we have a three-pronged effort in mind. First, we will send Mr. Burke to see them and he will try to make them understand the error of their ways. Second, since this world has become dependent on the American dollar for its welfare, we will use all our economic clout to persuade the wayward nations that only peace leads to prosperity. Thirdly, we will use the enormous power that our creative technologies have placed in my hands to destroy the continuing manufacture of explosives of all kinds. Another question? Yes, Mr. Singh."

"Mr. President, I'm with the Trans Indian Broadcasting Company. My question is, why are you instituting this program at this time? I mean, you could have done it before, or perhaps it would be better to do it five years from now."

"I think we've all studied enough history to know that in various periods of time, and in different locations, groups of the peoples of the earth have come into ascendancy. During these periods when one group leads or controls the others, much progress is made. I salute the Greek period for its contributions to philosophy, theatre, and medicine, and the Romans for architecture, engineering, and governmental achievements, and the French for emphasizing the concepts of liberty, brotherhood, and equality, and the Germans for music, mechanics, and science, and so forth. Every nation can cite its time in the sun. This happens to be the time of American ascendancy, and we want to impress on the world the ideals of peace, tolerance, freedom, and democracy.

"We must do this while we still have the chance. Right from the start the international bodies have been long on talk and idealism, but short on action. One hundred and eight nations, for example, have failed to report to the U.N. on the actions taken against terrorism in their countries. It's obvious that the United States will have to do the heavy lifting. There are times in history when trusting the leader is the best policy. We've been like children playing with dangerous toys. There have been too many accidents, shall we say, and it's time to put a stop to it by taking away the dangerous toys. Our strategy is to use unconventional tactics while dealing with conventional weapons, because once WMDs enter the picture it will be too late. Another question? You there, in the last row."

"Hamid al Sharif, Al Jazeera. Mr. President, how can you justify supporting Israel when the Palestinians have legitimate claims on their land?"

"The gentleman from the Arab media suggests that there is only one correct view of the Palestinian Israeli situation, but there are really at least two. Our plan is to bring this conflict to a peaceful resolution through negotiations. When there is no longer a military solution, perhaps the militants will be as clever at negotiating peace as they are at creating methods of wreaking havoc and causing violent death in their region."

"I have a follow-up question, Mr. President."

"Whatever made me think you would?" the President said, with a hint of ironic amusement in his voice. "Go ahead then, ask your question."

"How can you say it's the Arabs who are the militants when it's your soldiers that are in Iraq, Afghanistan, and other Islamic nations?"

"American troops are in Afghanistan and Iraq at the request of democratically elected leadership. We entered Iraq to rescue the population from a murderously harsh dictatorial regime, and when that was accomplished we were asked to remain by the succeeding freely-elected government to help protect them from those who continue to try to seize power at gunpoint.

"In the Middle East we've been fighting lies even more than armed men. Organizations such as the one you represent have been cynically inciting violence through slander and distortions about America's and Israel's intentions. The Arab dictionary has been rewritten to suit the insurgents. Suicide bombers are now defined as *freedom fighters*, sane people seeking peace are called *puppets*, and American military actions are described as *atrocities*. Perhaps when there is no more gunpowder to fire the bombast of the Arab Press we can get down to the business of negotiating peace. That should be everyone's ambition, and I think this plan to take the weapons out of the negotiating theatre will make it clear to the world which nations support peace and which do not.

"Those reporters here present may put an exclamation point on their journalistic efforts when I tell you that we are all alive at this very moment only because of the courageous efforts of the Security Forces and the Secret Service officers of the United States. Needless to say this includes our friends, the Arab journalists. Yesterday a suicide bomb attempt was thwarted, which was why this press conference had to be moved from the White House Press Center and rescheduled to take place here at the United Nations. Had the attempt succeeded, I dare say it would have made front page headlines, but it would have been written by others, as you and I would have been dead. The attack was meant to assassinate me. But the people who planned it didn't mind sacrificing *all* of you in order to get me. Wasn't that generous of them? I trust you will bear this in mind when you send in your reports. I believe that if there was ever a time for the killing to stop, it's now. May God go with you, and may he continue to bless the United States of America."

The news of the President's moratorium on explosives was punctuated by his revelation of the intended bomb attack on the press conference. The reporters were hurrying to get back to their desks so they could submit their stories to their editors. The mood among them could be described as stunned animation. They were grateful to be alive, and at the same time, being newshounds, they were anxious to get to work on the biggest story of their lives.

Margo Watson was perspiring with relief that her life had been spared, and simultaneously she was cognizant of the effect that reporting on this ground-shattering event would have on her career as a journalist. Yesterday she had been sitting next to the very woman who must have been the bomber. The woman had been escorted out before the conference began by a very tall guy who must have been a Secret Service man. She could hardly wait to get back to her editor to tell him about the events of the day, and to ask if she could be given by-line credit for the story she would write. She also thought that she might be able to pry a little sympathy from him because of her brush with death.

CHAPTER TWENTY-ONE

Laura Murphy took Brad's arm as they approached the main entrance to the White House. It wasn't her first visit to the famous building, but it was the first time she had ever been there on the invitation of the President.

She couldn't hide the fact that she was very excited to be at the White House for Bradley's installation ceremony as Ambassador Plenipotentiary to the Nations. She looked up at him proudly as they entered the familiar edifice. His job would be to explain, negotiate, and judge the problems incurred by the adherence to the President's War on Weapons and moratorium on explosives. He would take on one of the most difficult diplomatic assignments in history.

"How do I look?" she asked Brad. "Am I properly dressed for my new role as wife-elect of the Ambassador?"

"You look perfect," he assured her. "Although I have to admit that I like you even better in your silky pink negligée."

Laura could feel his strong arm around her waist as they entered the White House, but his reference to her negligée made her yearn to be alone with him again. She hoped they could go straight back to his suite after the ceremony.

"I'm so proud of you," she whispered, as she clung to his arm. "I'm sorry I made it difficult for you to allow your appointment to stand, by wanting to keep going with our environmental project. I know you understood and shared my feelings, but the President's appointment is akin to the Catholic Cardinals' unanimously electing a Pope. There was no way you could have refused to serve."

"Listen, darling, I think this new job of mine is going to mesh perfectly with your work. First of all, I discussed this with the President, and it was his idea that you accompany me on my travels, which are obviously going to be extensive. He said the strongest plank in his platform for reelection was going to be a *Declaration of War on Pollution.*"

"Really?" said Laura, her eyes sparkling.

"That's right," Brad said, pausing at the entrance to the White House. "The President is going to ask you to hire a small staff to travel with us. You and your staff will take inventory of the world's pollution problems. You'll be the chief auditor of the world's air, water, and land quality. Eighteen months from now you'll be asked to submit a report with recommendations as to how to proceed with a clean-up on a scale never dreamed of before. For what it's worth, I'll be on hand to act as a resource person. You'll be at least as busy as I am."

"I didn't know you had spoken with the President. Why didn't you tell me?"

"If I had told you it wouldn't have been a surprise. Besides, it's all Ivan Welland's fault. He was the one who hatched these ideas in the first place."

"Wow! He's got to be the world's best civil servant. Too bad there aren't more like him. That day in his office when you fellows shipped me off to the cafeteria with Brooklyn, she told me an interesting footnote about Ivan."

"Oh? What was that?" he asked, leading her inside.

"She said that his family name, Welland, is the name of the chief armorer in *Beowulf.* I think that literary allusion seems apt. Just before the press conference got under way, I saw him escort a woman out of the auditorium, and I'll bet you anything she was the bomber. So I think we may owe him our lives, as well as our new jobs!"

"If Ivan can keep the President alive, and if we can do what he's asked us to do, then in the near future we could see some genuine leadership coming from the free world. It's about time. Look! Here come Ivan and the President now."

"It's nice to see you both again," said Ivan, as they formed a group together. "I'm expecting Marina to come along any minute for the occasion."

Laura assumed the occasion he referred to was Brad's installation, but Brad had an additional surprise for her.

"Mr. President," Brad said, "I'd like to introduce you to my fiancée, Dr. Laura Murphy."

The President looked at Laura and smiled.

"I'm aware of your work in the field of environmental sanity, Dr. Murphy. I'm assuming that Brad has warned you about my designs upon you?"

"Not in those terms, Mr. President, but he told me what you'd like me to do about environmental planning," Laura replied in a slightly shaky voice, knowing she was speaking with probably the single most important person in the world.

"Well, will you take on this job for me?"

"Yes sir. It will be the culmination of my life's work as a scholar. I'm lucky. Academics almost never get to see the practical results of their scholarship, and I'm grateful for the opportunity. Your speech yesterday was so inspiring to me. Brad and I want to be a part of the team that brings these needed changes in our policies into fruition."

"Well, you and Brad will have a big part in it, I'm sure. And it will be cost efficient for the taxpayers too, having both of you traveling together and sharing accommodations. I must make a note to include that detail in my State of the Union speech," the President said wryly.

Laura blushed when the President spoke about their private living arrangements. What could he be thinking?

Just then Marina approached, accompanied by the Chief Justice of the Supreme Court, dressed in full legal regalia.

"Thank you, Chief Justice, for coming on short notice. I'd like to get Ambassador Burke installed in his new position and functioning as quickly as possible. Oh, and by the way, since statistics show that married men are healthier than unmarried men, I thought it best to host what may be the last shotgun wedding before the ammunition runs out."

Laura thought it strange that Brad's special installation was to be shared with somebody else's wedding ceremony. She even felt a bit annoyed to think that the focus wouldn't be entirely on him that day. She wondered what kind of a President would make personal remarks about her living arrangements, and then have two ceremonies take place side-by-side so that the spotlight was divided. She didn't want to judge the President, but it seemed to her that he could have refrained from the comment about her and Brad, and planned the timing of the two ceremonies a bit differently.

"Mr. Burke," said the Chief Justice, interrupting Laura's thoughts. "Would you stand here, please?"

The people attending the installation moved apart to let Brad take his place in front of the judge. Then they formed a semicircle around him, and the ceremony began.

"Put your left hand on the Bible, raise your right hand, and repeat after me."

The austere gentleman proceeded to administer the oath of ambassadorial office to Brad. When the ceremony was over, the President and the other witnesses extended their congratulations.

"Dr. Murphy," the Chief Justice said suddenly, "would you stand next to Ambassador Burke, please."

Laura put her hand to her chest as much as to say, *Me? Are you talking to me?* Brad saw her confusion, so he took her by the hand and gently pulled her to his side.

"This is the first time in all my years on the Supreme Court bench," said the Chief Justice, "that I've been called upon to swear someone in, and then marry him immediately afterward. It might even be the first time in history that such a thing has happened. But I enjoy making history, don't you, Mr. President?"

"I do, Chief, I do," said the President.

"Well, don't try to steal the spotlight, you old publicity hound. It's not you I want to hear the *I do's* from," he said. Then he launched into their marriage ceremony while Laura stood staring at him with eyes as wide as saucers.

When the old jurist got to the point where he asked Laura if she took this man to be her lawful wedded husband, it suddenly dawned on her that Brad had never actually asked her to be his wife. Now the question was being asked by the Chief Justice of the United States, with the President as a witness. Who could say *no* under these circumstances? Fortunately she didn't want to say *no*, so she said, *I do*.

Brad produced a ring that had been his grandmother's, and soon Laura was being addressed as Mrs. Ambassador. It was not exactly the ceremony that little girls dream about, but it was a wedding that most big girls would envy. After the nuptial kiss and the congratulations were over, the President invited them to his house for a celebratory drink. The Chief Justice, probably the only man in the country who would dare to speak to the President as a friend and equal, was amused by the suggestion.

"You old fool," he chuckled, "we *are* in your house, only you don't own it. I'm just hoping I don't end up having to evict you after your speech yesterday."

"How did this guy get appointed to the court, anyway?" the President laughed. "And what bunch of senatorial fools ratified *his* appointment?"

Laura knew that one thing was sure – she would never forget her surprise wedding as long as she lived. She had been married without expecting it. She had been appointed to a position for which she hadn't applied. Her academic life had imploded, and she was loving every minute of it. She felt more alive than ever before and was looking forward to the future, beginning with her wedding night.

Things were going well for Ivan Welland at home. Marina's long-awaited book had finally been accepted for publication by a prestigious academic press. His lovely baby, Julia, was plump and good-natured. The front of his house, so badly damaged by the bomb explosion, had been repaired and looked no worse for the experience.

The peace of his home life was in complete contrast to the turmoil at his workplace. Maybe the position of Security Advisor was just a natural magnet for confusion. Much of Ivan's post graduate education had been in the field of mathematics, particularly in the area of chaos theory. When it came to the President's proposal for his *War on Weapons*, Ivan used Heisenberg's uncertainty principle as a guide, but ever since the President's press conference announcement, the general result had been both chaotic and uncertain.

"What's on the agenda today, Brooklyn?" Ivan asked, as he passed her desk on the way to his office that morning.

"You have a meeting first thing with Brad Burke."

"Okay. Send him right in when he gets here."

"He's already in your office, waiting for you. I gave him some coffee, and I'll bring yours in as soon as it's ready."

The meeting had been set up so that Ivan could be brought up to speed about the two whirlwind tours that Brad had taken to the Middle East. Since it was the location of the greatest number of man-made explosions in the world, it was natural for him to concentrate his first efforts on that area. His purpose was to explain the President's plan, assure the leaders of Islam of his purely peaceful motives, and tell them what they should do to comply with the plan.

"But I've got to tell you," Brad said to Ivan as he sipped the fresh coffee that Brooklyn had given him, "there wasn't one country in the Middle East where there was any kind of support for the President's plan to end the use of weapons by calling a halt to the manufacture of explosives. They gave me all sorts of reasons for their lack of support, but the opposition to the program was unanimous."

Brad listed the nations he had visited, the individuals he had talked with, and the objections enumerated in each case. He hastened to add that the reasons they offered for their refusal to comply were likely not truthful ones. As he saw it, the real objections among secular leaders were also pretty low on the morality scale. They included a lust for power on the part of government leaders who didn't want to lose their sovereignty; fear that a caliphate was waiting in the wings to take over; and fear that their cultural heritage would be supplanted by an immoral, westernized, glitzy Hollywood version of what a free-wheeling life on earth should be like.

"It was crazy," Brad went on. "I mean, when I wrote down their reasons for objecting to the moratorium, I came up with a list of character flaws as long as my arm. Stuff like selfishness, pride, vanity, dishonesty, prejudice, and a whole host of other imperfections. I'm not trying to say that these flaws only exist in the Middle East. They don't, of course. They're absolutely universal, but their ugliness is multiplied when they infest the leaders of nations."

Ivan wasn't surprised when he heard Brad's description of the situation in the Middle East. He had encountered the same low instincts among people in high places everywhere he went, including the United States. Those who looked at the total canvas were unfortunately in very short supply.

"It all reminds me of a comedy sketch I once saw," Ivan said with a chuckle. "Chris Rock was speaking from the perspective of an African-American from the ghetto, who was complaining about drive-by shootings. He claimed that the best solution was to raise the price of bullets to $5,000 apiece. If bullets got that expensive, no one would waste them by shooting random people a dozen times each. He had a point. The best way to lower the supply is to raise the cost. That's the President's plan in a nutshell."

"That story is a good illustration," Brad agreed. "Maybe I should take Chris Rock with me on my next tour. The problem is, though, that nothing short of an intercontinental missile striking the belly of a chemical explosives factory would make enough of an impression on a would-be warlord to make him give up his violent ways."

The men both agreed that the threat approach was heavy-handed, but unfortunately it was necessary in the cases of certain rogue nations. The worst of these rulers would most likely require a more tangible indication of seriousness from the President before they abandoned their weapons programs.

The idea was to get a vast majority of nations to agree to the President's plan for the cessation of hostilities. Once that was accomplished, the pressure of the sheer weight of world opinion would be brought to bear on the rogue nations. If that peaceful initiative failed to move them away from the use of violent methods to attain their objectives, then the dogs of missile warfare would have to be unmuzzled. The President, of course, hoped it would not come to that, but for the first time in recent history, the U.S. had a Commander-in-Chief with enough intelligence to formulate a workable plan, and gumption enough to clip the horns of those who would like to stampede their way over the rest of the world.

But the President still had a couple of peaceful ideas that he wanted to implement. Strong, unpleasant medicine was needed to cure the world's violence before nuclear weapons metastasized. The role of Oncologist to the World was not one the President had sought, but it was thrust upon him because no other leader could do what was needed to stop the genocide. Before using force, however, he wanted to be sure that he had exhausted all other venues.

Brad and Ivan discussed every aspect of the President's initiative in minute detail, making changes wherever necessary. International satellite monitoring of explosions would begin at once. Military intelligence units were to be put on high alert. Inspection teams were assigned to each of the known producers of chemical munitions. They were to verify that production had ceased, and they were to monitor these plants to ensure they produced only non-weapons grade materials. Beefed-up efforts were to be exerted to halt arms smuggling. It would certainly be a long while before attrition wore down the opponents of the President's plan, but weapons lose their effectiveness over time, and leaders die or are replaced by others. The addiction to solving disagreements through warfare, having been given the cold turkey treatment, would be replaced in time by sincere diplomatic negotiating.

Following the President's instructions to make a final effort to convince the Islamist extremist leaders to go along with his plan, Ivan passed Brad a small file folder.

"This is a comprehensive media campaign that will help to convince the naysayer at home, as well as those abroad, that they should approve the President's plan."

"Thanks, Ivan. I'll take it on my next trip to the Middle East. If this doesn't do the trick, I don't know what will. But I certainly am looking forward to the time when we can beat our swords into plowshares."

"My sentiments exactly. But if the jihadist extremists insist on living by the sword, they'll have to die by the sword before any new plowshares will be coming off the assembly line."

Ivan's team had produced a computer-enhanced film to simulate the damage to an ammunition dump in Hezbollah-controlled Lebanon if a nuclear submarine fired a missile into the weapons storehouse. The film, with its recognizable underground storage site location just outside of Beirut, and the factory site near Damascus where the munitions were being produced, was to be given to the Syrian President to prove that the U.S. knew exactly where the Syrian weapons in Lebanon were made and stored. It gave a vivid, accurate portrayal of what was to be expected if the President ordered such a strike on these targets. At the same time it was a purely graphic concoction like a scene in a war movie, and no one would be hurt.

Each of the defiant heads of state would receive a similar film. A voice-over in the local language would advise any would-be foot-draggers that an intercontinental ballistic missile had been aimed at the target illustrated in the film, and if complete, immediate compliance to the President's requirement was not met, the resulting damage would be as it was portrayed in the film.

A back-up plan had also been prepared as the absolute last warning in case the DVD didn't have the desired result. This was a virtual reality 3D performance of a simulated attack on the specific offices and homes of the leaders who hadn't responded to the first, more general DVD. Computer enhanced but clearly recognizable replicas of the intransigent individuals and their families being blown to bits in graphic scenes were to be made as a final admonition to sign the President's weapons initiative. There would be nothing so convincing to these obstinate leaders as witnessing their own deaths in virtual reality.

Ivan, his team, and the President himself believed that if Brad showed these men their unromantic digital deaths, the realistic performance would perhaps alter their attitudes toward life. Dispatching some poor, brain-washed devil on a suicide mission was one thing, but giving up life as a king, emir, or president and getting your family killed was another.

If this last effort failed to bring the outlaws into line, it was obvious what the next step would be. Once he had made up his mind that he must be the police chief to the world, the President had become resolute. Anyone at home or overseas caught firing a weapon at a human target for any reason other than provable self-defense, would have to face capital punishment. Ivan had persuaded the President to agree to this by giving him a copy of Isaac Asimov's *Three Laws for Robot Behavior*, and asking him if he thought humans should be held to a lesser code.

Prince Umar and his paramour DeeDee had just completed a session that left no page of the Kamasutra unturned. They were lying naked on the Prince's pillow-bedecked bed.

"Well, at least one good thing has happened," DeeDee said gleefully.

"Only one?" the Prince replied, with a pout. "I counted two new tricks and three new positions. Didn't you even notice?"

"I'm not talking about that, fool. I'm thinking about my husband, Peter. He's is in charge of Paramount Petroleum now, and Brad Burke is out of the way for good."

The Prince was secretly disgusted with this infidel Western slut. Who did she think she was, calling him a fool? And why pick this particular moment to be talking about her husband? Well, her time would come. Umar began thinking about the subject of assassinations, and he grew even angrier. His hirelings had tried and failed to terminate Ivan Welland, and their plan to assassinate the President had failed, too. DeeDee knew nothing about these botched attempts, and Umar had no intention of telling her.

"Now we both control Paramount Petroleum," DeeDee said smugly. "You own the controlling interest, and I control the Chief Executive Officer."

Prince Umar didn't try to convince her otherwise, but the truth was that the stock ownership was in the hands of various members of the royal family, and not all of them shared his violent political views and personal ambitions. He had to live with these dissenters, however. In addition, the powerful green movement was agitating to reduce and eventually cut out the use of fossil fuels in favor of cleaner fuels. So although they controlled the company, its future was far from rosy in the long run, and in the short run the most profitable part of Paramount's business – chemical explosives manufacturing – was being threatened by the American President's war on weapons. The Prince went back to thinking about new and more effective ways to get rid of the President, Ivan Welland, Bradley Burke, and his new wife, Laura, all of whom had recently become big items in the Western media.

Ivan knew that many high officials in the U.S. government were bitterly opposed to the President's program. He also knew that some of them recognized who had been the real author of most of the President's plans. Many businesses thrived on political chaos and did all they could to see that it continued. Lobbyists for these special interests badgered Congress to oppose the President's war on weapons.

Several members of the Cabinet had resigned in protest. Included in the resignations were the Secretaries of State and Defense. Ivan was called into the Oval Office.

"Mr. President, you sent for me?"

"Yes Ivan, I've just received resignation letters from two important Cabinet members who evidently feel our War on Weapons is either foolish, naïve, or dangerous."

"I'm sorry to hear that, sir."

"No need to feel sorry. I can't afford to have anyone in these high positions who doesn't support our peace program 100%. We expected opposition, and we're getting it. But if I'm not reelected we won't be able to fully implement the most important peace initiative in history. We both know that the better part of this plan was yours. We both know that unless we make the *do it or die* clause a reality we'll never even begin to see peace in the world. I hope we never have to apply that clause, but if we do, I need men of courage around me who'll support me and do the necessary. In my judgment we've reached a crossroad in our relations with the Islamist extremists. Religious doctrines can be matters for discussion and debate, but once the Islamist extremists demand adherence to their precepts under penalty of tribute or death, they leave us no choice but to confront them. Do you agree with me, Dr. Welland?"

"I do indeed, Mr. President."

"Then, Dr. Welland, I'd like you to consider being the next Secretary of Defense."

Ivan was taken aback. "I'm honored by your offer to make me part of your Cabinet, sir, but I'd like to have some time to think it over and discuss it with Marina."

"Very well, Doctor, but I'll need your answer in twenty-four hours. Is that satisfactory?"

"Yes sir, you'll have my answer by tomorrow," Ivan said.

CHAPTER TWENTY-TWO

Ivan was worried when he looked over the draft of the report his staff had prepared. Lincoln's admonition that a *house divided against itself cannot stand* kept echoing in his mind. It appeared to him that petty political squabbles were rife in the U.S. and were causing Americans to fritter away a perfect opportunity to crush the jihadist insurgency.

He took a particularly dim view of the media, whose tactics had morally deteriorated over the years. Much of what he read in print and saw on TV would have been declared treasonous during WWII. What had changed? The Fourth Estate had inflated its importance to the point where it could publish or broadcast anything it wished. Slander and libel laws seemed no longer able to contain the vituperation of the media against those of whom it disapproved. The national interests were growing subservient to the economic interests of the media. The politically divided Congress fiddled while truth burned.

Emperors, kings, queens, and dictators had enjoyed unlimited power at different times in history, but never had the rhetoric of a few anonymous citizens so influenced the minds of ordinary men and women. If these media barons were paragons of virtue, or the wisest of the wise, it would be different, but they were just greedy, self-aggrandizing, morally deficient business tycoons, using their media power to further their own private interests. They deprived ordinary citizens access to the accurate information they needed for proper political decision-making, substituting their own personal opinions and agendas for impartial news reporting. It got worse as Ivan read further.

The media barons had invaded Hollywood, and truth and fiction had been blurred. Pouring money into the hands of movie producers, the media corporations gradually acquired the controlling interest in many studios and folded them into their empires. It wasn't long before Warner Bros. became Time Warner, and The News Corporation controlled Twentieth Century Fox. Through stock purchases on the New York Stock Exchange, ownership of these American companies became truly international.

In time oil rich Arab sheikhs, representing companies like the Kingdom Corporation from Saudi Arabia and the Emirate of Dubai, bought into these media companies. They learned the media business this way and then transferred the knowledge to the Arab media companies they formed, such as Al Arabiya and Al Jazeera, which are not regulated by an FCC and have no rules but the ones they make themselves. Their purpose is to produce propaganda for the Arab leaders, spreading the messages of Al Qaeda, Hezbollah, and Hamas while posing as independent media entities.

Welland was impressed with the work of his staff. They had linked all the various foreign subsidiaries, divisions, and associated media companies that operated in the United States. They had found the stockholder lists of the companies and cross referenced the major investors, finding many conflicts of interests. The team had discovered the FCC regulation that demanded that the owner of any TV station be an American citizen. It was surprising how many cynical media moguls had acquired United States citizenship in order to comply with this requirement. Ivan wondered just how loyal these citizens of convenience really were.

As one of the principals of the Kingdom Corporation, Prince Umar had been the point man in the move that put Arab leaders in financial control of some of the large international media enterprises. The time had come for him to leave his palace and go to the United States to attend annual meetings. His agenda was packed, for his family members were the largest single holders of publicly-traded stock in the U.S. As his family's representative, Umar sat on many boards of directors of American corporations. On this trip he'd have the added pleasure of telling Peter Dunbar that the Kingdom Corporation was now the majority shareholder in Paramount Petroleum, so Dunbar would be only a figurehead from then on, and the real control rested with the royal family of Saudi Arabia. He'd also do a little show-and-tell with DeeDee, so the infidel executive would know he'd been cuckolded.

DeeDee was expecting her Prince to reward her richly for her services as concubine and co-conspirator in the takeover of the Paramount Petroleum Company. She had, since her first tryst with Umar, pumped Peter for insider information about the company's projects, and had passed the information to Umar during their secret rendezvous.

Being an industrial spy came as naturally to her as being an unfaithful wife. She was charmed by chicanery and seduced by her own subterfuge. She would never have been able to explain exactly why she got so much pleasure from cheating, but deceit was integral to her nature. As soon as she had discovered that Peter was an innocent guy, she had set her cap for him. He was her ticket out of the Hollywood chorus line and into the solo spotlight of the corporate rich and powerful. She hated Brad because he was onto her gold-digging tricks, and she feared that he would be able to talk her innocent husbandly prey out of marrying her. Peter was able to detect oil under the ground, but he couldn't smell a rat in his marriage bed. She had once bragged to Umar that she had been unfaithful to Peter even on their wedding night. He had always wondered how she had managed that one.

Men like Bradley Burke and Ivan Welland were the types she couldn't abide. They were honest to a fault, which was a severe defect in DeeDee's eyes, and to top it all off they were in control of their sexuality and impervious to her tactics. Her failure to bed Brad was nettlesome to her. She had to see him at company functions at least twice a year, and she was therefore continually reminded of how she had been spurned. She was glad when she heard that he'd finally married a serious, hard-working professor. In her twisted mind she thought he would get tired of that type of a woman, so in time she'd renew her efforts to seduce him. Welland was too young for her – not that she cared about that, but he was a newlywed and a new father. His turn would have to wait, but she did have a question about whether his other measurements were proportional to his height.

Now that Brad had surrendered his position to Peter and had emeritus status at Paramount, DeeDee was freer than ever to do as she pleased. She had, through her husband's efforts, reached the top of the corporate pile. She ranked herself with Grace Kelly, Princess Diana, and Jacqueline Kennedy, but no one else thought as highly of her as she did.

Umar was en route to New York in his silver Boeing 767 at that moment, and she couldn't wait to see him again. Apart from his title and money, this Arab Prince fascinated DeeDee because he was the only man she had ever met who matched her in his Machiavellian schemes. She wasn't sure, but he might even outstrip her in the nasty tricks department, but then he had the advantage of being brought up in a royal family that had six thousand members. He had seventy-two siblings and half siblings to practice on, while poor DeeDee was raised in New Jersey and only had one younger sister from whom she was voluntarily estranged from birth. Her father and mother always took the part of the little sister, so DeeDee expunged them all from her life as early as possible.

To keep peace in the family Umar took his four wives on occasional shopping sprees. Under the guise of doing business, these trips afforded the Prince a chance to revisit his foreign concubines, or find new ones. Along with his wives came his older children. In New York the Prince occupied a whole floor of either the Waldorf Astoria or the Plaza hotels. During his trips to New York the royals played one hotel against the other in order to obtain lower prices or extra services. The personnel at the hotels hated these visits because the royal children were badly spoiled and created a daily mess for them to clean up. The Prince didn't care, as he was engaged elsewhere. As for the wives, they regarded the staff as childcare workers, so they were unconcerned about the trouble caused by their offspring.

As a lover DeeDee found Umar satisfactory, although as a looker he was only average. He kept his thick, black-and-gray beard meticulously trimmed. DeeDee wasn't sure that she would recognize him if he were clean-shaven. His dark brown eyes twinkled with a worldly-wise expression as they peered out from beneath his lush black eyebrows. What made him such a good lover was not his appearance but his experience. DeeDee guessed that with all his responsibilities as an inseminator he had learned to raise his sexual creativity in order to escape the boredom that comes with obligatory, repetitive mating.

He had promised to come to DeeDee's apartment as soon as possible after his plane landed. She had stopped caring about Peter's feelings in the matter long ago, but out of respect for Umar's position, DeeDee had been prudent about her relations with the Prince. She knew that Umar yearned to psychologically emasculate Peter by making him watch as he took his willing wife right before his eyes. The scenario by which he planned to do the deed was still unknown to her, and she could hardly wait to hear about it from the consummate conniver, Prince Umar.

La Víbora had thought long and hard, carefully considering all his options, and had finally decided on one. Most people would have tried to make a murder look like an accident, but it is never an accident when a viper strikes. More than anything else, he wanted Prince Umar to know that he was the one responsible for his death. Anonymous revenge is no revenge at all, or so he believed. The girlfriend would just be collateral damage. That would have to be her penalty for taking up with that *maricón* Arab. Rafael Alvarez was not to be taken lightly, and many an enemy, debtor, and traitor had found that out the hard way.

To achieve his purposes, Alvarez decided to assume the role of a wealthy foreign businessman. He pretended to leave the Viper behind, but beneath the soft exterior that he now projected dwelled the hard-hearted, clever killer that inwardly remained the same as always. He made periodic trips to New York and other U.S. cities where his illegal operations were thriving. It was dangerous to leave his citadel in the Colombian jungle, but he trusted no one and had to take risks if he wanted to evaluate his businesses for himself.

As usual he flew in his helicopter to the Ecuadorian border, where he passed across using forged documents and an assumed name. Border guards and customs officers were on his payroll. Alvarez understood the character and make-up of these men, who hated being posted to the remote areas of their countries. The only attraction of these places was the money to be extorted from the petty smugglers who used this crossing. La Víbora and his ilk provided the wherewithal for these petty officials to purchase relief from boredom through the use of liquor and prostitutes.

The Viper would make his way by car from the floor of the rainforest to the altitude of the highest capital city in the world – Quito, Ecuador. From Quito's airport he would fly first class to New York City on a commercial airliner. Along the way he would meet with his drug transporters. These men were moving cocaine on the backs of llamas, donkeys, and horses through the jungles to the Pacific coast of Ecuador. Next, his merchandise made its way north to California via hundreds of ever-changing smuggling tactics designed to avoid the attentions of the DEA. Traveling at the same time as Prince Umar, the Viper relaxed in the plane that would take him to the JFK airport.

A voracious reader of the Wall Street Journal, the Viper had learned that the Prince would attend board meetings in the city. From his New York connections he learned where Umar stayed when he was in town. He was particularly interested in what his people told him about the Prince's dalliances. Most interesting of all was the report that his quarry was having an ongoing affair with the wife of an executive at one of Prince Umar's oil companies.

As a result of that delectable piece of information, Alvarez scheduled his business meetings to coincide with the Prince's visit to New York. The Viper was insistent upon being efficient in his dealings, so making his trip at the same time as Umar enabled him to kill two birds with one stone. Being in New York now would conveniently give him the opportunity of recouping the honor he had lost when the Prince had spoken to him disrespectfully.

It is instructive to understand that both the Viper and Prince Umar had a great need to protect their masculinity. Neither of these proud men realized that the source of their feelings came from the same cultural influences. Alvarez was a man living totally in his time and culture. He didn't care that he had received his attitudes about what it means to be a respected man indirectly from the Arabs who had occupied Spain for seven hundred years. But it was the same Arabs who impressed their ideas of gender relationships on the Spaniards of that day and age. Eventually the excessively proud Arabs were forced to leave the Iberian Peninsula, but they left behind their arrogant ideas concerning masculine honor and the subjection of women. When the Spanish Conquistadors invaded the New World they passed on the concept of *machismo*, or male chauvinism, where to this day it clings to La Víbora's Latino male society like overripe Middle Eastern fruit that hasn't yet fallen from the tree.

Successful criminals are more observant than the average person. They have to be, as it's their business to take advantage of opportunities. Small time thieves and burglars in New York City were gentlemen compared to the drug smugglers of Colombia. Rafael Alvarez had managed to become the head of a crime syndicate in his country not because he was the most mannerly of the job applicants. He had risen through the ranks and had paid his dues on the streets of Cali and New York. His story was not unlike that of the gladiator who eventually rose to become a general, but without the uplifting aspects of heroism. His leadership was based on instilling fear in the hearts of those who followed his orders. His unquestioned bravery and calm under fire were legendary, but his real genius was seen in his ability to cold-bloodedly calculate the results of the pure violence he unleashed.

The advantage of the element of surprise rested with Rafael Alvarez, as the Prince didn't know he had become the Viper's intended prey. Umar had no idea that Alvarez was in New York or that he was being hunted by him. If he had known this, he would not have slipped away from his bodyguards to visit DeeDee at her Park Avenue apartment.

Both the New York police and the federal authorities were very experienced in handling and protecting foreign dignitaries and diplomats. They had been advised of the Prince's arrival and his plans, except for the side trip to DeeDee's pad. This one little omission was to have a far-reaching effect on the Prince, his paramour, the Viper, Bradley Burke, Ivan Welland, and the President's war on ammunition.

CHAPTER TWENTY-THREE

Laura Burke was having just about as much difficulty gaining support for greening the world as her new husband was having in the Middle East when he tried to convince Islam that the reduction of munitions was in their best interest. The first and basic obstacle was that she was a woman. Most, though not all, of the men at the table simply didn't take her seriously. The vast majority of Arab bureaucrats involved in governing the environment had very little interest in the subject to begin with. Usually they had been given their jobs as a sinecure from an important relative who wanted to keep them out of the way. Retaining their jobs required only that they not interfere with the status quo, and not get embroiled in any controversial matters that were bad for the oil business. They were just as uninterested in discussing the environment with a woman as they were obdurate about not straying from their job descriptions.

It became obvious that as long as Brad and Laura were working and traveling in the not-as-yet liberated world, her womanly work would be best spent supporting her husband's disarmament campaign. A culture that reduced its own effectiveness by fifty percent before it even began to involve itself in today's competitive world economy was bound to be less successful. A one-gender work force is approximately as effective as a one-armed boxer. Laura had no doubt, however, that the situation for women would change in time, even in Islamic countries.

What really concerned her just then was that countries which produce crude oil also export most of their pollution, since they don't refine the raw product into diesel, gasoline, and other volatile fractions, but ship the crude oil to refineries in industrialized nations. The refiners and the industrial economies that depend on the internal combustion engine create most of the world's green house gasses. But Arab protestations against incrimination on the basis of their relatively small consumption pattern would gush out as soon as Laura raised any pollution issues.

In the end, the clean air argument put forward to consumers in the Middle East was entirely smothered by the fact that the price of fossil fuels was so cheap. No amount of hot air spent in debating the morality issue could overcome the materialism of the moment. Laura's only hope was that the rising price of oil on the world market would eventually trigger a massive switch to clean-burning fuels. But market conditions would have to be the driving force behind it, because politicians and businessmen would never agree to it. The need for alternate fuels was almost as pressing as the need for arms control in the Middle East.

Brad was having his problems, too. The oil rich Arabs had developed large subsidiary companies that had for the past few years been extremely successful in manufacturing the petroleum derivatives used in producing munitions, and they weren't about to give this business up just to appease the American President.

One could not avoid noticing the proliferation of arms in the Middle East. The best customers for explosive chemicals were the militant insurgents and terrorists who could be seen on TV every day, with their omnipresent black ski masks, RPGs, mortars, and automatic weapons.

It was very much to the advantage of the oil interests in the Middle East to keep their customers supplied, especially those who were nearby and could turn their violent attentions on them if they ever became dissatisfied with the service or the product. Besides, the Arabs slyly reasoned, if the U.S. unilaterally ceased making explosives, the Arab market share would be even greater. Long-term thinking in the Middle East was poles apart from America's democratic idealism.

Burke was forced to come to the conclusion that he would have to use some of the visual aid tools that Ivan had given him if he was going to achieve any results. He was certain from his long experience in the oil business that no amount of blather would convince the Arabs to pay attention to the wishes of the infidels. They had many centuries of experience in negotiating, lying, and bluffing. Their culture presupposed that unbelievers used the same ploys and tactics as they did, and that the underlying purpose was malevolent.

Brad was losing hope that he could verbally convince these governments to peacefully suspend the manufacture and the expansion of munitions and explosives. The only thing short of selective missile attacks was to present a clear visual example to them of the military consequences for non-compliance with the President's war on weapons program.

Ivan believed that the DVD simulating the missile attack should be shown separately to the top leaders of each country. Brad had suggested that the video simulation be shown to the Arab leaders during one of their meetings, so the message could be given to all dissenters at the same time. Ivan vetoed this strategy on the theory that a group of hardliners would strengthen and unify one another. It was better to isolate and divide them, overcoming their objections one by one. That was Ivan's considered opinion.

Brad was eventually persuaded by the fact that the DVD material was so cleverly specific, as far as people and locale were concerned, that only a suicidal fanatic or a fool would fail to be swayed by it. Convincing an Arab leader that his house will be burned down and his family killed by showing him the image of his burning house and the simulated but recognizable corpses of his loved ones, was the strongest way to make the point that everyone could be spared simply by obeying a perfectly reasonable request to discontinue the production of gunpowder. Brad wondered if Hollywood technology would at last end up having some useful purpose. How ironic that Islam's most hated disseminator of infidel perversion should end up being its best hope for peace!

Brad was scheduled to visit Syria next. If simple logic failed to produce results, he resolved to show the DVD to the Syrian Head of State. There was little to lose, as the relations between the Syrians and the Americans had been strained for many years over policies concerning Israel and Arab support for insurgents in Lebanon and Iraq. Not being one of the oil rich nations had had a deleterious effect on Syrian politics. To stand tall among their richer Arab brothers, the Syrians became more militaristic and extreme in order to get respect. It would be difficult to sell them on disarmament.

Brad was counting on the Syrians to remember what had happened to Khadafi in Libya in the 1980s when the U.S. shot a missile down his palace chimney that nearly killed him, and did kill his daughter and thirty-six others. Seeing the DVD would certainly remind the Syrians of their vulnerability. Brad would also demonstrate how much better Libya had fared since Khadafi had shown some contrition, how much more secure he was on his throne now that he was no longer trying to be an international outlaw, and how this scenario could also play out for Syria, too.

Laura was packing and preparing for their trip to Damascus when Brad came into the bedroom to remind her that he had a meeting scheduled with Ivan to discuss last-minute details concerning the President's proposed war on ammunition. He turned her around and gave her a big hug.

"Don't forget my black silk socks, darling. They're in the back of the top dresser drawer."

"Got it."

"But most important of all, remember to pack that pink negligée of yours, okay?"

"Oh, get out of here, you sex maniac," Laura laughed.

Brad gave her a lingering kiss, then left for his meeting with the Secretary of Defense and the Secretary of State. He shook his head as he went out the door, hoping he would remember the details he needed to know in his discussions with people at the highest level of government.

Brad and Laura had continued to live in the Marriott Hotel. As one of the perks for serving on the Board of Directors of Paramount Petroleum, Brad was allowed to use the company suite in Washington. Things had happened so quickly that the newlyweds hadn't had time to find a home, nor at this moment did they particularly care. They were traveling so frequently that they were spending more time overseas than in the U.S.

For Laura it was like the honeymoon they had never taken. She was excited about going to exotic places for the first time, and although Brad had been there before, it was all new and exciting to her. Her zeal for tourism in the area, however, was dampened somewhat when Brad reminded her that the wife of an American ambassador was a target for kidnapping or even beheading by some folks in this part of the world.

The doorman whistled for a cab to come to the front of the hotel. Brad climbed in and told the driver to take him to the Pentagon. He was shown immediately into Ivan's new office and was told that the Secretary would be with him in a minute. Brad looked around the huge room while he waited. It seemed to him that the hawkish character of the office didn't quite suit the current occupant's personality.

Ivan smiled knowingly when he came into the office and found Brad looking quizzically at the room's furnishings.

"My predecessor hasn't moved his belongings out yet," Ivan explained. "I think he was a throwback to the time when the job was called *Secretary of War*."

Park Avenue, like Fifth Avenue and Central Park West, was crammed with condominiums in high-rise buildings standing flank to hip with one another. For those with a liking for wide-open spaces, Manhattan seemed like a warren that housed fur-clothed humans living in elegant closets on top of, next to, and under the nearest neighbors. But for those who relished city life, these apartments represented the apex of civilized living.

Umar belonged to the first group. He could not imagine living in a situation that prevented him from seeing enemies approaching from the distance. When his limo dropped him off at the front entrance of DeeDee's building, he felt a twinge of foreboding. It passed quickly as the uniformed attendant held the door open and admitted the Prince, in his full Arab regalia, into the elegant lobby.

Mrs. Dunbar had told the doorman to announce the Prince's arrival, and she gave instructions that he be shown to the elevator without delay. While she waited for the elevator she dialed her husband at work and demanded that he come home immediately, as she was experiencing an emergency.

Peter was furious. He had work to do to get ready for the annual meeting the next day. He decided to have it out with his wife at last. She couldn't expect him to drop important business matters in order to attend to her eternally selfish whims. He had never complained before about her completely self-centered behavior, but he was determined to do it this time. He agreed to come home, as he always did, but this time it was with the intention of taking her to task.

As usual, DeeDee didn't care what he thought. She knew it took him exactly half an hour to get home from his office. This was to be a special time. She would humiliate him in the extreme by seeing to it that he caught her red-handed with the Prince, and the next day Umar would have the second pleasure of a business cuckolding when he took over Peter's company.

Umar, who hardly ever went anywhere without bodyguards, felt vulnerable as he approached the only door on the penthouse level. Before he could knock, the door opened and DeeDee silently and demurely ushered him into the entrance hall. Once he was inside she closed the door and flung herself at him. She grasped him around his thick neck, putting her legs around his hips, and kissed him many times.

One of the things that Umar liked about DeeDee was her unpredictable spontaneity. One of the things that DeeDee liked about Umar was his reserved, cool, manly royal bearing which in their private moments she dearly loved to disturb. Umar found her wild, Western sexual attitudes exciting. There was no element of submission in this woman, whereas all his other wives and concubines could be counted upon to serve his wishes and whims without comment.

DeeDee's list of needs and appetites, on the other hand, were just as important to her as his were to him, and she didn't mind enumerating them. Umar could never tell what stage of the battle they were in. It was thrust and parry, attack and retreat, and never surrender with DeeDee.

She led the Prince through the immaculately furnished apartment that was predominantly done in red tones. The antique French sofas and chairs were dispersed around the room in a studied attempt to be casually creative. Thick carpeting in neutral beige covered every surface of floor throughout the apartment.

The contrast in the styles of home furnishings in Umar's palaces and in the apartments of wealthy Americans was mood-altering for him. The seraglio style, with its tent-like qualities, suggested that Arab owners were ready to move on to the next oasis at a moment's notice. The permanent structure of the Arab palaces was immovable, of course, but the decor still suggested mobility, while the American style was derived from European and Asian influences, suggesting a false permanency.

The bedroom was dominated by a canopied four-poster bed, supposed at one time to have served Cardinal Richelieu. DeeDee began to undress. She was wearing a conservative blue silk shift that clung to her hips, custom-made for her by her favorite designer. The dress was lovely, and like so many elegant clothes, was simple, well sewn, and flattering to her female curves.

DeeDee loved the dress and wanted to remove it before Umar could get his clumsy hands on it. Besides, underneath the dress she had on what she regarded as the sexiest underwear ever seen. She had a favorite lingerie shop in New York that catered to wealthy woman of taste, and she had acquired the outfit just for this occasion. The tiny semi-transparent garments were made with seduction in mind. Each element was designed to reveal and at the same time to tantalizingly withhold their contents until just the right moment. DeeDee was confident that the sight of her wearing these white lacy undergarments would arouse her Prince.

As to her own arousal, she had developed a fetish about the Prince's garments. In their previous meetings he had worn Western business suits, but DeeDee had been secretly thrilled when he had shown up one day in a floor-length white-belted Arab aba that was more like a dress than anything else. From then on she had demanded that he wear his aba with all the accoutrements. His headdress had a reddish rope that held it together, and a wide belt was cinched at his waist. Deedee had been delighted to find out what a sheikh wore under his robes, and having that knowledge made her unique among the ladies in her circle. Even his wives had never seen Umar naked, and certainly never performing a striptease. It was like finding out what a Scot wears under his kilt, but she already knew that.

The dark figure on the garden roof opened the door just as the gigantic helicopter descended on the United Nations. It was New York, and at any given time something special was going on in the city. Like any New Yorker, he paid little attention to the events at the UN as he entered the building. His soft, black Italian shoes made no noise as he descended the stairs to the penthouse living area one floor below. His movements were stealthy but exuded confidence, as if he were in his own house.

He listened intently at the door that was used by servants and delivery people. Hearing nothing, his gloved hands turned the knob slowly. It was locked. His hands slid inside his jacket and withdrew a leather folder the size of a wallet.

Inside were the small tools of a locksmith. The lock was not a difficult one to pick, and in a minute his skilled hands had turned the lock's tumblers to the open position.

The intruder pushed the tool folder back into his pocket and removed a black 9-millimeter pistol from a shoulder holster. He carefully inspected the weapon, gave the silencer a twist to make sure it was on tightly, and clicked the safety off. He had chosen to use hollow point bullets that would splatter when they contacted the target. He turned the knob and silently opened the door a crack.

He was sure that on this day the woman of the house would have given any employees the day off, and he was right. He passed through the doorway and found himself in the spacious kitchen, luxuriously equipped with institutional-grade stainless steel appliances and sinks. Gun in hand, he moved stealthily across the kitchen, past the laundry room, and toward the sound of voices coming from another area of the apartment.

His feet had moved from the hard tiles of the kitchen floor to the deep pile of the carpeted areas. He moved along a hall toward the familiar sounds of people engaged in sex. He came to a bathroom adjoining the room from which the sounds were emerging.

He could tell instantly that it was the bathroom used by the woman who occupied the bedroom. The shelving was loaded with vials, flasks, jars and bottles of every size, shape and color. The intruder was now faced with a decision: should he burst into the bedroom, using the element of surprise to accomplish his mission, or should he wait in the bathroom for one of them to come to him? He decided on the latter course of action. He leaned against the wall, listening and waiting.

Next door, things reached an inexorable crescendo, and then went quiet except for the sound of heavy breathing. The intruder readied himself behind the bathroom door. One or the other of these fornicators would sooner or later decide to use the bathroom, and then he would spring into action.

As it happened, the Prince decided to urinate and walked over to the lavatory. He opened the door, stepped inside, and when he turned to close the door the hidden assailant jumped out and grabbed him from behind. He put the pistol against Umar's temple, pushed the door shut, and whispered, "Make no sound, or you die."

With one strong arm around the Prince's neck, the gunman half pushed, half guided Umar to the edge of the huge pink-tiled bathtub.

"Dunbar?" the Prince hissed.

"No, you idiot. It's Alvarez the mediocre murderer, now *your* mediocre murderer."

He pressed the barrel of his gun into the back of Umar's neck at an upward angle so that when it discharged, the soft bullet went into the Prince's cerebral cortex and continued on into his brain. The Viper guided the slowly slumping naked body of the moribund Prince into the tub.

DeeDee heard the unusual whooshing sound of the silenced pistol firing, but didn't recognize it for what it was. Rafael flushed the toilet and turned the water on hard in the sink, believing that the normal sound of running water would allay any suspicions that the woman might have. His ruse worked. Mrs. Dunbar stayed put, lying bottom up with her head facing the windows and away from the bathroom.

Allowing the water to keep running in the sink, La Víbora opened the door and peeked into the bedroom. Then he sprang into action, moving rapidly across the room and arriving at the bedside before DeeDee could change her position. With one strong hand he shoved her head face down into the pillow so she couldn't turn to see him. With his other hand he pushed the silenced barrel of the gun against the back of her head.

"Umar, what are you doing? You're hurting me!"

Rafael Alvarez was not a man to concern himself about hurting a woman, especially a *gringa puta* like this one.

"Umar, stop that," DeeDee said. "You're killing me."

"I'm not Umar, but yes I *am* killing you," and with that the Viper fired his weapon into her skull. DeeDee's body seized, stiffened, and then went still.

His venomous work done, his honor avenged, the Viper turned away from his second victim and silently retraced his steps toward the service entrance. On his way he passed a room that was obviously Peter Dunbar's home office. On the spur of the moment he walked to the large teak desk and tried the center drawer. It was locked.

To the son of a locksmith this little fastener presented only the slightest impediment. He withdrew the wallet with the tools in it from the breast pocket of his jacket. In a few seconds he'd opened the desk, and quickly searched through its drawers. He found nothing of interest except an envelope containing a considerable number of hundred dollar bills in the top drawer. He pocketed the money.

In the lowest drawer of the right pedestal he discovered a pistol. Intuitively, almost as if he had planned it, the Viper exchanged the pistol that he had used to kill Umar and DeeDee for the one in the drawer. He quickly relocked the drawer, and resumed his path to the service entrance.

Smiling at his own cleverness, he latched the door so it would lock behind him, and climbed back up the stairs to the roof above. He ran across the rooftop to the adjoining building, opened the roof door, and stealthily descended the many flights of stairs to the lobby.

He pocketed his rubber gloves and peeked out of the door. Waiting until the elevator discharged some tenants, the Viper fell in behind them and walked out of building. Neither the doorman nor the tenants paid any attention to the well-dressed, black-haired gentleman. He went to the corner without looking back, hailed a cab, and left the scene of his brutal crime.

Moments later a cab pulled up in front of the Dunbar's apartment building, and Peter got out. He walked into the building, hardly acknowledging the doorman's greeting. He was furious with his wife and fully intended to give her the first serious dressing-down that he had ever mustered. Fuming about how she had summoned him home for what he believed was a fatuous reason, he was primed to explode at her. He opened the fancy rococo carved mahogany front door to his apartment – the one that DeeDee insisted they buy to replace the plain but perfectly serviceable old one.

"DeeDee, where are you?" he shouted in a loud, angry tone of voice.

Getting no answer, he started looking for her. In the farthest room he found her unresponsive naked body lying face down on the bed. He approached the bed.

"What's wrong with you?"

He directed his question at the tousled head of red hair on the bed. When he got no answer he went up to her and prodded her. When she didn't move he became alarmed and quickly called 911.

CHAPTER TWENTY-FOUR

Detective Bill Lynch and his partner at the New York Police Department had been called by one of the two uniformed officers that had been sent to the Dunbar apartment at the behest of the medics who had reported the suspicious death as a possible homicide.

Lynch was typical of the new breed of detectives. He had a degree in criminology and had been accepted to law school, but he had decided he wanted a more active life than the practice of law could provide. Fourteen years on the force in New York, most of them in the homicide section, had furnished him with the active career he was looking for. Lynch's partner, Dalton Fry, was an ambitious junior detective on his way up the ladder, fresh from his previous assignment in the Harlem Division.

Lynch examined the corpse, the bed, and the crime scene. It was obvious from the bullet wound in the skull of the dead woman that this was a clear-cut case of murder. It would be a high profile case, the detective thought, judging from the ritzy address and the information the uniforms had given him about the husband being held for interrogation in the next room. He instructed the cops to cordon off the crime scene. Then he got out his cell phone and punched in the number for the Coroner's office.

"Find Dillon," he said, in an authoritative, peremptory tone. He waited for a few seconds.

"Dillon here."

"This is Lynch. I've got a stiff for you."

"Okay. Give me the address. I'll be right there."

The Assistant Coroner knew from Lynch's attitude and the address he was given that the case would be interesting at worst, and at best a career maker for a pathologist.

"Fry, call the Crime Scene Investigation unit and tell them to get over here," Lynch barked. "I'm going to poke around a little, and then I'll speak to the grieving husband."

Lynch walked around the room without touching anything. He noticed the pile of white cloth on a chair near the bed. On closer examination he saw that the material was an Arab man's clothing, probably removed in considerable haste, judging from the way it had been tossed over the chair.

"So where's Alladin?" he said to Fry.

"Huh?"

"The guy who was wearing these." Lynch pointed at the chair. "What do you say we look for him?"

They walked slowly into the bathroom. The shower curtain had been drawn closed. As Lynch opened the curtain, he had the feeling he was in a scene from the movie, *Psycho*. There it was, right in front of his eyes – the naked body of a guy shot in the back of the head and then dumped into the bathtub.

"Now we've got two corpses, and one's an Arab. Probably an important one, considering his clothes and his location in this part of town. What's your take, Fry?"

Lynch was interested in what his partner thought, but it was mostly a training exercise, as the senior detective had already guessed what had taken place in the posh apartment.

"Off the top of my head it looks like a jealousy killing. The husband comes home, finds his wife in bed with another guy, and shoots them both," the junior detective said.

"We'll have to wait for the Coroner's report before I tell you what I think. Have the cops round up the doorman and the building staff. Now let's go talk to the husband."

The two detectives approached Peter Dunbar.

"Mr. Dunbar, I'm Detective Lynch with the NYPD and this Detective Fry. We'd like to ask you a few questions."

"If you must," Peter replied, looking up at them.

"Did you kill your wife, Mr. Dunbar?"

"No, I did not."

"Did you kill the man?"

"What man?"

"The man in the bathtub."

"What are you talking about?"

"I'm talking about the corpse we found in the bathtub."

"I don't know anything about a corpse in the bathtub. Your questions make me think you regard me as a suspect. If that's the case, I'd like to call my lawyer."

"If you were in our position, Mr. Dunbar, what would *you* think? If you didn't kill anyone, you have nothing to fear from us. But the fastest way to get things cleared up is for you to tell us the truth right now so we can catch the one who did this. You said you came home from work and found your wife dead on the bed. Do you usually come home from work at this time?"

"No. As I told the officers, my wife called me at work and asked me to come home at once. When I got here I found her on the bed, dead. That's when I called 911."

"Both doors to this apartment were locked?"

"Yes. Who doesn't lock their doors in New York City?"

"Who, besides you, has a key to this apartment?"

"As far as I know, my wife and I have the only keys. Oh, and the concierge has a passkey."

"Mr. Dunbar, do you employ servants?"

"A woman comes in three days a week to clean."

"Doesn't she have a key?"

"Not as far as I know. My wife may have given her one, but I doubt it. She didn't trust Maria or anyone else."

"Would you mind writing Maria's name and address down, please? Detective Fry will contact her," Lynch said. "So, if what you say is true, how do you explain how your wife died? The doors were locked, you have the only key, the locks don't appear to have been tampered with, and you came home early."

"Regardless of how it looks, I didn't kill my wife. I didn't look in the bathtub, and I never saw any other body."

"Well, let's go look. Maybe you can identify it for us."

"Very well, I'll look at it."

Dunbar walked to the bathroom and seemed to be taken aback by the sight of Prince Umar's naked body.

"Do you know this man?" Lynch asked.

"Yes. It's Prince Umar of the Royal House of Saud."

The minds of both Dunbar and Lynch were thrown into overdrive. Lynch was angry, as he thought the diplomatic corps of the Saudi embassy would be coming down on the NYPD for not protecting such an important man, the son of the King. They'd want to take the body before he could get the path lab results. He had to work fast. When the Saudis got the news, the political pressure be on. The Muslims bury their dead the next day, and he was sure the Saudis would not allow him to work the case without interference.

"Is Dillon here yet?" he called to anyone within earshot.

Peter hadn't wanted DeeDee to die, but he wasn't entirely sorry now that she was gone. He knew he'd been unhappy in his marriage for a long time, but he hadn't wanted to face divorce proceedings. His wife was the type who would have had no mercy about taking him to the cleaners if he had initiated an action against her. She would never leave him either, as he was too good a provider.

He began to think about the effect of the Prince's death on Paramount Petroleum. The Royal Prince was killed in the apartment of the CEO of the company whose majority holdings were now controlled by the Kingdom Corporation. To the conspiratorial minds in Islam, only the worst-case scenario would be considered a possibility, namely that the infidel had murdered the Prince for gain. It occurred to Peter that the Arabs would call for a fatwa.

The questioning was interrupted when Dillon, the Forensic Coroner, arrived. Lynch explained the situation.

"Give this your full attention," he concluded, "and give the Arab a thorough autopsy, DNA, the works. You won't have a second chance. As for the woman, I need a cause of death and time of death as soon as possible."

By this time the apartment was swarming with forensic crime scene investigators, several police photographers, and the Coroner's staff pushing gurneys to be used for taking the bodies to the morgue. Lynch went to Dunbar's office to continue his questioning, but in his absence the suspect's lawyer had arrived. Lynch had run into him before, and found him cocky and egotistical. The attorney handled cases for the rich and powerful whenever they got tangled up in criminal affairs, and he had a good grasp of the law.

"Are you laying charges against my client, Detective?"

"I haven't decided yet. I still have some questions."

"Go ahead, if they're not incriminating."

"Very well, then. Mr. Dunbar, do you own a gun?"

"I keep a handgun locked in my desk. It's registered, and I have a permit for it. Would you like to see it?"

"If you don't mind."

Dunbar got up and went to the desk. He took a key out of his pocket and began to unlock the desk. Fry moved around so he could see Dunbar's hands, on the odd chance that he might get the gun and try to use it. Peter pushed the swivel chair back and reached down to retrieve the pistol.

"Move away from the desk," the Detective said.

Dunbar obeyed, and Fry moved closer. He reached into the bottom drawer of the desk and found a 9-millimeter handgun with a silencer attached to its barrel. He put a pencil through the trigger ring and lifted the weapon out of the drawer to show it to everyone. He smelled the barrel.

"This weapon has been discharged recently."

"That's not my gun," Peter Dunbar protested.

"Mr. Dunbar," Dective Lynch said, "I'm arresting you for suspicion of murder and I'm taking you to the station. You have the right to remain silent." He read him his Miranda rights as the police led him away.

Ivan Welland was about to begin his meeting with Brad and Julia Montcalf, the Secretary of State, when Brad's cell phone began to chirp like a scared bird. He excused himself and answered it.

"Hello, Burke here."

"Brad, it's Peter Dunbar. I need to talk to you."

"I'm in a meeting with the Secretary of Defense and the Secretary of State. Can it wait?"

"No. Use the speaker. Welland needs to hear this, too."

Burke switched the speaker on and turned to Ivan.

"It's Peter Dunbar, my successor as CEO at Paramount Petroleum. He says it's urgent, and he wants you to listen."

"All right."

"Go ahead Peter, Dr. Welland and the Secretary of State are listening, too."

"Okay, I'm calling from the detention center in the NYPD Midtown Precinct. I'm being held on suspicion of murdering my wife. They found a gun in my desk that doesn't belong to me, but it might be the murder weapon. Anyway, I want you to know that I had nothing to do with DeeDee's death. I just discovered her body in our apartment and I called the police right away. My lawyer has been here and he's doing what he can. But the real problem is this. The police are also saying I killed Prince Umar of the Saudi Royal House. They found his body in my apartment, too. I have no idea what he was doing there. I didn't invite him, nor did I know he was there, either alive or dead. His body's in the morgue now. This whole mess is going to have terrible repercussions for the U.S., Ivan, so I wanted to warn you."

"Thank you, Mr. Dunbar," Ivan said, trying to collect his thoughts.

"Brad, the annual meeting of Paramount Petroleum is set for tomorrow," Peter continued. "Prince Umar is the top gun in petroleum and he was here to represent the Kingdom Corporation, which has a huge stock position in Paramount. As the CEO I was planning to run the meeting, but obviously I won't be able to attend. So Brad, I was hoping you could go in my place. I know you're an ambassador now, but as the previous CEO you're the only person with know-how and presence enough to head off an international crisis."

"Don't worry about it, Peter," Brad said. "I'll be there. Just take care of yourself."

"Thanks, Brad. Thank God you can make it."

"Thank you, Mr. Dunbar, for the heads up," Ivan said. "I'm so sorry about your wife. You were right to call us. We'll put our heads together and move on this matter at once. Is there anything else we can do?"

"I'll let you know. I have a good lawyer, but I'll be in touch if anything else comes to mind."

"Peter, I'm sorry for your loss," said Brad. "We're here for you."

"Thanks Brad. God, it's good to have friends at a time like this. Thanks for sticking by me."

The cell phone went dead.

"What can you tell me about Dunbar?" the Secretary of State asked Brad.

"I've known Peter for a long time," Brad said. "I started at Paramount Petroleum after I got my MBA from Harvard, then I recruited Peter away from a competitor a couple of years later. We've been friends ever since. I introduced him to his wife, DeeDee, but that wasn't my most successful merger arrangement. I don't believe he could have killed DeeDee or anyone else. There must be another explanation."

"Madame Secretary," Ivan said, "what do you think we should do to suppress the pent-up outrage that's just waiting for an excuse like this to spill over onto the globe?"

"It's a bad situation," she said. "Umar hated Americans, and he showed his dislike for us during oil negotiations. Many people here will be glad to be rid of him, but this is going to look bad. Umar's combative hate-mongering will make it seem as if we were the ones who wanted him out of the way. It's a tricky situation, and I don't see any immediate solution. We may all find ourselves in Brad's position – we look guilty because we seem to be the most likely suspects."

"That's true," Ivan agreed. "But for now, though, I think we should do the following: Brad and I should do some fact-finding while we're in New York. At the moment all we have is the testimony of the one who's being held for suspicion of murdering the Prince. Even if Peter Dunbar is everything Brad claims he is, we still owe it to ourselves to find out what the police have to say, and what evidence they have for holding Peter as a suspect."

"That sounds good to me," Brad agreed.

"I do think that you should cancel your trip to Syria, Mr. Ambassador," the Secretary of State said. "Being there when this hits the media could be dangerous for you and your wife. The President's War on Ammunition program must not be impeded by this incident, either. It's so ironic. The successful implementation of his program would have insured the absence of bullets, and therefore the Prince and Dunbar's wife would still be alive. I'll take it upon myself to advise the President of this unfortunate incident and what we're doing about it."

"Good, then. We'll stay in close touch," Ivan said.

The Secretary of State returned to her office to speak to the President and to develop some ways to head off the expected outrage that would emerge from the Middle East.

Ivan called his assistant, Brooklyn, and told her that he was going to New York and why. He asked her to call the team and alert them to the circumstances, and to stand by for emergency service. He also asked her to call his wife, Marina, and tell her he wouldn't be home for a day or so and he would call her when he could. He grabbed the suitcase that always stood at the ready for occasions such as this.

Brad was making his arrangements at the same time. He called Laura and told her the trip to Syria was off until further notice. He asked her to cancel all their appointments in Syria. He would explain everything when he could, but she must not talk to anyone about this. Something urgent had come up, and he'd be traveling with Ivan Welland. He told Laura he loved her, and not to worry.

The two men virtually flew out of the Pentagon. They boarded Marine One, and for the second time they were both transported directly to New York. On their way north Brad told Ivan all he knew about Peter Dunbar and his wife, DeeDee. He explained how, after accumulating oil revenues for many years, the Saudi royal family had sought safe, profitable investments for their enormous profits. They had acquired large equity positions in the biggest petroleum companies, and among these was Paramount Petroleum.

In a short time the noisy chopper landed on the NYPD's helicopter pad. They were met there by a Secret Service limousine and driven to the Midtown Police Precinct, where Detective Bill Lynch came out to meet them. He escorted them into his tiny, cramped office, where they sat facing each other.

"I know you're busy, Detective," Ivan began, "so we won't keep you very long. This is your city, and the crimes committed in it are yours to solve, but this particular one is special because of the effect it could have on world peace. Therefore I ask only two things of you. First of all, that you consult us before releasing any information to the media, and secondly, that you keep us completely informed of your progress."

"That shouldn't be a problem," Detective Lynch said.

"We can supply you with background information that could save you a great deal of work," Brad told him. "If you'd be willing to share your evidence with us in return, we could probably head off an international brouhaha that could sink the President's new peace initiative."

"Can you give us a status report?" Ivan asked.

"Sure, but I don't have the Coroner's statement yet. All I can tell you is what we found when we arrived on the scene."

"Okay, let's have it," said the Secretary of Defense.

"We found the body of a naked woman, face down on the bed. Mr. Peter Dunbar, the only occupant of the apartment at that time, identified her as his wife. When the Coroner arrived, he officially diagnosed the death as murder by gunshot. After conducting a crime scene examination, I discovered the body of a naked man behind the shower curtains in the bathtub. He had been shot in the head, same as the woman. Mr. Dunbar denied having anything to do with the murder of his wife, even though he was alone in the locked apartment. He didn't know about the corpse in the bathtub. We then found a 9-millimeter pistol in Dunbar's locked desk. The gun had a silencer on it and had been fired recently. We questioned the doorman, who told us that Dunbar had entered the building quickly and looked very agitated. He took the elevator up to the penthouse. This information left us with no choice but to take Mr. Dunbar into custody."

"I understand, Detective," Ivan said. "We aren't here to criticize your police work. The Ambassador and I are mostly interested in keeping a tight lid on the potential for an international incident of major significance. As soon as you allow it to be known that you have the body of the Prince in the morgue, you can expect a delegation from the Saudi Embassy to retrieve the body immediately. You'll want to make sure you've done every possible test, taken all the essential photos, and collected all the evidence you can before you turn the corpse over to the Saudis. They'll send it to Riyadh, and we'll never get near it again. As a measure of respect for their customs, I suggest you call in the imam from the nearest mosque and let him prepare the body."

"That's a good suggestion. I'll arrange it," Lynch said.

"Ambassador Burke, maybe you could tell the detective everything you can about Peter Dunbar. While you two confer, I'd like to see the weapon that you confiscated."

"Certainly, sir, but we've sent it to our ballistics experts for testing and tracing," Lynch replied.

"As you can imagine, we in the Defense Department have a lot of experience with weapons, so it might pay to coordinate our efforts with regard to the source of the gun. If you could have someone take me to ballistics, I'd appreciate it greatly."

A young detective took Ivan to the ballistics lab. During Ivan's conversation with the chief of the laboratory, it became obvious that NYPD was only interested in matching the weapon with the bullets that had resulted in the deaths of two victims. The chief was part of the construction of the legal case for the prosecution of Peter Dunbar, so it was his job to establish that the weapon found in Dunbar's desk was the one that fired the fatal shots.

Ivan was more concerned about the source of the pistol. To whom was it sold after it left the manufacturer? Welland was inclined to believe Dunbar when he claimed the gun was not his. If Ivan's team could trace the gun back to its origins, they might be able to establish the identity of the murderer. The serial number, model type, and the manufacturer's name were what he needed to put his team to work on the problem. When the chief had given him that information, he called Brooklyn and told her to put the crew to work to establish the identity of the owner of the weapon.

When Ivan was convinced that all the details of the murder investigation were being well handled, he let his mind dwell on the political aspects of the case. Who should tell the King that his son had been assassinated? Should he be told in person, by telephone, or through the embassy and diplomatic channels? Whatever procedure was adopted, the King had to be told the truth in all its details. He must be made aware that the death of his son was not political, religious, or business-related, and that nothing good could come of letting the case be built up into fodder for terrorist propaganda.

The method he chose to release the news of Prince Umar's death to the Arab media would be critical if an international incident was to be avoided. The Americans would have to be seen to have clean hands in the matter of the assassination. It also might be helpful to do everything possible to persuade the King not to allow his grief and anger to push him into irrational behavior that might give the extremists all over the world a focal point for their usual violence.

Ivan was anxious to find incontrovertible evidence that the Prince's death was in no way attributable to American political ambitions. Welland knew this was the case, but convincing the King that the United States had nothing to do with his son's murder might take more than just the plain truth. Unfortunately all this was coming right after the President's announcement of his *War on Weapons*, which was not a popular idea in Saudi Arabia in spite of the fact that the Saudi kingdom would be one of the largest beneficiaries of such a plan. Simply put, the idea of any plan that didn't include Islamic input was too much for a paternalistic Arab society to accept, no matter how profitable the long-term results might be.

CHAPTER TWENTY-FIVE

Detective Bill Lynch went over the Coroner's report as soon as he received it in the morning. Apparently Dillon had taken his advice and put on a full court press to get his report in quickly. Brad and Ivan had stayed overnight in New York and went back to Lynch's precinct office the next morning to see the pathology report. The men waited with anticipation to hear what the medical examiner had to say.

"To summarize, the M.E. says that the Prince and Dunbar's wife were killed at the same time, by the same gun," Lynch read. "One unusual fact was that the victims were killed with hollow point bullets. This is not the kind of ammunition used in ordinary guns. Customized bullets are not usual, and their use in these murders indicates that the perpetrator had knowledge of, and access to special rounds. It also indicates some degree of premeditation."

"What else do we know?"

"There were no fingerprints on the weapon, so the killer must have worn gloves. We didn't find any suspicious gloves in the apartment."

"Which means what?" Brad inquired.

"Probably not much. Dunbar could have flushed them, or if someone else committed the crime he or she was professional and prepared for eventualities," the detective remarked. "He probably took the gloves with him."

"Anything else?" Ivan asked.

"The couple had engaged in sex. The lady had semen in her vagina, and the male had traces on his organ as well. It's too soon for the DNA report, but I think we can assume that the semen was the Prince's."

"Go on," said Ivan.

"We checked the phone records and found that a call was made to Dunbar's office about half an hour before the time of death. This coincides with what Dunbar told us. He said his wife had called him and told him to come home."

"I can support that in a general way," Brad interjected. "She'd frequently call him at the office with unreasonable requests. He sometimes grumbled to me about them."

"If we piece together the evidence and the information he gave in his statement, it sounds as though he's telling the truth about his late appearance on the scene," Ivan said.

"His story is certainly possible," Detective Lynch agreed, "but we still have the weapon to contend with. Dunbar said he owned a gun and kept it in his desk, but that the pistol we found was not his. It's hard to believe that someone else switched the murder weapon for Dunbar's gun after the shooting. The killer would have had to open the locked desk and exchange guns instead of making his escape quickly. He would have had to be able to pick the desk lock, and relock the desk after the switch was made. Detective Fry and I saw Dunbar unlock the desk when we were questioning him. If the killer was not Dunbar, then there's the question of how the perpetrator could have known there was a gun in the desk in the first place."

"Perhaps he was looking in the desk for money or something," Brad suggested, "and he just came across the gun and decided to do the switch to throw us off the track, or even better, to implicate Dunbar in his wife's death."

"There are an infinite number of possibilities, and some probabilities, but I have to deal with raw evidence and not be thrown off the scent by random speculations. The apartment showed no evidence of robbery. If someone else had been in the apartment, other than the husband I mean, he would have had to be part locksmith to have unlocked and relocked both a door and the desk. So I guess I'll hold onto my original suspect for the time being."

"May I see Dunbar?" Brad asked.

"Sure. We've got him in a holding cell in the basement."

The three men walked down the stairs, turned right, and found the detention cell. Dunbar was sitting on a cot that hung down from the grey wall. He looked small and lonely. He smiled at Brad, pleased to see a familiar face.

"Mr. Ambassador, I'm sure glad to see you. I didn't kill anybody. You believe that, don't you?"

"I believe you," Brad said. "Let me introduce you to Dr. Ivan Welland, our new Secretary of Defense."

The two men shook hands.

"Is there anything I can do to help?" Brad inquired.

"Other than telling them that I'm innocent, I can't think of anything for the moment."

"Detective Lynch," Brad said.

"Yes, sir."

"I've known this man for twenty-five years, and he's never lied to me. If he says he's innocent, I believe him."

"Mr. Dunbar, may I ask you a question?" Ivan inquired.

"Certainly, Mr. Secretary."

"The police believe the intruder didn't steal anything. According to your statement, he must have left the apartment shortly before you arrived. If that's true, what do you think was his motive for killing two people?"

"I wouldn't exactly say that nothing was stolen, unless you consider $10,000 in cash to be nothing."

"Why didn't you mention that to the police before?" Ivan asked, looking puzzled.

"My lawyer told me not to speak to the police unless he was present. So that's why I didn't mention it."

"Where was the money?" Ivan asked him.

"It was in my desk drawer, with the pistol," Dunbar said. "I noticed the envelope was gone when I removed the weapon. The cops were so excited to see the gun, and so anxious for me not use it on them that the money issue went by the board. Is this important in some way that I don't understand?"

"Well, Detective Lynch and his colleagues were quick to tell me that there was no evidence of robbery as a motive for the crime. But now there *is* such a motive. It gives credence to your contention that someone else committed the murder."

Ivan could tell that the detective was anxious to get back to his desk, so he concluded the meeting.

"Mr. Dunbar," he said to Peter, "Brad and I will investigate further and do our level best to substantiate your version of the events. We'll also get in touch with your lawyer and use our influence to see that he devotes himself fully to your defense."

"Th-Thank you both for coming," Peter stammered.

Ivan and Brad followed Detective Lynch back through the maze of corridors to the exit of the building.

"The Ambassador and I will do everything we can to help you clarify the evidence in this case," Ivan said to the detective. "I have a distinct feeling that there's a great deal more to be known about these murders. I promise we'll keep you posted. There may be political, diplomatic and offshore business details that the local police may not be privy to, and we can be helpful with these. I expect that in the best spirit of reciprocity you'll let us know your findings, too. This crime is in your jurisdiction and we don't dispute that, but it also has serious international ramifications, and we must be involved in those as well. Do we understand each other?"

"Yes sir, perfectly," Lynch replied.

"Please let me know if you turn up any DNA evidence to indicate the presence of an unidentified person in the apartment or its entrances, and don't overlook the roof door and stairway. In the meantime, the Ambassador and I think you've done the right thing by holding Mr. Dunbar in detention. It may be that he was also a target for death, but luckily for him he wasn't in the apartment at the time. But he should be safe in jail."

"Right now the clearest explanation is that it was a crime of passion committed by an enraged but calculating husband," said Lynch. "I agree, however, that every piece of evidence must be examined so I can turn it over to the District Attorney, who will decide if he has enough of a case to convict Mr. Dunbar."

The men shook hands and went their separate ways.

Ivan had the Secret Service car drive him and Brad Burke to Paramount Petroleum's New York office. Brad, of course, still knew everyone on the executive floor. He was expected to attend the annual meeting the following day as a member of the board and Chairman Emeritus. He had fully intended to resign his board membership at that meeting, on the grounds that there was a conflict of interest between his old and new jobs. At that moment he was glad his resignation had not yet been tendered, as he wanted access to company files, materials, and some desk space for Ivan and himself. A conference room was made available, and the two men settled down to work.

Brad wanted to review the agenda and all the pertinent information about the annual meeting scheduled for the next day. It had occurred to him that it might not have been purely coincidental that Prince Umar, who carried the proxies for many of the company's largest shareholders, had been murdered just before he was due to attend the same meeting as the suspected perpetrator. Brad wanted to explore the ramifications of this overly obvious coincidence.

Ivan had several important details on his mind. All of them bore heavily on his wish to ensure the success of the President's *War on Weapons*. His own war on weapons, however, had narrowed itself down to one particular weapon, the one that had killed the Prince. He called his office.

"Brooklyn, it's me. Have you got any information for me about the gun?"

"Yeah boss, I was going to call you. The guys jumped all over the manufacturer of the gun and got him to search his sales records to see who purchased it. It turns out that the pistol was part of a large shipment sold to the police department in Cali, Colombia several years ago. I followed up with them, and their *commandante* told me that he remembered ordering those weapons for his SWAT team, but that they had been hijacked by parties unknown, and never received by the police. Does that help?"

"Well, a little, maybe."

"I'm checking now to see if any other guns from that shipment have surfaced anywhere in the country. I've got the ballistics guys in the FBI crime lab in Quantico checking to see if your gun could have been used in other shootings. According to the manufacturer, that model wasn't machined to accept a silencer. That means someone in the aftermarket must have adapted the gun. The boys are trying to run down the source of that kind of customizing. A different company made the silencer on the murder weapon, and we're checking to see if they do this kind of work, or if not, who does?"

"Good. Keep me posted. Anything else?"

"We're getting some information from Abdul's Arab contacts to indicate that the dead man, Prince Umar, was a heavyweight sponsor of some pretty violent terrorist groups, including the one that was headed up by Ibn Mansurallah, the guy the Israelis killed not long ago. I don't know if this has anything to do with your situation in New York, but we know the Prince was also big in petroleum-based munitions."

"That would explain why Ambassador Burke was not too popular with the Prince," Ivan remarked. "He probably wasn't too fond of the President, either."

"Yes, and he probably wasn't one of your fans, either."

"Speaking of popularity, have you heard anything about the investigation into *my* assailants?"

"I'm afraid that when you changed jobs and moved into the Pentagon, the boys around the White House lost some interest, although I'm sure they'd deny that. Maybe they figure that now that the entire military reports to you, they don't need to worry about your safety anymore."

"Brooklyn, I'm not going to speculate about that, and yes, I'm wearing my protective vest. Keep the boys going at full speed and on course. I'll be checking in frequently, and you should call me any time you have news."

When Brad went over the agenda for the annual meeting of Paramount Petroleum, he noticed that the last item up for consideration and approval was far too sketchy to suit his idea of what a standard annual meeting should be. Apart from the usual items, such as the appointment of auditors for the coming year and executive compensation disclosures, there was an item called "management policy decisions for the future." Brad tried to get more information about this item from the headquarters staff, but they seemed to know nothing about it except that the discussion was supposed to be led by Prince Umar.

As in most public corporations, the board of directors is divided into various oversight committees, each of which is responsible for seeing to it that the company's officers are discharging their duties honestly and effectively. The Prince was the head of the stockholder relations committee. This meant he would probably be addressing ownership issues. Questions involving mergers and acquisitions often arise in this way, so Brad's instincts were alerted to the possibility of some sort of financial wheeling and dealing that would effectively be a bid for a hostile takeover.

After Brad and Ivan had called their wives, they decided to have a meal together and discuss the case before getting back to work on the world's weapons issues. The men were well aware that the President's program to halt the manufacture of explosives and ammunition should not suffer or be delayed by anything. They also agreed that they must find a way to make certain that the murders didn't serve as a sort of catalyst for a new round of violence in the world that would obviate any peace efforts. Time was of the essence, as the Prince's murder and his burial were issues that required immediate diplomatic and political unanimity in the way the facts of the case and its announcement were presented. Some of the facts were not in yet, which made it risky to concoct political positioning policies that might subsequently be blown out of the water when the whole truth was later revealed, but they still had to tell the King something *now*.

As they sat together in the restaurant, the two men appeared to be businessmen discussing some sort of venture. Brad, with his elegant suit and distinguished executive appearance, looked like the senior in rank. Ivan, because of his great height, youthful appearance, and slightly rumpled academic hair and clothes, might have appeared to a casual observer to be Brad's assistant, but to the participants of this conversation there was no hint of hierarchical importance either given or taken. The nation was fortunate to have placed the handling of this sensitive problem in the hands of these two men. Brad, with his patient nature, vast experience and skillful abilities in negotiating important matters, and Ivan, with his creative mind, sharp analytical talents and lofty moral standards, were the ideal decision makers for the problem at hand.

"It seems to me," Brad remarked, "that we're going to have to make some kind of announcement before we have all the facts."

"It's always best to stick to the truth," Ivan replied. "What do you think the Saudi King will do if we just tell it like it is?"

"In my experience the truth to an Arab is just a negotiating tool. If it helps their cause, fine. If it doesn't, a lie will do just as well."

"Brad, what do you think are the negatives if we just ask the President to call the King and tell him man to man exactly what happened?"

"I think the King will accept that on the personal level. I'm guessing that a man with seventy sons won't miss one as much as a man with only one son. But he'll talk to his counselors and they'll advise him to use the death of Umar in our country as a bargaining chip to make us give them something they want."

"Any idea what that might be?"

"We probably should ask the Secretary of State what she's got on the table with them right now," Brad answered.

"Good idea," Ivan said. "Call her and see what she says. I don't know if I'll ever get used to dealing with Islamists. Most of my success with them has come at the end of a gun."

"I don't think Islam will figure into this too much. Sure, they'll want the body back at once. We can give them that with no regrets. I don't think this particular Prince was well liked by his family elders, any more than we liked him."

"What's the number one concern of the Royal House?"

"My guess would be job security," Brad said. "They want to protect what they've got. It's not easy to hang on to a monarchy in the world of democracies, communists, and theocracies."

"Hmm. I guess you're right. Does that mean they'll favor the President's War on Weapons?"

"Well, I'm hoping they'll like being the ones with fewer guns, if their rivals have even fewer still. The problem with Umar was that weapons were his bag, and he would have lost money, power, and more importantly *respect*, if his government accepted the President's program."

"So," Ivan said, "can level with the King about the circumstances of the Prince's death?"

"I think so. If the news is presented right, we can keep a lid on the extremists. He won't want the news to get out that his son Umar was killed while he was having sex with an infidel adulteress. He may even suppose that the murder was Allah's penalty for Umar's sin."

"We agree that our advice to the President is that he should personally tell the king the truth about the murder?"

"Well, first we should consider what the real purpose of Umar's visit to the United States could have been. I'm sure he didn't come all the way over here just to enjoy DeeDee's charms. I know that he was supposed to take the floor at the

Paramount Annual Meeting scheduled for tomorrow. It's possible he was using DeeDee to spy on Peter. I'm trying to find out what he was going to say at the meeting, but so far nobody at the company seems to know."

"I don't suppose you could cancel the meeting until we get all the facts?"

"It would be rare for an annual meeting to be cancelled. It's scheduled for tomorrow morning, and many of the attendees from distant places have no doubt already arrived in the city. But with the CEO in jail and a dead board member to contend with, I suppose I could use my role as Chairman Emeritus and propose a postponement."

"How would it be if you held the meeting, but just dropped the last item that Umar was to have addressed?" Ivan asked.

"That's a good idea, Ivan. It would keep the corporate status quo, and give me more time to investigate. The legal requirement for public corporations to hold an annual meeting would have been met. I'll just advise the Board that a special meeting can be called for a later time. Hopefully we can have Peter Dunbar's name cleared by then so he can continue on as Chairman, or if he's unable to go on in his position, a substitute can be found. Whatever Prince Umar was going to propose can wait until someone else brings it forward. Yes, Ivan, that's exactly what I'll do."

"Suppose we skip dessert. I'll call the President and see if he'll go along with our proposal that he call the King and tell him the truth about the death of his son. Then I'll check with my investigators, and the NYPD to see if there have been any new developments in the case. Perhaps you can use this time to prepare for the annual meeting in the morning."

"Sounds like a plan," Brad said.

CHAPTER TWENTY-SIX

No sooner had Brad and Ivan settled into their seats in the conference room they were sharing, than Ivan's cell phone beeped for attention.

"What's up, Brooklyn?" Ivan said into the tiny instrument lost in his oversized hand.

"Hi, boss. We've been working the case hard, and we've turned up some items of interest."

"Okay, shoot," Ivan answered.

"A mob informant put us in touch with a gunsmith in Dallas. We spoke to him, and he remembered making a silencer for a 9-millimeter pistol that had been ordered by a Latino hood. Naturally he was paid in cash and has no receipt and no address for the purchaser."

"So how come he remembered the transaction, then? I imagine from what you've told me so far that this was a routine transaction for someone in his business."

"I asked him that myself," Brooklyn said. "All he could say was that nobody could possibly forget the man who picked up the silencer. I also took the liberty of asking the CIA to examine their overseas phone tapping records to see if Prince Umar had ever made any calls to Colombia. We struck pay dirt. It seems there were two conversations. A long one, then a short one a few weeks later. The subject matter was in some sort of code, but without too much of a stretch it could have been interpreted to be the placement of a hit order, and in the case of the shorter call, the cancellation of the order due to the failure of the hit man to complete his contract. We studied the timing of the calls, and they coincide precisely with the attacks on you. We think that they were talking about the assassin who was shot during the attempt on your life that day, and the henchman who subsequently tried to blow you up at your door in Georgetown."

"I'm not sure I see the connection between the Prince's murder and the attempts on my life," Ivan said.

"As strange as it seems, we think it was Prince Umar who ordered the hit on you. We believe he hired a South American organization to do the dirty work so if anything went wrong it would be blamed on the drug cartel, and not the Arabs."

"But I've never met Prince Umar. Why would he want to have me killed?"

"We're speculating here, but Abdul and Damian think it was Umar's way of sabotaging the *War on Weapons* plan by killing its author and chief promoter."

"How would he have discovered that the President's plan originated with me?"

"We're not sure about that yet, but there's another linkage."

"Oh? What's that?"

"The gun that killed the Prince."

"Yes?"

"Ballistics reports that it's the same gun that was used in the unsolved murder of a Chicago drug lord a year ago. This killing was drug related and involved the leader of a gang that was under surveillance by DEA agents. The MO was exactly the same, even to the wound to the back of the nude man's head, and the presence of a naked woman's body, killed in the same way as was Mrs. Dunbar was. The one thing we don't know is how the killer knew that the drug lord had given his bodyguards the night off so he could be alone with the woman. The DEA could never figure out how the assassin had gained entrance, since the doors were all locked from the inside. Does any of this sound familiar?"

"Indeed. So it's possible that the attack on me was carried out by criminals in the drug trade in order to take the attention off the true perpetrators – the Arab oil interests."

"Exactly. At least that's how it looks to us," Brooklyn said.

"It certainly explains a lot, but it's not altogether reassuring to me, since the killer is still on the loose. Believe me, I'm going to keep my clothes on from now on."

"You might try wearing a helmet too, boss."

"Any other good news to tell me?"

"David and Damian are working up some stats that could prove some connections existed between Umar and terrorism. I'll let you know when we've got something definite."

"Good work, Brooklyn. Give my best regards to the crew."

Bradley Burke had just finished a long telephone conversation with the CFO of Paramount Petroleum when Ivan approached him.

"How are you making out, Brad?"

"I've just had an interesting and informative conversation with Peter Dunbar's Chief Financial Officer. He reiterated something he warned me about when I was CEO of Paramount. He says that he believes there's a conspiracy going on to take over the company by illegal stock manipulations."

"How would that work?"

"Well, gradually a number of large foreign investors have combined to acquire a majority stock holding in Paramount by using blind corporations, off-shore banks, and small brokerages fronting for dummy companies. Large publicly held companies, in order to keep their ownership status as diversified as possible, are required to make public their shareholder registers. No one entity is allowed to own any more than 10% of a U.S. public company without making it known to the SEC. The Arabs are getting around this proviso by hiding the true ownership of the securities held by overseas shareholders, and by not registering their ownership as required by law. In the case of Paramount, and probably most other international petroleum operators as well, the super rich Russians, Arabs, Nigerians, and other OPEC recipients of the oil windfalls in their countries are investing their wealth in large cap American companies such as Paramount. On the surface, having all this foreign cash pouring into the U.S. stock markets has buoyed our economy, but we're losing control of our economy slowly but surely, because we no longer own it."

"I'm not a financier, but that doesn't sound good to me," Ivan remarked.

"It's not good at all," Brad agreed. "The smart operators are economic neo-colonialists. They realize the foolhardiness of war, especially when they can get what they want by buying it with their surplus cash. It may be that the terrorists, warriors, and warmongers are not our biggest enemies. The violent ones only present a highly annoying, temporarily bloody problem. Combating them saps our military and economic strength, but it only hastens the advent of a *financial* reign of terror. The real dilemma is the bloodless economic takeover that will put us into a permanent state of Islamic dhimmitude."

"I can imagine how hard it's going to be for the President to convince the spoiled, short-sighted American public of that. So many of our liberal-minded citizens seem to believe that U.S. greed is the cause of the present day terror attacks. I really fear that the nation will march off into a modern form of slavery like a horde of lemmings. *By a sagacious and persistent use of propaganda, heaven itself can be presented to a people as hell, and inversely, the most wretched existence as paradise.* That's a quote from Adolf Hitler's *Mein Kampf*, and he should know."

"It's hard to imagine, isn't it? Yet the signs are all around us. We're using our resources of money, labor, and energy to show mercy, keep the peace, and work for justice, but the very recipients of our mercy deny it to others, make war with us, and spurn our system of constitutional law. So I agree with you that our President has a monumental task ahead of him. I pray that he has the courage, stamina, and will to see it through, because he's the only leader who can do it."

"Well, it's up to us to do everything we can to help him. To start with, what do you think we can do about the Paramount situation?"

"I'll conduct the annual meeting, and keep any questions about illegal ownership off the table using the Dunbar situation, and the Prince's funeral as the reason for not handling those matters just now. If I do it right, they won't expect that I'm stalling until the CFO and I have a chance to prepare the case that their proxies are illegal, since they haven't made public their oversized holdings. I'll prove that their shares exceed the allowable percentages of voting stock blocks, which makes their proxies invalid. In the meantime I'll have an auditor from the Securities and Exchange Commission get over here right away to look into the register and verify the irregularities."

"Good, you do that, and I'll call Detective Lynch to see if he has any new evidence to report before I call the President," Ivan said.

Brad called the CFO and had him come to the conference room to collaborate on the financial details pursuant to the annual meeting, the securities investigation, and the interim management of the company until Dunbar's innocence could be established.

Ivan dialed Detective Lynch's number.

"Hello, Lynch, this is Welland. Listen, I'm about to call the President to advise him of the Prince's death, as protocol demands that *he* be the one to inform the King, and I need to have the latest facts before I contact him."

"I'm afraid there's no unexpected new evidence, Dr. Welland. DNA testing was expedited, and the semen extracted from the woman's body belonged to the Prince, but that was as expected. We found a black hair in the bathroom that didn't belong to the Prince or to Mrs. Dunbar. We're searching the FBI files of all the available open cases of murder to see if we can find a match of DNA in crimes with a similar MO. The hair could establish the presence of a third party in the room. We are also running DNA tests on the housekeeper to make sure the hair isn't hers."

"Have you coordinated activities with my assistant? She's given me some interesting details about the murder weapon, and I want to make sure that we're sharing evidence completely and promptly with your department. I'd like our dealings with each other to mirror the new climate of cooperation between security and policing agencies under the Homeland Security Act."

"I've had several conversations with Ms. Brocklyn, who by the way, is one terrific coordinator. She told me about the killing in Chicago that was evidently done with the same MO and the same weapon. The Chicago PD and the DEA are also cooperating with NYPD to scour their drug informants for leads. So far the only one that seems to have any weight came from an undercover cop in Manhattan. He says he knows of a gang boss named Rafael Alvarez, a Colombian who worked in New York for a time, and was much feared by dealers and drug peddlers on the street. They refer to him as the Viper."

"I'm glad to hear that you're working well with *Brooklyn*, my assistant. Everyone in Washington calls her *Brooklyn* in spite of the fact that she hails from the Bronx. Go figure. Does anyone know the current whereabouts of this Viper?"

"He seems to have no record that we know of. There's a sort of urban myth surrounding the guy, but no one has ever seen him. The consensus is that he's in Colombia running the Cali drug cartel," the Detective said.

"Hmm. My investigative team and the Secret Service are also working to discover the perpetrators of two attempts on my life in Washington D.C. The leads in this case seem to be pointing in the direction of Colombia, too. The CIA, using their ear in the sky, have documented a couple of calls between the dead Prince and an anonymous cell phone user in Colombia. Their feeling is that the drug and gun smuggling kingpin was hired by the Prince to do away with me. I'm beginning to feel the coils of a South American snake tightening around me. This Viper they speak of seems to be both constrictor and venomous striker, a new hybrid perhaps, with drug, gun smuggling, and murder for hire operations. Anyway, Lynch, if you've nothing else to report, I'll call the President now."

"Good luck, sir. Between us we'll catch this guy I'm sure."

Ivan Welland was less sure.

Ivan waited for the familiar voice of the President of the United States.

"Mr. Secretary?"

"Mr. President, I'm afraid I have some distressing news. The Saudi Prince Umar has been murdered in New York."

"Which is the distressing part, that he was murdered, or that it happened in New York?"

Ivan was a little taken aback by the President's attitude.

"In this case, the latter," Ivan said. "We were put on the defensive right away. Comments about how the most powerful nation in the world was unable to protect a royal visitor are going to come pouring in from everywhere in the Middle East. The inference, if not the outright accusation that we are the murderers, will be heard and seen in the Arab media, unless we handle this matter very carefully. I understand your lack of feeling for Prince Umar, who was certainly no friend of our country, but protocol requires that *you* must inform the King, so I'd like to tell you exactly what happened, and help you work out what you're going to say to him."

Ivan described in detail the circumstances surrounding the death of the Prince. He advised the President that the husband of the dead woman was being held by the NYPD and suspected of being the murderer. Ivan made the point that the Arab press would blame the U.S. oil companies in the event that they couldn't attach the blame to the American government. He then quoted Bradley Burke's opinion that the Arab oil sheikhs had long desired to vertically integrate the petroleum business, thereby monopolizing top to bottom control of the world's vital energy supplies. The U.S. and Britain had wisely refused to let that happen, by keeping the refineries in their countries or in places over which they had control, instead of placing them near the source of the raw material. This would have been cheaper but riskier, as the Arabs would probably have nationalized and seized them."

"And the bottom line?" the President said. "Where exactly is this going, Ivan?"

"You'll see, sir. I'd like to get you there step by step."

"All right. Keep it coming."

"Well, the Arabs have been left with the crude petroleum which isn't useful until it's refined into diesel and gasoline. According to Brad Burke, the Arabs had bitterly resented being hamstrung in this way. They tried unsuccessfully to build their own new refineries, but this turned out to be technically difficult without American support. It wasn't financially cost effective either, because it duplicated facilities that were already built and functioning elsewhere, so they began using another blueprint. With the huge profits they had made from selling the crude to the refiners, they secretly began to acquire enormous blocks of stocks in the publicly traded refineries owned by the U.S. and the United Kingdom."

"I'm beginning to see where you're going with this," said the President.

"I'm glad you're with me, sir."

Ivan went on to explain how, beginning with Paramount Petroleum, the Arabs had conspired to acquire the controlling interest in the large, publicly-held corporations, using blind trusts and dummy corporations. Brad Burke suspected that the murdered Prince Umar had come to New York to attend the annual meeting for the purpose of installing a new pro-Arab board of directors. Ivan claimed that evidence to this effect was being gathered even as they spoke. If this raid on Paramount were allowed to succeed, the same methods would be used to gain control over all the major oil refining companies in the United States. Ivan explained to the President how Brad was going to foil the Arab takeover at Paramount by using the legal prohibitions of the SEC that were put in place to prevent such surprise corporate stock ambushes.

"This intriguer Prince," Ivan continued, "was the front man in the effort to gain complete control of the world's oil, but he couldn't do it alone. He had to have at least the tacit support of the oil sheikhs, and of the OPEC monopolists, and therefore the King. We know Umar had direct contact with known terrorist leaders. We believe he financed large-scale terror attacks on selected targets chosen not only for their vulnerability, but also for the political damage and embarrassment that they could cause to America."

"In the light of these revelations, how do you suggest that I handle my conversation with the King?"

"I believe you should handle him firmly. We mustn't let the ghost of Umar rule the day. My advice is that you tell the King straight out that his son was an enemy of peace, but that no U.S. government agency was involved in his assassination. You must threaten to release the details of his death with photos, DNA, and any other evidence that would embarrass the King, his extremist supporters, and his domain if it were made public. The idea would be to convince him that he should let his son go gentle into his good night."

"And what do you think will be the King's reaction to this news?" the President asked.

"I believe the King is nothing if not a pragmatist. He wants what he wants, but he also puts a value on what he has. This lost son was not a favorite son. He was too close to being an impatient successor to the throne. He was also a notorious womanizer, a political conspirer, a supporter of violence, and a constant source of potential embarrassment to his family. Umar will not be missed, as the King has a host of other clone-like sons who are anxious to move up the eligibility ladder. But the King won't say any of these things. He'll play the grieving father and deftly move on to other matters, hoping to find a more subtle conniver among his progeny to replace Umar, in the same way that a white shark supplants a lost tooth."

"If you're right, the King won't want us to release any of the details to the press. Can we keep this from them?"

"I hope so. Their Embassy staff will collect the body and fly it home for the prompt burial required by Islamic tradition. We can refer any media questions to them."

"What about the NYPD, will they keep quiet about the details of their investigation?"

"The investigation is being led by a Detective Lynch. He seems like a good man, and I believe I can persuade him to keep a lid on it as long as we don't get in the way of the perpetrator's being brought to justice. He can continue searching for the murderer of Mrs. Dunbar, and the guilty party can be brought to trial for that crime. The conviction for one gory murder carries sufficient penalty to satisfy the Detective, I should think."

"Very well, Ivan, that's the way we'll handle it, then. I'll call the King at once. You see to it that the transportation of the body is done with dignity and dispatch."

"Yes sir, Mr. President."

CHAPTER TWENTY-SEVEN

Rafael Alvarez was amazed, to say the least. Not a word had appeared in the newspapers or on TV about the murders of the Prince and his mistress. Not a word had been released about the attempt by his henchmen on the life of the Security Advisor to the President, either.

This was clearly not normal, and Alvarez was suspicious that there was some kind of conspiracy under way to cover up these crimes. Although he didn't understand who wanted these events silenced, he knew it had to be someone very powerful to be able to accomplish it. He didn't fear that he would be linked to the murders because he had been very careful to leave no clues as to his identity. Nevertheless, he couldn't shake the feeling that he was like a field mouse being observed from afar by a patient owl.

The Viper, like his namesake, knew his health depended upon his stealth. His recent troubles in Chicago had resulted in his having to rid the drug trade of one of its local heroes, and this had resulted in a backlash. He knew from experience that a small war would have to be fought to reestablish his hold over the market in the Midwest.

Alvarez was weary of the struggle for supremacy in an illegal business that was fraught with lethal violence on both sides of the law. He had entered the business to make money, and he had reached that goal many times over. One of the secrets of his success was that he trusted nobody. He was a fair number of points above his contemporaries on the IQ scale, but many equaled him in their predilection for violence. Sooner or later the Viper knew he would have to fight again to keep his place as king of the drug mountain, and like the leaders of most unstable realms, he had an exit strategy.

Retirement was not a common option for people in his business, but Rafael was determined to change that. For many years he had squirreled away cash in various locations under different names. He had properties in a number of the less-policed areas of the world. He knew that false identities set up over time would be difficult to trace. Documents, some legal and some forged, were kept handy in case he had a sudden need to disappear into anonymity.

Whether it was guilt, or suspicion, or merely a hunch, Alvarez decided that the time had come for him to go on the lam. There was almost no place on earth that didn't have a stash of cash and weapons awaiting his arrival. Over the years the Viper had learned to fly both helicopters and fixed wing aircraft, and he kept fast cars at most of his properties. He had suitable wardrobes and disguises to match the photos of his numerous passports. His swarthy complexion, ability with languages, and worldly presence would allow him to pass as a citizen of many nationalities. Anyone on his trail would be led a merry chase, and if by chance he was ever cornered, his skill as a locksmith and a crack shot would, combined with his *sangfroid*, make him difficult to arrest.

After telling his associates he was going to Sao Paolo to do a deal with some customers, he pointed his plane toward Panama, arriving there hours before he would be due in Brazil. He donned a parachute, set the automatic pilot to take the plane over the Caribbean and into the Atlantic when it ran out of fuel, and he bailed out. Covered by the night darkness, he landed on a beach in the nearly deserted Archipelago de Bocas del Toro, near the town of Almirante. He buried his chute and walked to the little town where he had a car waiting. He drove through the night, crossed into Costa Rica, passed through customs using a U.S. passport, and drove to Puerto Limón, a small city on the eastern coast.

Limón is a nasty little commercial port believed to have sheltered Columbus during his fourth and last visit to the new world in 1502. It's hot and unpleasantly humid, and has its fair share of mold and mosquitoes. It's not any kind of a tourist attraction, and has earned a disagreeable reputation for frequent muggings and robberies. It is, however, the best deep port on the Caribbean coast of Costa Rica, and it's from this port town that millions of pounds of bananas are shipped north every year. Rafael Alvarez bought a cup of coffee and some pastries from a nearby bakery, and sat down on a bench to rest and have a nice little picnic breakfast along the seawall in the Parque Vargas.

Before his paper coffee cup was even half empty he was accosted by a young local hellion with a knife. He demanded the Viper's money. Rafael had noticed the man approaching and had marked his intentions long before he got close to him. He had withdrawn his pistol and had placed it under the waxed paper that contained the pastry that he was holding on his lap. When the would-be robber spoke, Rafael smiled back at him, uncovered the handgun, and displayed it prominently so the young thief could not miss it.

"One step closer and you die," the Viper hissed.

The thug stepped back and walked quickly away.

Rafael had lived among men like this all his life, and he knew them well enough to read their minds. The cowardly robber would either disappear into the general population, or in rare cases he would go and find a few friends and return, assuming that anyone carrying a gun must have something worthwhile to protect. Alvarez placed this young man in the former category, so he calmly finished his breakfast while he watched a black sloth move in slow motion in a nearby tree. He took the sight of the sloth to be a pleasant harbinger of his leisurely life of retirement.

The Viper's battered old four wheel drive vehicle was in perfect mechanical condition, having been maintained to Alvarez's specifications, so it was operationally much better than its exterior would indicate. It was a long drive to reach his secluded hideaway. He drove over rutted and pot-holed roads that meandered across the country from east to west, from the Atlantic over the central mountain ranges to the Pacific coast. Up and down, through clouds of mist and patches of sunlight and rainbows, he progressed happily toward his long anticipated Shangri-la.

Some years earlier he had acquired the title to a house and land that had formerly been the vacation cottage belonging to a family of coffee barons. Like the prodigal son in the Bible, the scion of the family coffee fortune had gone to the far country, in this case to New York City, to sow his wild oats. Unlike the prodigal son, however, he became addicted to drugs, thanks largely to the ministrations of the ever-helpful Viper. The son eventually ran out of money, but before he could return to his father he died from an overdose. When his father received the news of the death of his son, he too died, and the Viper took over the cottage. He adopted the identity of the dead son and planned his retirement as Antonio Jiménez.

His destination now lay outside the little town of Golfito on the north side of the Golfo Dulce, at the foot of the lush green mountains in the rain forest. The town itself had become a draw for the sport fishing cognoscenti that are attracted by the marlin and sailfish that swim just beyond its bay. Rafael was able to keep his fast cruising boat in those waters without drawing too much attention to it. A small airport also provided an escape route, should one be needed.

The town itself had its own rustic charm, with its seedy "downtown" consisting of a duty free zone that attracts bargain hunting Ticos from the capital city of San José. The country of Costa Rica has wisely decided to keep much of its magnificent land in primary forests and nature reserves, so it is a destination for eco-tourists, campers, and outdoor types seeking world class hiking opportunities. Rafael depended on these attractions to provide a reasonable supply of women that were easily met in the evenings in the bars of Golfito. His world-weary eyes lost some of their animal wariness, and Rafael settled down to life as a Central American squire, convinced that he had made his escape and that he would never again have to worry about being the subject of a man hunt.

Brooklyn, David, Abdul and Damian had been working flat out to connect the dots between the murders of Prince Umar and DeeDee Dunbar with the attempts on Ivan's life. In conjunction with Detective Lynch, they had begun to create a scenario in which one perpetrator could have committed the crimes, or at least conspired to do so in both cases. The fly in the ointment was that the motive in each case seemed to be almost completely different. It looked as though it were a crime of passion in the case of the Prince and the adulterous DeeDee, and a paid political assassination in the case of Dr. Welland. The events or would-be events seemed to have absolutely nothing in common.

   The weapons used in both crimes were different, and although the pistol used on the Prince and Mrs. Dunbar were the same as the one in the Chicago drug dealer killing, it appeared to have nothing to do with the attack on Ivan in Washington, which was carried out with an AK 47. Team Welland had established a connection to Colombia through the relationship it found between the shipment of weapons and the police in Cali. That shipment had subsequently disappeared in Colombia, and it was believed to have been stolen by gang members in the drug trade. The team had previously established that drug dealers in Latin America were also the largest smugglers of guns. The assassin that the Marine shot dead after he fired on Dr. Welland had been a Colombian, affiliated with drug traders.

   Brooklyn and her crew were working the Colombian connection for all it was worth. They poured over the passenger lists of travelers going to and from Colombia, searching for a man named Rafael Alvarez. No one by that name had entered the U.S. during the time that interested them. He could have been using an alias or a foreign passport, of course, but up to that point the Colombia connection, although far from solid, was really all they had to go on.

Brooklyn called Detective Lynch to inquire about the hair they had picked up in the murdered woman's bathroom. Had a match been found? She was told that unfortunately they had nothing to match it to. All they knew was that a dark-haired unidentified man, other than the Prince and her husband, had sloughed off a hair, but they didn't know how long ago that hair had appeared, or to whom it belonged.

In her discussions with Interpol, the local Cali police, and Colombian diplomatic circles, all that Brooklyn could glean was that a mysterious crime syndicate boss named Rafael Alvarez, aka La Víbora (the Viper), was reputed to be the head of a large illegal drug and gun smuggling business. For many years the Colombian authorities had been seeking unsuccessfully to find him and bring him in for questioning. The wily Viper had taken on an almost iconic status among the lawful and the unlawful elements in the country. He had always managed to elude them, and even putting an extra high price on his head hadn't worked. No matter whether the Colombian citizenry sided with the good guys or with the bad guys, Alvarez was a mysterious cult figure akin to a comic strip action hero. Like the Invisible Man, he was thought by many Latinos to have the ability to materialize and disappear at will.

The Viper's reputation for being an escape artist of sorts was only an added incentive for the team that had solved much larger international riddles than simply finding a criminal in hiding. If there were such a person as the Viper, the team was confidant it could ferret him out. Having access to every piece of intelligence gathered by U.S. sources was going to be of inestimable value, but it was the application of superior minds in combination with computer technology that made Ivan's team the most fearful enemy that the Viper had ever had to face.

A virtual electronic blanket was thrown over Colombia's entire geography, and every occurrence there was analyzed for its possible relationship to the search for the cunning Viper. David Feingold's ability to create algorithms for data analysis was legendary. In the course of a few days he had devised programs that would compare information received from hundreds of sources, putting the data into interrelated categories that could flag interconnected events instantly. Tools like these, in the hands of brilliant investigatory minds, were certain to make things very difficult for the likes of a common criminal.

A few days after the murders in New York, a mysterious incident occurred that under normal circumstances would have gone unnoticed. Hundreds of miles out in the Atlantic Ocean, a U.S. Naval vessel on patrol reported a radar sighting of an apparent small jet plane crash. The ship had investigated, but found no physical evidence of an accident at sea. Such an isolated occurrence, if it was not specifically a part of a missing aircraft search, would have received scant mention beyond the ship's log.

However, when David Feingold's computer tied these details to an incident involving a missing private aircraft that had left Cali, Colombia bound for Sao Paulo, Brazil on the same day, David decided to look deeper into the matter. He thought it strange that the plane had not only failed to arrive at its destination, it had never been reported missing, either. At first glance there seemed to be no commonality between the Viper and an unreported plane crash many thousands of miles from Brazil. And yet if there had been any mention of a plane crash anywhere on the planet, there would have been a search. Feingold was left with a haunting suspicion that the unreported disappearance of a private plane was an indication that it was probably up to no good.

Perhaps the cargo was contraband goods or persons who were thought to be legally expendable. The Colombians had assumed the plane had crashed in the jungles of Brazil, and like so many crashed planes before, would never be found again once it was lost in the vast jungles of the Amazon.

David didn't like open-ended assumptions like that. He resolved to get to the bottom of the missing plane incident. He had one of his contacts in the transportation safety board phone the Colombian in charge of flight information for aircraft in the Cali region.

Shortly thereafter he received word back that the aircraft was an expensive new Learjet, model 40XR, the type used by corporate executives and the super rich. The flight plan registered with the authorities called for a direct non-stop flight to Sao Paulo. A chartered aircraft company based in Miami leased the plane from Bombardier in Canada, the manufacturer, and the CEO of that company was listed as Ricardo Asunción. Feingold observed that the initials R.A. were the same as those of Rafael Alvarez.

The address listed turned out to be non-existent, and the name was unknown in Miami airplane circles. Flight specifications for the make and model of the plane indicated that fully fueled, the plane could have covered the distance to the point reported by the U.S. warship. But once out of Colombian airspace, it would have been possible for the pilot to alter the flight plan.

David figured that although the unscheduled flight would have appeared as a blip on some radar screens, the majority of air traffic controllers would probably have paid little notice to it. Traveling at the 525 MPH cruising speed for that aircraft, and heading away from the North American coast at a cruising altitude of 41,000 feet out over the open ocean, the unidentified plane might not have aroused much concern among the guardians of the airspaces through which it was traveling.

Feingold numbered himself among the most suspicious of men, and since he had been working for Dr. Ivan Welland he had grown even more paranoid than ever. Accepting the obvious was just not an option anymore. If the Viper had been flying the airplane, he would like nothing more than to have everyone believe that he had crashed and perished at sea. David was therefore unconvinced. If the plane that had gone missing in Brazil, or turned seaward and crashed hours later, was the same plane from Colombia, then where was the pilot? No mayday alarm had ever been broadcast. No hysterical wife had turned up seeking her husband.

Feingold's fine mind considered the escape options and found them worthy of the Viper. Few could afford the loss of an elegant jet plane just to cover his tracks. The Viper could, but David suspected he never would, and that explained why it had been leased from the manufacturer and not purchased. David would have bet his paycheck that the Canadian company was being set up to eat the loss right from the beginning.

Who was after the Viper? It must have been a powerful force to pry him away from his precious jungle headquarters. Obviously the master criminal wanted to give the impression to his enemy that he was dead. Perhaps he *was* dead. But bailing out of a jet plane was out of the question, wasn't it?

The most common assumption would be that the plane had lost cabin pressure and all aboard had died of hypoxia. The plane, flying under automatic pilot controls would have flown until it ran out of fuel and crashed into the sea, as had happened to several private jet planes in recent history. That would certainly be the most popular opinion, the one that a surviving incognito Viper would want people to believe.

David's suspicious mind didn't think that the Viper was suicidal, or that he was stupid. He contacted the NTSB and was told that they couldn't do much of anything for him unless some physical wreckage was found. They did check the maintenance records of the plane and found them to be in order, which proved that it was in good mechanical condition at the time of its last inspection a month earlier.

On a hunch, David Feingold decided to delve into the registry of pilots licensed to fly jet aircraft. The name Rafael Alvarez did not appear on the list, but Ricardo Asunción's name was listed as having obtained the necessary training and the hours of flight time required to qualify for the license that had been granted three years earlier. If Ricardo and Rafael were the same person, it still didn't explain how he could have exited the plane and lived. At a speed of over 500 MPH and at an altitude requiring that oxygen be supplied, he couldn't have parachuted safely to the ground.

Solving *the how he did it* problem wouldn't tell Feingold where the Viper was, but it might narrow the search down a bit and it would be comforting to know that there was a way for him to have jumped out of that plane and lived. A fireman's oxygen-breathing equipment might have enabled him to breathe until he had fallen to 10,000 feet or so, that is, if he could have kept the mask on in the powerful air current that the plane's speed and the five-mile fall would have created.

David went on line and called up the jet plane's specs and the diagram of its conformation from the Bombardier website. Looking at the measurements, he could see that trying to exit in flight from the side entrance door would almost surely result in the parachutist's being blown back into the tail structure by a combination of the aircraft's thrust and the Honeywell jet's exhaust. He studied the sketch closely and found the baggage hold was located in the underside of the fuselage.

"Aha!" he said aloud.

He reasoned that it would be possible for a person to make a successful jump out of the baggage compartment. That didn't make it safe to do so, however. The stress on a human body as it is wrested through the air at over 500 MPH and then suddenly exchanges forward motion for gravity's downward force, is akin to hitting a concrete wall in a speeding car. Breathing at 40,000 feet in almost oxygen-free air must be figured into the equation, and the question of whether assisted-breathing equipment would remain affixed to a man's face in wind conditions exceeding those of four combined hurricanes was a practical problem for anyone contemplating such a rash exit. Even if the Viper could have figured out a way to overcome all the practical problems, it didn't solve the main riddle. If he'd managed to successfully jettison the plane, then where was he now?

Assuming that the radar sighting was indeed a Learjet leased by Rafael Alvarez, this reduced the search area to several million square miles of land mass. It was unlikely that such a calculating individual would eject over the sea. The chances of being picked up at sea, even by someone expecting it, were far too risky.

No, David was certain that the Viper would have ejected over terra firma, but that still left millions of miles of jungles, mountains, and coastal areas. Rafael Alvarez could be almost anywhere, and every day that went by enlarged the possibilities. His conclusions were supported by the reports from the police in Colombia to the effect that the Viper had simply disappeared. His trafficking empire was in chaos and they suspected that a rival gang had killed him. In spite of the guesswork of the Colombian police, David called Ivan to tell him that his hunch was that the Viper had made a clean but unusual getaway.

Dr. Ivan Welland, the Secretary of Defense appointed by the newly elected president, had many responsibilities that extended beyond the solving of murders and bringing one perpetrator to justice. The same was certainly true for Ambassador Burke. As interested as they were in the results of the investigation into these crimes, both men had duties to their country that trumped these inquiries. The President had asked that Ivan be a silent listener to the conversation he was about to have with the King, and of course Ivan had complied.

"Your Highness," said the President when the telephone connection had been completed, "I'm afraid I have terrible news for you. Your son, Prince Umar, has been murdered, and there is nothing I can say to sweeten or change that, except to say that I'm very sorry for your loss."

There was a temporary delay on the other end of the line as the King absorbed what the President had just told him.

"Mr. President, how did it happen?" the King said, as the shock of the news changed to incomprehension over the way this could have occurred.

"I'm afraid the details are rather sordid, but please bear with me," the President replied. "The Prince was found shot in the back of the head. His naked body was dumped into the bathtub of an apartment in New York that is owned by the CEO of Paramount Petroleum. Also found at the same time was the naked body of Mrs. Dunbar, the CEO's wife. We know that they had just had sex when the murder occurred. We have taken Mr. Dunbar into custody under suspicion of committing the murders, but his guilt is yet to be proven."

After an even longer pause, the King spoke. "If I heard you correctly, you told me that a Prince of the Royal House was assassinated in the home of the CEO of an American oil company with whom our nation conducts much business, and you are not sure who did it, but you are sure that my son had sexual relations with the man's wife?"

"Yes, that's about all I can tell you at this moment, except that we're conducting a thorough investigation into the circumstances, and we hope to bring the culprit to justice quickly."

The President was taken aback by the cold-blooded response of the King, which showed almost no feeling at all.

"There are two matters that I must discuss with you," the President continued. "First, the return of the body to your care, and second, the announcement we shall have to make to the public at large."

"I will have our Embassy make the arrangements with your Secretary of State to retrieve the body," the King said. "I don't see the necessity of making all the sordid details available to the public, however."

"In a democracy where there's freedom of the press, it would be dangerous to withhold information lest later it be discovered and blown out of all proportion as a scandal that would embarrass both our nations."

"Nevertheless, if everything you have told me is true..."

"And it is..."

"Then I must insist that the details of this matter be kept quiet and be concealed from the Western media. There are forces operating in the Middle East that would use this incident to foment hostilities against my realm and your country as well. I can keep this quiet, and you must too. The life of one Prince can't be valued equally with the worth of a dynasty and the peace of the world."

"I sympathize with your position, but there is only one way that I could be tempted to try to keep this incident quiet."

"What way would that be, Mr. President?"

"If Your Majesty were willing to sponsor and advocate my *War on Weapons* program in your part of the world, then perhaps I could justify covering up this international event."

There was silence at the other end. "Are you sure," said the King at last, "are you quite sure it wasn't your own CIA that assassinated Umar? Maybe it was their plan all along to do this in order to force my hand and make me accept your so-called War on Weapons."

"That's not true. The Prince may not have been popular here in some quarters, but no one in my government was authorized to kill him. I must have a decision about this matter at once, as I will have to clamp down on the police before the story gets out. I think if you accede to my request you'll go down in history as one of its leading peacemakers. As the ruler of the land containing the holiest places in Islam, your nation's participation in my explosives and ammunition abatement program will be a beacon of hope to the rest of the world. Other Muslim nations will follow in your footsteps, and the economic benefits of international trade and tourism will enrich all the children of Islam. Naturally some elements may hate the idea of peace, but these are your enemies as well as mine."

"Very well, Mr. President. I can see your point, and I agree that making something good come from Prince Umar's death would be beneficial to all."

"Excellent, Your Highness. I promise you won't be sorry. Perhaps you could also convince the other Arab monarchs that an initiative such as yours would also be in their best interests. A popular government is not one that is likely to be overthrown. If there were to be a number of forward-looking, peace-making hierarchical rulers coming out in favor of my *War on Weapons,* it would suggest to the world that good kings still make fine rulers, which would be a message I imagine that the kings would like to transmit."

"I must speak to my advisors about your proposals, but if you keep your promise to make sure that Umar's death remains a secret, I will support your weapons plan."

"Thank you, Your Highness. I shall send Ambassador Bradley Burke to you next week to work out the details. I'm very sorry about your son."

CHAPTER TWENTY-EIGHT

Ambassador Bradley Burke and his wife embarked on a whirlwind tour of the Middle East. Beginning with the King in Saudi Arabia, Burke presented a document to be submitted to all the leaders in the Middle East, which in essence was a contract between the President of the United States and the various independent Arab states. The leaders were to sign a statement that they had received the document and had agreed to its terms, or to sign that they had received it, but didn't intend to adhere to its stipulations.

Those who took the latter course were warned that non-compliance carried risks, and the names of those countries were made public. In the forum of the United Nations, heroic efforts were made to bring these countries into compliance. Ivan's team watched carefully. In the end only three of the twenty-two Middle Eastern countries refused to comply. The Defense Department was informed about the situation and readied its response.

Brad made one last visit to the three dissenting nations. He showed the leaders the DVDs that had been prepared to give them an idea of the specific damage that would be done to their military armories if they didn't cooperate. The simulated attacks were presented in 3D and with a newly-developed virtual reality mode.

The leaders squirmed, postured, bluffed, lied, objected to threats, and argued from every possible angle, but in the end Brad's patient, wise counseling persuaded only one more nation to sign up. Two outlaw countries decided to disregard the wish of the majority of nations and defy the might of the United States rather than comply. They flatly refused to go along with the plan, no matter how carefully Brad explained that putting an end to the manufacture of ammunition and explosives would leave them no worse off than before. They reiterated the point that they were following the will of Allah, and that no man-made treaty could trump the Koranic imperative that all men should bow down and worship the one true God, Allah, as revealed to the Prophet. Those who died in defense of Allah's plan would immediately go to the paradise prepared for them, so the bona fide worshippers of Islam had nothing to fear from temporal powers. No matter the odds against them, Allah would enable them to emerge victorious.

On this note Brad was summarily dismissed and sent back to his country to report the disappointing news to his President and to the world at large.

Ivan's team was convinced that Prince Umar had been killed by Rafael Alvarez, the Viper, even though the evidence was not as incontrovertible as they would have liked. They all agreed that the hunt for the murderer must go on, however, and so the case was kept open. Sooner or later a lead would turn up and his whereabouts would be discovered, then the Viper's DNA could be matched to the sequences obtained at the crime scene. But for the time being the file would remain open, along with other cold cases that were dormant pending new evidence.

While Bradley Burke was touring the Middle East, Ivan Welland had been dispatched by the President to visit the New York City Chief of Police at his headquarters. His mission was to bottle up the incomplete evidence in the case of the double murders in the Dunbar apartment.

Using the power of the presidency, Ivan was able to make the Chief see the logic of suspending the release of the details to the media. The Chief admitted to Ivan that he often withheld information about ongoing investigations if he felt that releasing it would impede the inquiry. Detective Lynch, who had reached an impasse in his investigation anyway, was ordered to cease work on the case. The files were impounded and secured in the Chief's office pending the discovery of new evidence from which a case could be made. The body of the Prince was surreptitiously sent home for burial. Dunbar was released on the grounds that the District Attorney had insufficient evidence to prosecute him.

Welland ordered the members of his team to focus on the wider issue of implementing the President's War on Weapons. It was time now for them to present to the Joint Chiefs of Staff all the information they had gathered about the location and the approximate size of the various facilities that were engaged in the production of explosives and ammunition worldwide. It would be their responsibility to judge if the factories were complying with the President's order to suspend the production of chemicals used in the manufacture of explosives, and to target for destruction those facilities that were non-compliant.

It became obvious that the task at hand was enormous. Ivan's job as Secretary of Defense had received an historic new focus. No longer would he be directing the powerful U.S. military forces in large-scale international conflicts. The emphasis now was on the removal of the materials of war rather than the dispatching of the wielders of weapons.

Ivan was frequently reminded of the folk tale about the fox and the hedgehog, who were trying to find a peaceful settlement. The fox berated the hedgehog for inciting trouble by displaying his defensive bristles in such an open fashion. The hedgehog, for his part, argued that he would give up his quills as soon as the fox gave up his teeth. What the President was doing was the equivalent of sending the fox to the dentist to have all his teeth pulled before the hedgehog would even consider relaxing his bristles. The dental procedure was not as risky as it seemed to some Americans, as the U.S. military had several generations of foxes in reserve, but it was a generous gesture nevertheless.

It was amazing to Welland to discover that all nations now pretended to be hedgehogs, including his own. Years earlier Ivan's title would have been Secretary of War, but now it was Secretary of Defense.

It was the same all over the world. No nation wanted to be seen as an aggressor. In recent times, however, the aggressive elements had become secretly embedded within many nations, and governments pretended that although their intentions were utterly peaceful, they had little or no control over the violent, organized minorities in their midst.

The truth, of course, was something altogether different. Whether through fear of reprisals by their violent cousins or covert support for their cause, most of the nations of Islam permitted extremist elements to exist, if not flourish, at the core of their societies. Until diplomacy succeeded, the fox's teeth had to be extracted. In this context Ivan's task was to do painless dentistry starting at home, and extending his services to patients all over the world. Dentures could be provided later as needed.

Damian, under Ivan's watchful eye, was working on a plan to use the law of supply and demand to create a seller's market. By simply increasing the price of the raw chemicals needed to manufacture explosives, the end price of bullets, shells, mines, and such weapons would appreciate, and consequently their use would decline.

As each large manufacturer of explosives chemicals mothballed their facilities, the price of their lethal wares rose higher. Ten percent of the factories on the list produced eighty percent of the ingredients used in the production of weapons. So they started with the largest producers first.

In an amazingly short period of time they began to notice results. Conservation of arms supplies was the first reaction to the shortages created by the seller's market. Gone were the usual scenes of hooded men in Arab cities gleefully brandishing their weapons and firing shots into the air. Weapons quickly disappeared from view as hoarders rounded them up and added them to the supplies already hidden in the basements of schools and mosques. The few remaining arms smugglers, when they were able to lay their hands on deadly illegal merchandise, were asking prices that no one could afford to pay.

Statistics created from research data proved that the number of bullets of various calibers produced in each year of the first decade of the 21st century exceeded the total population of the entire world. In other words, there was a bullet produced every year for each person on the planet. Ivan was determined to make sure that these bullets never reached their targets.

Under the direction of its new Secretary, the United States Defense Department underwent a total revision in its methods. The curriculum in the military academies was reconfigured to place more emphasis on police work. Fortunately the military's Special Forces had been working on infiltration, intelligence, and surveillance for a number of years, so from day one these units were prepared to clamp down on those who refused to obey the President's orders. First at home, and then in the hotspots of the world, raids were conducted to clean up the arms caches of the dissenters. Since the Middle East was the source of most of the illegal armaments, the focus of military police actions began there.

Large, unexplained explosions were unleashed around the Middle East in weapons caches that had not been revealed to the government as required by the authorities. When the hidden weapons were discovered, the innocent children in the schools and the well-meaning worshippers in the mosques were quickly evacuated, after which the mini-armories were annihilated, using air-to-ground missiles whenever possible.

In the more difficult cases commando raids were employed. The dramatic explosions served as a warning to everyone that the easy availability of explosives for the manufacture of IEDs and suicide bombs were coming to an end. It was hoped that the two holdout nations would observe the destruction of arms in neighboring countries and come to terms with the President's War on Weapons and Ammunition program.

This was not to be, however. The tradition of religious martyrdom continued its irresistible sway over the self-serving young hotheads of the world who were determined to secure eternal bliss in the arms of heavenly virgins at the expense of a host of distinctly unenthusiastic earthly victims.

The President was left with no choice but to persuade the cynical, equally self-serving leaders of said hotheads that their choices were not in the best interests of their people, nor yet of their beloved Allah. America was forced into the unsought and unwanted position of policing the world. Extremist combatants had found a way to compel the referee to fight, but their purpose in doing so remained unclear.

The irony didn't escape America's leaders. Ivan referred to it as the elevation of the sixth commandment (*you shall not make wrongful use of God's name*) to the number three position (*you shall not murder*). The President preferred to think of it as a merger of the two – the Islamist jihadists were committing murder in the name of Allah.

Once again the forces of democracy were going to be called upon to sacrifice their men to preserve sanity and promote peace in parts of the world where freedom was desperately needed but fiercely resisted by dictatorial leaders and misled religious zealots. No three men ever wanted peace more than the President, Ivan and Brad. But no men were more determined to implement their conviction that the beginning of planetary peace had to start with disarmament. They knew it would be many years before a completely weaponless world existed, but the longest journey always starts with the first step, and they were committed to making that first step. They were not unaware of the irony of having to take up arms in order to be able to lay them down, but they had faith that this first small step would eventually lead to a giant leap for mankind.

Many future world leaders would recognize the wisdom of the American President, and in time he would come to be known in the history books as "The Peacemaker."

If you enjoyed reading *Cruise Control,* you will also like the first book in the series, *Council of Caliphs,* by the same author. First editions are available and can be purchased at www.erserandpond.com, or you may send a check or money order for $24.95 (please add $1.50 sales tax plus $4.00 for postage and handling) to Erser and Pond Ltd, 1096 Queen Street, Suite 225, Halifax, Nova Scotia B3H 2R9, Canada. Checks and money orders should be made out to Erser and Pond Ltd.

Aidan de Vries

Cruise
Control

If you enjoyed reading *Council of Caliphs,* you will also like the second book in the series, *Cruise Control,* about an attempt by Islamist terrorists to sink the world's largest cruise ship on her maiden voyage. It is available at www.erserandpond.com, or you may send a check or money order for $22.95 (please add $1.38 sales tax plus $4.00 for postage and handling) to Erser and Pond Ltd, 1096 Queen Street, Suite 225, Halifax, Nova Scotia B3H 2R9, Canada. Checks and money orders should be made out to Erser and Pond Ltd.